To S

Girls Who Dare, Book 2

By Emma V. Leech

****

Published by Emma V. Leech.

Copyright (c) Emma V. Leech 2019

Cover Art: Victoria Cooper

ASIN No.: B07P19585K

ISBN No.: 978-1096195658

Table of Contents

To Steal a Kiss

Members of the Peculiar Ladies' Book Club

Prunella Adolphus, Duchess of Bedwin – first peculiar lady and secretly Miss Terry, author of *The Dark History of a Damned Duke.*

Alice Dowding - too shy to speak to anyone in public and often too small to be noticed.

Lucia de Feria - a beauty. A foreigner.

Kitty Connolly - quiet and watchful, until she isn't.

Harriet Stanhope – serious, studious, intelligent. Prim. Wearer of spectacles.

Bonnie Campbell - too outspoken and forever in a scrape.

Ruth Stone - heiress and daughter of a wealthy merchant.

Minerva Butler – Prue's cousin. Not so vain or vacuous as she appears. Dreams of love.

Jemima Fernside - pretty and penniless.

Matilda Hunt – blonde and lovely and ruined in a scandal that was none of her making.

Chapter 1

My dear Prue,

I'm so happy for you. You and Bedwin are a perfect match. I shall miss you while you are away. Do write, if you can tear yourself away from your handsome husband for long enough! No, by the way, I never did complete my dare. At least... not yet.

—Excerpt of a letter from Miss Alice Dowding to Prunella Adolphus, Duchess of Bedwin.

13th June 1814, London.

"They looked terribly happy, didn't they?" Alice said with a wistful sigh as the carriage rumbled through London.

Alice was returning home with Matilda after the marriage of their dear friend Prunella to the Duke of Bedwin. That Prue was now a duchess was extraordinary and so at odds with her friend's character she could not help but smile. What a bold young woman she was. She would not be your everyday duchess, that was for sure.

Alice turned to look across the carriage to her friend, who was staring out the window with a frown creasing her brow.

"What?" Matilda looked around and then sat up a bit straighter, as if tearing her thoughts from a dream. "Oh! Yes," she said, smiling now. "Yes, indeed. They did. I think that marriage will be a great success. Lucky Prue."

Alice nodded and gave a wistful sigh. She wasn't jealous. Not really. That would be unworthy of her. Prue deserved her happiness and Alice was completely, wholeheartedly delighted for her.

Dash it.

Well, maybe a tad envious, then.

"Chin up, Alice. Your time will come." Matilda's voice was soft, her expression warm. She would make a good mother, Alice thought. The young woman had certainly taken to mothering the Peculiar Ladies, taking everyone under her wing. Alice especially.

With a disparaging sound, Alice indicated her thoughts on the likelihood of that prediction.

"Oh, it will indeed," she said, surprising herself a little with the bitterness of her words. "In the form of the Honourable Mr Edgar Bindley."

Alice didn't bother hiding her dejection over the idea. Matilda had become one of her closest friends over the past weeks, and an ally in the war to thwart her parents' plans. They were social climbers of the most ferocious kind and saw their daughter as fair game for their own advancement, no matter her ideas on the subject.

The *honourable* Edgar Bindley, youngest son of the Earl of Ulceby had shown an interest in Alice, and they were keen for her to make an advantageous marriage. That Alice not only found him physically repugnant, but could find nothing good to say about him, seemed of no importance. There was something cold, something lacking in Edgar Bindley, and Alice had no wish to discover what it was.

Matilda grimaced and shook her head.

"No, no. We're not giving up yet, Alice. They gave you to the end of the season."

Alice gave a snort and shook her head. "It's the middle of June, Tilda." A fact which was driven home to her each evening as she crossed another day from the calendar. "Time is running out. I can't even get up the nerve to speak to a man in public, let alone tempt him into completing my dare. What chance do I have of getting one to propose?"

"Faint heart," Matilda scolded, wagging a finger at Alice.

As a member of The Peculiar Ladies' Book Club, an establishment for wallflowers, oddities, and the unmarriageable—Alice had been one of the first to take part in a series of rather outrageous dares. Not that she had yet completed her dare, only taken one from the hat in a rare display of courage, or perhaps insanity.

Her actions had shocked her as much as the other ladies of their number. Alice was shy. So shy she had trouble speaking to people outside of her immediate family or friends without stuttering, blushing, and making a fool of herself. That she had been the second to pipe up and take a dare from the hat was still something she was a little perplexed by. Yet, she was desperate: desperate to change her life, to change herself, to *live*.

Prue's dare—to dance in a garden at midnight—had culminated in marriage to the Duke of Bedwin, the man with whom she'd danced. Silly as it might have seemed, Alice clung to the hope that such a romantic fate might await her.

Alice's dare was to kiss a man in the moonlight. A lovely idea, if there were a single man of her acquaintance, outside of the revolting Mr Bindley, willing to do the honours. As she could hardly accost a man in the middle of a ballroom and ask him to help her complete a dare—even if she had an ounce of the nerve required for such a feat—she was rather stuck.

"Did you mean what you said?" Matilda asked, drawing Alice's attention away from such gloomy musings.

"What was that?" Alice frowned, trying to recall, and then felt a jolt of apprehension as she remembered her rather spur-of-the-moment comment earlier at Prue's wedding.

"You said you weren't going to sit on the sidelines any longer, but that you would go out and get your happy ever after."

Anxiety stirred in Alice's chest at the thought of doing anything other than sitting about and waiting for her fate to change, but she had so little time left. Her parents had determined she would have Mr Bindley if no better offers were forthcoming, and she had until the beginning of September. Little more than six weeks. She had to do something.

"I-I," she stammered, before taking a deep breath. "Yes," she said, wondering if she ought to stop the carriage. She felt rather ill.

"Excellent," Matilda said, beaming at her. There was a look in her friend's eyes she couldn't quite like. A glint of determination. "And you're ready to complete your dare?"

Alice swallowed hard. She felt ready to run away and hide, but she kept that to herself for fear Matilda would think her a wet blanket. She *was* a wet blanket. If she were totally honest, wet blankets had a deal more weight to their characters.

"Well?"

Do it. Do it. Do it, a little voice in her head repeated, the words in time to the desperate thudding of her heart.

Matilda had offered to help her with her dare weeks ago, but Alice had been too afraid to agree. The idea that Matilda would arrange for a man to kiss her... a complete stranger....

Alice shivered with apprehension.

It was not that she didn't trust Matilda, she did. She knew the beautiful young woman had a good and kind heart and would never set her up with an unpleasant fellow, or someone who would compromise her or take advantage, but... but Matilda was *ruined.*

She was wealthy and beautiful and from a distinguished family, but her father's fall from grace, her brother's notoriety, and her own reputation rendered her unmarriageable to any decent gentleman. The family had fallen on hard times due to their father's excesses, and her brother had established a notorious gambling club to recover their fortune. Recover it he had, too, in grand style. It was not a respectable occupation for a gentleman, however, and then… there was the matter of Matilda being caught alone with a man.

It had happened through no fault of her own, it was true, but still, was she really the person Alice ought to trust with this particular dare?

"Kitty has only given you this final full moon to complete your dare, Alice," Matilda warned. "You've already had two months. You were only supposed to have two weeks."

"I know, I know!" Alice wailed, wringing her hands together. "I wish…."

I wish I'd never taken the stupid dare.

No.

For heaven's sake, Alice, grow a backbone.

Do something.

Anything.

For if she didn't, she might as well resign herself to being Mrs Edgar Bindley.

Alice shuddered.

"Yes!" She squeaked more than spoke the word, forcing it out before good sense could remind her of all the reasons this was a ridiculous, terrible, and dangerous idea. Yet, Prue had been brave, and she'd gained everything she ever dreamed of. Surely Alice could do the same?

Matilda beamed at her and shuffled along the carriage bench to take Alice's hand.

"Wonderful. Well done you, Alice. Now, are you going to the Ransoms' ball?"

Alice nodded. She felt light-headed; her skin clammy. Perhaps she was going down with something. Something that would consign her to her bed until after the full moon, with a bit of luck. Then she'd be out of time, and unable to complete her dare through no fault of her own. No shame in that.

Nonetheless, shame overwhelmed her. Alice was no fool. She knew kissing a stranger in the moonlight would not change her fortune. Yet it had become somehow symbolic. If Alice could do this one reckless, daring thing, surely there was more to her? A painfully shy wallflower would never do such a dreadful thing, so if *she* did it… she'd no longer be a painfully shy wallflower. Would she?

It made sense to her, at any rate.

"That's the perfect time, then," Matilda said, giving Alice's hand a squeeze. "A full moon, and the Ransoms' place is vast, full of balconies and romantic gardens. Now, don't you worry about it. I shall arrange everything."

Alice felt her stomach twist and wanted to laugh or possibly sob at the idea she could stop herself worrying. She'd be able to think of nothing else between now and then. She'd make herself ill with it, not get a wink of sleep, and be red-eyed and blotchy by the night of the ball. A delightful prospect for any young man. She swallowed a groan of misery and, as Matilda let go of her hand, she pressed it to her stomach, which was threatening retribution.

"W-Who?"

She couldn't ask more than that, too afraid she'd cry or vomit or do something equally repulsive if she tried to speak further.

Matilda gave her a reassuring smile and reached out a hand to tug at one of Alice's red curls. "Someone I trust, darling. Someone who will be sweet and kind and respectful. You have my word."

Alice nodded. She couldn't have done anything more if she tried, and she was too concerned with keeping the contents of her stomach in place to make the attempt.

"Look at you," Matilda said, frowning and shaking her head. "Why has no gentleman snatched you up? You're perfectly lovely."

Alice glanced up at Matilda to see sincerity in her eyes.

"You're like a lovely porcelain doll, fragile and perfect."

Alice grimaced. Her father had often described her thus, thinking it a grand compliment, as Matilda obviously did. Alice didn't want to be fragile and breakable, though. The idea that she needed protecting and shielding from the harsh realities of life was something she came across from every quarter. If a gentleman ever approached her, it was this that drew them. She was petite and slender, waiflike, a description she'd heard all too often. Yet her inability to speak to people she didn't know, let alone men, and her annoyance at being treated like a child, soon had them giving up and moving on to more convivial company.

No one realised there was a fire burning in her heart, fuelled by frustration and the desire for more, even when her wretched nerves would not allow her to speak her mind. She'd inherited her red hair from her grandmother, a woman of grand passions and determination. Why hadn't Alice inherited more than just her fiery locks? Why couldn't she have had inherited the spark that had driven the woman on and made her rather a scandalous creature, known for her sparkling wit and a string of much younger lovers? Alice wished she'd known her, but she'd died when Alice was a baby.

She snorted at the idea that such a description could ever be levelled at her. No doubt she'd end up like her great aunt, Agatha.

A faded little creature who spoke in a whisper, smelled strongly of peppermint, and was forever searching for her handkerchief.

Please, God, no.

Alice's mother always refused to speak about her outrageous parent, her lips thinning and a look of deep displeasure in her eyes when the subject arose. Mrs Dowding was a stickler for propriety and had instilled her daughter with an unhealthy terror of doing anything she ought not. Yet her grandmother's portrait hung in one of the lesser used guest rooms, gathering dust, and Alice often went to look at it... perhaps in the hope the woman would lend her courage.

"Come home with me," Matilda said, giving Alice a conspiratorial grin. "We'll discuss what you're to wear for the ball. I have an idea how you should arrange your hair. Those tiny little curls make you look about twelve. I'll have my maid try it and you can see what you think."

With a soft laugh, Alice agreed. It would make little difference. No amount of primping ever gave her the nerve to speak up and make herself heard, but there was little point in trying to thwart Matilda once her mind was made up. She was a force of nature. So, with a nod of agreement, she allowed her friend to redirect the carriage and they headed off to Matilda's home.

Chapter 2

My dear Lucia,

Do you think Alice has the nerve to go through with it? I do hope so. If ever a girl needed an admirer to boost her confidence....

My wretched brother had better do the job.

—Excerpt of a letter from Miss Matilda Hunt to Senorita Lucia de Feria.

The evening of the 13th June 1814. Half Moon Street, Mayfair, London.

Once Alice had departed, Matilda stared into the empty hearth and rather wished there was a fire burning there. It was so much easier to think when there was a merry fire to focus one's attention on. Midsummer was not the time to be heating the already stuffy room, however. Her brother's home was an elegant space, the entire house decorated with taste and in the height of fashion, no expense spared. Matilda had seen to that.

The walls of the room were a delicate robin's egg blue, and heavy silken grey-blue curtains fell in lavish drapes at the large windows that looked out onto an elegant and fashionable street. A richly patterned rug in golden tones covered the polished wood floor, the warm colours bringing a softer feel to the cool blues and accentuating the many gilt frames of the artworks that festooned the walls. All the most modern furniture designs by the most sought-after makers were arranged about the stylish room.

Above the fireplace was an impressive gilded bronze and black marble French clock with a large *putto* holding a bird. The clock struck both the hour and the half hour, and Matilda had come to resent it more every day. She felt the sweet-faced *putto* was measuring out her life chime by chime. Perhaps she would replace it. Nate wouldn't care, despite the fact the thing had cost an unholy fortune.

Her brother was always on at her to spend his money, encouraging her to buy new dresses, jewellery, whatever she desired. They both knew why that was, but Matilda let it go without comment. She didn't take advantage of his generosity, but neither did she feel any compunction about spending when she wanted to. He owed her that much.

He owed her a great deal.

She moved to the window, turning the latches and pushing up the sash to let a welcome breeze flutter into the room. Movement farther along the road caught her eye, and she noticed the glossy carriage belonging to her brother coming along the street.

Thank goodness.

As the owner of one of the city's most exclusive and notorious gaming clubs, Nathaniel Hunt kept rather unsociable hours. Usually he was away all night and slept most of the day. He had said he'd be home early this evening, but what Nate said and what Nate did were not always compatible.

She had plans for her brother, however, and she would ensure he played along. No matter what he said. If a bit of blackmail was required to achieve her ends… so be it.

Poor, sweet Alice. Such a little mouse of a girl. If she wasn't very careful, she'd find herself married to the odious Mr Bindley. Alice had pointed the man out to Matilda a few weeks back and Matilda's heart had clenched. She had a sixth sense about men, and her instincts told her Bindley was a snivelling little rat, the kind to bully those over whom he had power.

Little Alice wouldn't stand a chance.

Well, her own future might be in ruins, but Matilda was damned if she'd let Alice make a bad marriage. The girl just needed confidence, that was all. The kind of confidence she might gain from hearing a handsome man tell her she was lovely, desirable, that he was inflamed by her. A man like Matilda's brother, for example. For Alice *was* lovely, and she did not understand the power that could give her, if she could only believe in herself.

Matilda had no illusions. Nate would refuse. He'd rage about the idea, and become utterly furious, and then Matilda would remind him of what he owed, and he would capitulate. His guilt weighed heavy, and it was for this reason she never used it against him.

To do so now was underhanded, she knew, but she had never played the card before, nor would she do so now if it wasn't something she felt so strongly about. Why, she didn't know. Only that Alice's happiness had become important to her. All her friends' happiness. The Peculiar Ladies had become a refuge, a focus in her life which seemed already so full of regrets. Matilda would not see her friends regret as she did. They deserved better. They'd get better, if she had anything to do with it. She would guide and nurture and advise them the best she could. She would see them all married and happy, and then perhaps her life would feel less empty.

Besides which, Nate needed a wife.

A smile curved over her mouth at the idea of Nate and Alice. Nate wouldn't see it. Not at first. She might be quite mistaken, of course, but....

Something told Matilda that Alice had hidden depths. Now and then she saw a spark of something in the girl's eyes, something hot and fierce like that red hair she always scraped back in such an unbecoming and childish style. Alice just needed the courage to let that spark flame like her fiery locks.

A handsome fellow like Matilda's brother, well… maybe he could provide the tinder? Though Nate would die before he admitted it, his current lifestyle was never one he'd longed for. Before their world had crumbled, Matilda had known that Nate would marry a nice girl and settle down and have a family. He was suited for it and, unlike many of his friends, had never made a show of trying to evade his fate. He'd welcomed it.

Then their father had squandered their fortune and their futures, and everything had changed. Nate had changed. He'd become harder, colder, his feelings forced down into some dark place where they'd not trouble him. Not obviously, at least. He'd become the epitome of the handsome young scoundrel, and many young men tried their best to emulate his nonchalant grace and devil may care attitude. Yet, Matilda felt certain the Nate she'd once known was still there, still longing for a home, for a wife and family. If only he'd acknowledge it.

Such a life would be a deal better for him than his present lifestyle, that was for certain. Besides, she'd never tried her hand at match making before and, if she was to ensure her friends were all suitably settled, she may as well begin with her brother. Her own life would hold no such romance, after all, so the least she could do was indulge herself in manoeuvring others into their happy ever afters.

Matilda looked up as the man himself entered the room.

"Evening, Tilda." He greeted her with a flash of a crooked grin before he took himself off to the decanter that had been left ready for him.

"For heaven's sake, Nate," she said with a sigh of reproach. "Can't you get in the door before pouring a drink?"

"I'm in!" he exclaimed, gesturing to the room about him. "Or am I mistaken, is this the garden? It is a bit chilly."

He nodded at the open window and Matilda rolled her eyes at him.

"It's stifling in here, as well you know. The whole city is stifling," she added with a sigh, waving a delicate hand-painted fan back and forth with more vigour than her usual understated style would allow. It was only her brother, after all. Matilda stared about the fashionable room—with not a thing out of place, no sign of wear or age—and a pang of longing for their childhood home in the country stabbed at her heart. She forced it down. No point in crying about that. The place had long been sold to cover their father's debts.

"Ah, well, that explains my raging thirst," her brother replied, raising the glass to her and taking a large swallow. With a sigh of satisfaction, he crossed the room to stand beside her at the window and dutifully kissed her cheek. "What's ailing you, sis?" he asked, casting a knowing eye over her. He knew her too well.

Matilda gave a huff of annoyance she wasn't really feeling. That was the trouble with Nate. It was so hard to be cross with him. Tall and broad and blond, with twinkling blue eyes, he cut a dashing figure. Add to that an abundance of charm and a devilish smile, and he could have most women eating out of his hand in no time. Matilda was immune to charm of that nature, being his sister and knowing all his worst traits, but still, it was never easy to scold him when he was such a lamb.

"You drink too much, you don't sleep enough, and you keep bad company," she said, folding her arms and feeling like the worst sort of nag, but someone had to say it.

"Ah, the life of a gaming club proprietor," he replied with a nonchalant shrug.

Matilda sighed and shook her head. There was no point in remonstrating. It made no difference, and he had a point. How else was he supposed to live, under the circumstances? That meant circumstances needed to change before he could, which brought her back to the point in hand.

"Nate, I want you to do something for me."

It was always best to attack Nate head on. He was too straightforward for subtlety and despised subterfuge.

"Of course, Tilda. Name it," he said, sitting himself down by the empty hearth. He frowned at the fireplace. "It never feels the same with no fire burning, does it? Not half so welcoming."

Matilda rolled her eyes. "It's the middle of June," she pointed out, despite having observed the same thing herself.

"What do you need then?" he asked, returning to the conversation. "A new frock? Hats? Or is it decorating? Surely you've done every room in the house by now? Twice, in fact."

Matilda felt a twinge of guilt over that debacle but retreated into irritation, knowing he was baiting her. "You know very well I only did one room twice, and that was because the colour of those curtains was not what I ordered. I had to redecorate the entire room to match. It was most aggravating."

Nate made a mild sound which might have been amusement, or possibly incredulity. Matilda ignored it.

"Very well. Not frocks or jewels or decorating. A horse?" he suggested.

"Oh, stop it, Nate. I'm serious; I want to talk to you." She settled herself down in the chair opposite him as he pursed his lips.

"Horses *are* serious business, Tilda," he said, a touch reprovingly. "Don't you even think about buying one before I've looked it over. Can't have someone selling you a miserable rip. I've got a reputation to think of."

"The less said about your reputation, the better," Matilda said, immediately regretting the tartness of her voice as guilt flashed in his expression. She sighed. "I don't want you to buy me anything,

Nate. I just need you to do something for me. It will only take a moment of your time, but it would mean a great deal to me."

Nate's eyes narrowed and he studied her, turning the glass in his hands back and forth.

"A favour, then," he said, and she could hear the suspicion behind the observation.

Well, there was no point in prevaricating.

"Yes, a favour. You remember I told you about my friends and the dares they'd accepted?"

Nate snorted and shook his head. Matilda scowled at him.

"Well, you remember I told you about Alice? She's a sweet girl, pretty as a little doll, but terribly shy. Her time is running out, Nate and…. Oh, I just want her to accomplish the dare. I know it's silly, but I think it would give her some much needed confidence, put a bit of fire in her blood."

Her brother's gaze darkened, and Matilda could see then the figure that others spoke of, the one she rarely saw. Nathaniel Hunt was a ruthless businessman, cutting off credit to dukes and earls alike if he had the slightest inkling they couldn't pay. He didn't suffer fools and was not one to be taken advantage of… by none but his sister, at least.

"What in blue blazes has that got to do with me?" he demanded.

"You're going to help her," Matilda said, putting up her chin and holding his gaze. His blue eyes were crystalline, glittering with indignation.

"The devil I will!" he exclaimed, surging to his feet. "A fine way to get myself trapped into marriage."

Matilda sighed, well aware of Nate's thoughts on that particular subject. They were akin to his thoughts about rising before midday, hangovers, and tripe. At least that was the impression he put about, like any self-respecting libertine. As his sister, however, she felt certain she knew better. She hoped she did.

"She has no ideas of marrying you. I can assure you of that. She's all but engaged to Mr Bindley, much against her wishes, but he's a repulsive creature and... oh, damn it, Nate. I won't condemn her to the likes of Bindley without, at the very least, completing her dare. And what's it to you? It's just a little kiss."

Nate snorted and returned a dark look. "It's never *just* a little kiss."

"I wouldn't know," Matilda retorted, hating the acerbic tone that escaped before she could check it.

Her brother flinched and a stilted silence followed.

"Bindley?" he said, frowning a little.

"You know him?" Matilda asked, brightening. Nate had become a very powerful man, not simply because of the debts he held over many of the most illustrious names of the *ton*, but because of the gossip and information that filtered through the club. If he had something on Bindley, something that would make him less of an inviting proposition to Alice's parents....

Nate shook his head. "No. Name rings a bell, that's all."

"He's the youngest son of the Earl of Ulceby."

"Ulceby?" he repeated, wrinkling his nose. "By God, if he's anything like his father, I pity the girl."

"So do I!" Matilda exclaimed, frustrated. "Which is why you will escort me to the Ransoms' ball tomorrow night. You'll meet Alice on a moonlit terrace, say a few pretty words, and kiss her."

"Damned if I will!" Nate exploded, heading to pour himself another drink. "You've got rocks in your head if you think I'd ever agree to that."

"Oh, for heaven's sake," Matilda shouted back, exasperated. "I'm not asking you to stick pins in your eyes. It's not as if she's unattractive. In fact, she's quite lovely. You should thoroughly enjoy it, or have you completely given up on the fairer sex? Your reputation would suggest otherwise."

Nate glowered at her.

"I don't go around kissing little innocents on balconies, Tilda. I don't know what kind of man you think I am—"

"Oh, yes," Matilda said, interrupting him and sneering a little. "What little affection remains is reserved for opera singers, or was it a dancer this week? I forget."

"Matilda," Nate said, with a warning in the way he spoke that she could not ignore.

"No, *Nathaniel.* I rarely ask you for anything, as you well know, but I am asking you for this." A thread of anger laced the words, pulling them tight. "I appreciate you think it silly, but nonetheless, it is important to me. I want Alice to be happy, or at least to… to have as few regrets as possible."

Nate stilled, and she knew she had him.

Unlike me, she didn't say. She didn't need to.

Matilda sighed. "Please, Nate," she said softly, moving closer to him and laying her hand on his arm. "It's only for a few moments. Just be your charming self, make her feel beautiful, desired, make it romantic. One little kiss, that's all. I shall stand guard and make sure no one interrupts you, so there's no danger."

She felt the muscles in his arm grow rigid with tension. He hated this, was furious that he felt he couldn't refuse her. Perhaps she ought to feel guilt at manipulating him so, but she'd changed too over the years. Her heart was harder.

"And what if she recognises me?" he asked, his displeasure obvious. "Won't she feel foolish when she discovers it's your brother you forced into meeting her?"

Matilda shook her head. "She's never met you, and it will be dark but for the moonlight. With the hours you keep, it's unlikely you'll meet her again anytime soon. Besides," she added, smiling, "if she ever discovers it, I'll tell her you needed no persuading. In fact, you leapt at the chance. It wouldn't be hard to believe, would it?"

"Naturally," Nate said. There was a flash of something in his eyes, something raw and hurt. He moved away from her.

Belatedly, a pang of guilt struck at her heart for using her brother so, but there was no one else she could ask.

"I just want her to be happy, Nate. That's all."

There was more emotion in the words than she'd meant to show. For all her thoughts of blackmailing him, she didn't mean to burden him with her unhappiness. Indeed, she took great efforts in appearing happy and vivacious, everything she'd always been before… before her father, her brother, and the Marquess of Montagu had stolen her future from her.

"I know, Tilda," Nate said, turning to look at her, his mouth quirking a little in a crooked smile. "Fine," he said with a sigh, clearly unhappy, but resigned at least. "Your Alice will have her kiss in the moonlight, you have my word, but you'd better keep a sharp eye out, for I'll not get leg shackled. Not even for you."

Matilda held her tongue, knowing he'd never ruin Alice like she'd been ruined, no matter how he despised the idea. Instead she let out a breath of laughter and nodded her agreement.

"Fair enough." She went to him and kissed his cheek. "Very best of brothers."

Nate gave a bark of laughter at that.

"Too much?" she asked, smirking a little.

"Far, *far* too much," he agreed.

Chapter 3

I have seen your brother, Matilda. If Alice finds herself indisposed, I might be persuaded to take her place. What a handsome rogue he is. If anyone's kiss could change a woman's life, I'd wager his could.

—Excerpt of a letter from Senorita Lucia de Feria to Miss Matilda Hunt.

The evening of the 13th June 1814. Half Moon Street, Mayfair, London.

Nate watched as his sister left the room, and sighed. Would it always be like this? Would he never be free of the guilt?

No.

A stupid question, in any case. He didn't deserve to be free of it. He never would.

Nate rubbed his eyes, dry and gritty from too little sleep and the smoky atmosphere of the club. Regret lay heavy upon him for so many reasons. He dropped back into the elegantly upholstered chair by the fireplace, and his thoughts returned to that fateful night. The night his father had lain dying.

Hunt Senior had taken to his bed and slowly but steadily declined, the doctor diagnosing pneumonia. During his illness, his father confessed to having run up something of a debt. Totally in the dark as to his spendthrift ways, Nate had cheerfully bade the old man not to worry, he'd sort things out. What a bloody laugh.

Soon enough it became clear that their father had not run up *something of a debt,* he'd ruined them. Sums the like of which Nate could hardly conceive of were owing left, right, and centre, with bailiffs hammering on the door at all hours of the day and night. They'd had to sell everything. All the land, the property— that which wasn't already mortgaged to the hilt—artwork, furniture, and even every piece of jewellery that mother had left Matilda. When all was said and done, they barely had the clothes on their back to call their own.

Added to that, their feckless parent didn't even have the decency to make a clean break but lingered on for weeks, adding doctor's bills to their endless list of debts.

Furious and sick at heart, terrified of what would become of them, Nate had gone out to drown his sorrows.

Feeling like doing much the same now, Nate got up and refilled his glass, moving to stand by the window that Matilda had left open. He leaned against it, resting his forehead on the cool glass and enjoying the breeze that ruffled his hair as he stared down at the darkening street.

Matilda had come to fetch him that night. His father was dying at last, and had been asking for him, wanting to beg his forgiveness. The servants had all gone by then, save a maid who came in for a few hours during the day. At that hour of the night, though, his sister had been alone, playing nursemaid to a dying man. The old devil had been selfish to the last, begging her to fetch Nate so pitifully that she went out into the night. Alone.

Matilda had taken it upon herself to come to the men's drinking club of which Nate had always been a member. He, at least, had no debts and his membership had been paid in full until the end of the year. He'd had every intention of remaining there until they kicked him out at midnight on the thirty-first of December.

Somehow, and Nate still didn't know how she'd done it, Matilda had begged the proprietor to let her in, and he'd shown her to a private room to wait, while they tracked Nate down.

Except the room had been neither as empty nor as private as they'd supposed.

Nate groaned. He regretted so much about that night. He regretted the fact he'd refused to go to her, once her message had been relayed. He'd hated his bloody father by that point, and he was damned if he'd give him leave to rest in peace when the bastard had condemned both his children to live in penury. He regretted that too. His father had been a fool and a spendthrift, but Nate had loved him, and he regretted never having told the old devil as much.

Too late now. Far, far too late.

So, now he tried to make amends. Matilda had lost her father and her future the very same night, and whilst his father's sins were not his, he might have saved her reputation. If only he'd not gone out that night, if only he'd gone to her at once... if only the Marquess of Montagu wasn't such a cold bastard, and far too powerful to touch.

Instead, Nate lavished his sister with every luxury she could possibly want, anything to ease the guilt at having stolen her future from her. She ought to have made a grand match by now, beauty that she was. She ought to be happily married with children at her feet, the only thing Matilda had ever really wanted.

Instead he'd condemned her to a life where she would never catch the eye of a respectable man, not as a wife at least. She never told him how many men had made indecent proposals, but he knew they did. Still, she faced them down. Wherever possible, she went out and mingled with those who shunned her, holding her head high, daring them to say it to her face. God, but he admired her courage, even as it broke his heart.

So, now she'd have him play besotted fool to her mousy friend, a creature too timid to find a man by herself. Well, if it was what Tilda wanted, he could hardly refuse. He just hoped to God the girl wasn't too insipid; he'd never been much of an actor.

With a grimace, Nate shook his head, and finished his drink.

**

14th June 1814. The Ransoms' Ball. London.

Alice clutched at the glass of ratafia in her hand, so tightly it was a wonder she didn't shatter it, though dropping it was more likely, given the way her palms were sweating. Less dramatic perhaps, but just as embarrassing and far more in character.

"Do stop fretting, Alice," Matilda said, low enough that only she could hear. "There's nothing to be worried about. It will be marvellous."

"Who is he?" Alice asked, finally getting up the courage to ask the question that had been plaguing her ever since she'd agreed to this madness. Whether or not she had the courage to hear the answer was another matter. Running from the room, from the building, and possibly from London seemed a far more appealing prospect.

Where could she go and hide? Grimsby, perhaps? She'd never been there but it sounded grim and awful, the kind of place that could swallow up a wallflower, so she'd never be seen again. Alice felt a rush of fondness for it.

She was losing her mind.

"Someone I trust," Matilda said, her blue eyes full of reassurance. "A good man, and a handsome one too. Just don't fall in love with him," she added, a teasing note to her voice.

Alice gaped at Matilda in astonishment.

"I'm more worried about stammering, fainting or possibly throwing myself off the balcony, though all three are a distinct possibility," she muttered. Of all the idiotic, hare-brained schemes—"

"Hello, Alice, Matilda."

Both women looked around as Kitty Connolly greeted them. She was a pretty girl with thick dark hair and laughing eyes and had gained a place among the ranks of the Peculiar Ladies by simple virtue of being Irish. No amount of dowry and beauty could make up for such a crime in the eyes of the *ton.*

"Is it true you're going to complete your dare tonight?" Kitty asked, clutching at Alice's arm.

"W-Well—" Alice stammered, wondering if this might be the time to talk her way out of it.

"Yes," Matilda cut in, giving her a stern look. "Yes, it is."

"How exciting!" Kitty exclaimed. "Tell me everything, who is...?"

She trailed off, eyes growing wide as they focused on something, or someone, across the ballroom. Alice thought she caught a flash of red hair in the crowd.

"Kitty?" Matilda asked as the colour drained from Kitty's face, only to be replaced by a bright flush across her cheeks. "Are you quite well?"

"I-I," Kitty stammered, breathing hard. "I thought I saw someone... I...."

Without another word, she took off, careering across the ballroom, knocking into people left and right, heedless of their exclamations and curses.

"Whatever was that about?" Alice asked as they stared after her.

"I have no idea and, really, who knows with Kitty?" Matilda added, shaking her head. "Of all our number, I feel I know her the least."

Alice nodded, frowning at the dark-haired girl as the crowds swallowed her up. Kitty was something of an enigma, but one thing Alice did know about her was that she was brave. To Alice, she seemed utterly fearless. No doubt she wouldn't think twice about meeting a strange man on a balcony. Alice, by contrast... thinking was the *only* thing she'd done, the only thing she'd ever do, as she simply couldn't go through with it.

"Matilda," she said, spurred on by anxiety and desperation. "I can't... I just—"

Matilda pressed a finger to her lips and shook her head. "Come along, Alice. I think we need to have a chat."

Propelled by a stronger force of will than her own—as usual—Alice hurried off in Matilda's wake as her friend sought a quiet corner. They found it in the form of a long picture gallery. Lamps illuminated the grand corridor and the spaces between paintings were studded with shadowy alcoves. Within these were displayed other works of art, such as vases and statuary.

"Oh, look at this one," Alice exclaimed, moving into an alcove to inspect a stunning Chinese vase. Anything to put off the inevitable.

Matilda lingered in the corridor, her gaze focused on a painting that Alice had instinctively avoided as it depicted a nude Venus in a reclining pose. From the fleeting glance Alice had cast it, she'd seen a beautiful woman, staring at herself in a mirror, making her as much a voyeur as the audience regarding her.

Alice turned away from the vase and back to Matilda, who was staring with rapt attention at the painting. In that moment Alice believed that Matilda, not Venus, was the loveliest work of art in the room. Her blonde hair, artfully arranged in loose curls, framed a face any painter would die to capture. A mouth as lush and soft and pink as any ever set to canvas was parted a little, her blue eyes captivated, shining with... with what? Alice wasn't sure, only aware that she ought not to intrude. She moved back into the alcove and then jolted as a man's voice broke the almost reverential silence.

"Alone, Miss Hunt? And regarding such a scandalous painting. Is that wise?"

Matilda's posture stiffened at once, her gaze flying to Alice's. Alice moved forward from her hidden spot in the alcove, to show the man Matilda was not, in fact, alone, but Matilda shook her head. It was a tiny movement, barely perceptible but Alice stilled, perplexed. Matilda's blue eyes held hers for a moment, as if confirming she should stay put, and then she turned, slowly.

Head back, shoulders squared, she stood as proudly as a queen to face whoever had spoken to her.

Alice's gaze fastened on the reflection of a shadowy figure in a glass fronted case on the other side of the gallery, and her breath caught. The figure was indistinct, but the man was still unmistakable. The Marquess of Montagu. The man who'd ruined Matilda with nothing more than his presence.

Matilda stared at him, her gaze icy with loathing. She did not curtsey as she ought in the presence of such a high-ranking man, neither did she acknowledge him.

"Of all the things you took from me, you have given me the freedom to act as I please. I need no permission from anyone, least of all you. You've already taken my reputation. I have little else to lose."

There was a pause, then he spoke again, his voice every bit as cold as Matilda's expression.

"I'm not sure that's true."

Alice could only see Matilda's face in profile from her hiding place, but she saw her friend arch one elegant eyebrow, a derisive quirk touching her lips.

"Oh, you're sure it isn't true," Matilda said in disgust. "You know nothing happened between us that night. Thanks to you, everyone else in the world believes it did, so what does it matter? You've ruined my life, and if you think I'll thank you for observations as to how I live it in the light of that fact, you are very much mistaken."

"I did nothing of the sort," the marquess replied, sounding bored, at best. "I did not invite you into that room and, as you said yourself, I did not lay a hand on you. You were there by your own volition."

"My father was dying. I was searching for my brother. It was my father's dying wish to speak with him one last time," Matilda shot back, the words bitten off, laced with fury.

"So, you left a dying man alone, instead of sending a servant?"

Alice gasped at the cruelty of that statement and saw Matilda flinch, just a little.

"We could not afford servants at that point, as I'm sure you're aware. My father had gambled away our inheritance and left nothing but debt. That's why he wanted to see my brother, to beg his forgiveness."

Even in the glass, Alice could make out the sneer of contempt, though she could hear it even more clearly in the marquess' voice.

"Ah yes, convenient of him. Who can refuse the wishes of a dying man? Even one who has condemned his family to destitution? So, as an act of contrition, he sends his daughter out into the night, alone. What a saint."

Matilda gasped at that, one hand flying to her throat.

"You're a cold-hearted, wicked bastard," she said, as Alice covered her mouth with her hand to muffle her own intake of breath.

How Matilda had the courage to face this loathsome creature down—and swear with such ease—Alice could not fathom, but she'd never been prouder.

The marquess greeted Matilda's words with nothing but a snort of amusement.

"*Not* a bastard," he drawled, sounding almost apologetic. "I'll own the rest of it, though. However, I'm still a better man than your father."

"How dare you—" Matilda began, but the shadowy figure in the reflection raised his hand to silence her.

"My family—my name, their inheritance—that is everything," he said, and the stunning arrogance behind his words was only diminished because Alice knew they were true. "Montagu is one of the oldest and most powerful names in the land. Everything I do is for the family good. I'd never bring shame or disrespect down upon us. Certainly not by marrying some nameless, penniless chit who has the temerity to visit a men's club in the early hours of the morning, just because she's witless enough to enter a room I'm already inhabiting."

"I never asked for that," Matilda flung back at him. "My God, I'd rather the position I'm in now a thousand times over than find myself married to a man more dead than alive."

There was a spectacular silence and Alice felt all the tiny hairs over her body raise as the atmosphere prickled with tension.

"What, then?" he said, and for the first time that ice cold demeanour seemed just a little shaken, a subtle thread of irritation discernible in his question.

"You could have helped me," Matilda said, the fury in her voice hot enough to singe every painting in the room, and even blistering enough to melt a little of the marquess' *froideur* and expose a glimmer of white-hot anger. "You could have silenced those men, refuted what had happened. If you're as powerful as you believe, you could at least have stood up for me, mitigated my shame, but you did not. You stood back and did nothing, said *nothing.* Someday, you'll pay for that. I'll make sure of it."

"How naïve you are," he said, that cold, disdainful voice making Alice's skin crawl. "If I'd done any of the things you suggest it would have been far worse for you. It would have indicated I cared. It would have suggested a sense of guilt, of duty. Now, at least, you have some who believe the truth of you. If I'd have given any such defence—as you pretend you wanted me to—they'd have been certain we were lovers."

"I doubt it," Matilda spat back at him. "I doubt anyone believes you capable of such a physical human act. I could believe you pay your mistresses to tell tales of your prowess for there's nothing in you that could actually ever feel *anything.* Are you frigid, my lord?" she asked, a deliberately mocking tone to the question. "I wouldn't have a problem believing it. Touching another must disgust you. After all, you might have to show a little emotion. All those stories about you, about your lovers and your skill…." Matilda made a disparaging sound. "I don't believe them."

"Oh, you believe them," he said, the words barely audible as he took one step closer and then paused. "And you're lying to yourself and me with this martyr act. If I'd offered for you that night, you'd have accepted without a second thought. I saw the look in your eyes when you discovered us alone together, dying father or no, and it wasn't fear or loathing."

"My God," Matilda whispered, breathing hard as she stared at him. "I don't believe a more despicable man ever walked this earth. I wish you joy of your name and your power and your fortune, but I know you'll never find it. Does every bite of food taste like ash? Does every day stretching out before you fill an endless landscape devoid of colour or hope?" Alice watched as Matilda stared at him and then nodded. "It does, doesn't it?" she said, the words surprised, as if a revelation had been given her. "I've changed my mind. I don't despise you. I pity you, and, for your information. I'm not alone. I have friends. Lots of them, and one of them is right here."

Matilda turned to Alice and gave her a warm smile. Her eyes were bright, her cheeks flushed from her confrontation, but she seemed calm now, serene. She held her hand out to Alice.

"Come along, dear," she said, almost grinning. "We'll find somewhere else for our little chat. The marquess wishes to be alone." Matilda looked back at him and Alice followed her gaze. "I'd like to grant him that wish," Matilda continued. "I suspect it's one he'll live with all his life."

With all the dignity and bearing of an empress, Matilda turned her back on the marquess and strode away.

Alice glanced back once more, at a man with a face that might have been chiselled from granite for all the warmth it held. He was tall and lean, broad shouldered, grey eyed, and utterly cold. Alice shivered and turned away, hurrying after Matilda and out of his toxic presence.

Chapter 4

Alice! I heard a rumour you're to complete your dare at the Ransom ball. I'm so cross I couldn't come. Did you do it? Was it dreadfully romantic? Tell me everything!

—Excerpt of a letter from Miss Bonnie Campbell to Miss Alice Dowding.

14th June 1814. The Ransoms' Ball, London.

Once they were out of sight of the marquess, Matilda hitched her skirts and ran, leaving Alice to scurry in her wake. They found a quiet room, the furniture ghostly with Holland covers, and Matilda closed the door behind them. She leant on it, her hands flat against the wood, and breathed hard. Then, to Alice's astonishment, she burst into tears.

Her shoulders shook and she trembled all over, clutching her arms about her chest as if she'd never be warm again.

"Matilda!" Alice exclaimed, hurrying to her. Putting her arms about her, she guided her to a shrouded armchair and sat her down. Kneeling before her, Alice took her hands, chafing each one to bring warmth back to her as they felt like ice.

"Matilda Hunt," Alice said, her voice stern and full of fierce pride in her friend. "That was, without a doubt, the most magnificent, impressive, glorious thing I've ever had the privilege to witness."

Matilda gave a little hiccoughing laugh and attempted to wipe her eyes on her sleeve.

"Here," Alice said, taking a handkerchief from her pocket.

"Thank you," Matilda said, her voice thick. "I'm not sure I feel very magnificent. I feel small and stupid and frightened. My God, Alice, he's a marquess. What if he retaliates? Whatever was I thinking?"

"You weren't thinking, you reacted," Alice said, staring at her in wonder. "I never react, Tilda. I only ever think. I think and think and think about all the things I want to say, the things I want to do, and I never actually do or say, *anything*." She squeezed Matilda's hands, staring up at her. "He deserved it. He deserved everything you said to him, the odious, appalling man, and I was never prouder. Heavens, when you said you'd rather be in the position you are a thousand times over than marry a man more dead than alive… did you see his face? It was like you'd struck him."

Matilda nodded, blinking back tears. "I saw," she whispered.

"Weren't you frightened?" Alice asked, so envious of Matilda's courage she was desperate to emulate it, to know her secret.

"Terrified," Matilda admitted with a wan smile. "I thought I might be sick at any moment. You'll never know how hard it was to stand there and face him. I wanted to run away, I wanted to cry, but I was damned if I'd let him see that. He's ruined me enough. I'd not give him the satisfaction."

Alice stared at her, stunned and intrigued. "Truly?"

"Truly."

She could see the truth in Matilda's face. Now they were alone, her eyes were shining with fear and misery, but she hadn't shown it to the marquess. Somehow, she'd forced those feelings down, out of sight, and gathered her courage. Could Alice do that? In some small way, could she push her fears somewhere out of sight? At least for a little while?

"What time am I supposed to be on that balcony?" Alice asked, her voice wavering only a little.

Matilda turned to her and smiled, wiping her eyes on the handkerchief Alice had given her.

"Midnight, of course."

"Of course," Alice repeated. "Well, then. Come along, Empress Matilda. You need to guide me to my illicit rendezvous."

Matilda snorted. "Empress?"

Tugging her friend to her feet, Alice nodded. "That's what you looked like, facing the marquess. You looked like an empress and, believe me when I tell you, he saw it too."

Matilda gave a mirthless laugh. "No, dear Alice. The marquess looks at me and sees something far beneath his notice, something to be ground beneath his heel because I'm unimportant to him. I'm worthless to a man like him, I can assure you of that."

Alice shook her head and grasped her friend's hand. "You're worth a thousand of him, Tilda. It's probably why he's so hateful. He knows it too."

***

"Through that door, Alice." Matilda gestured to a shadowy room that lay beyond the half-open door. Gauzy curtains billowed on the warm breeze, the rippling fabric beckoning her forward. "You'll find the glass doors open out onto a balcony overlooking the side of the house. No one in the gardens can see you because of the trees. I'll go to the end of the corridor. I can see the stairs from there, so if anyone comes up, I'll have plenty of notice."

Alice nodded... at least, she thought she did. Her body seemed rather numb, a little slow in obeying commands. As she moved, one foot in front of the other, her limbs felt awkward and heavy, as though she'd forgotten how. Her heart appeared to be shaking her ribs, rattling her bones like a monkey fighting to escape the bars of his cage.

Deep breaths. Deep breaths. Don't forget to breathe, Alice, she instructed as she slid past the open door and closed it behind her. Was he already here? Was he waiting? Who was he, this nameless, faceless man who was to be her first kiss?

When she'd been younger, Alice had imagined her first kiss. It had always been sweet and romantic, rather chaste really. This could be nothing like that. How was there any romance in meeting a man she'd never even seen before and giving him her first kiss? There wasn't, she knew that, and she regretted it, but that wasn't the point. Not anymore.

Alice would never know what romance was if she didn't stop hiding. If she didn't learn to show her face, her heart, and her soul to another, how could anyone ever fall in love with it?

Matilda had done it. She'd shown the depth of her character by facing a man that frightened her and holding her own. In a small way, for Alice, that was what this was. An exercise in courage, nothing more. A foolish but daring act to bolster a weak-willed creature too ready to allow the world to buffet her back and forth as it desired.

No more.

No. More.

She walked onto the balcony and let out a breath of relief to discover she was alone. A momentary reprieve, at least. It was a lovely night, with a hint of warmth still to the breeze that fluttered her skirts and cooled her burning cheeks.

Alice put her hands to the railings, curling her fingers about the painted iron. She closed her eyes and drew in a deep, deep breath, steadying her heart. *Breathe, Alice.* Slow and steady she drew the night air into her lungs, letting go of each exhalation until she felt languid and a little dizzy.

Something changed and Alice stilled. She'd not heard a sound—there had been nothing to give him away—but he was there, behind her. Alice could feel his presence, feel the weight of it in the air.

"Hello," she said, a little surprised to discover her voice steady. All that breathing had done something to her: she felt giddy with it, lightheaded and almost tipsy.

"Hello."

Shivers chased over her skin at the sound of his voice. It was deep and warm, and she wondered how he could make that simple word sound so seductive, or perhaps she was doing that? Perhaps it had been the same sound she'd heard a thousand times before, but here, beneath the moonlight, alone on a balcony, she heard it differently.

Alice moved, about to turn and face him.

"Wait," he said, as she stilled at once. "Don't turn around."

"Are you scared to look? I'm not as unappealing as all that," Alice said, startling herself with the clipped tone of her voice. Good heavens! Where had that come from? She panicked at once, about to apologise. Of course he might think she was unattractive. She was nothing special compared to Matilda, but—

He chuckled, the sound wrapping about her, sliding over her skin like a caress.

"I can see that much from here," he said, the reassurance soothing her. "That's not why I asked."

Alice wanted to ask why he'd asked, but her last outburst was still ringing in her ears, her nerves all a jitter.

"Don't you want to know why?" he said, reading her mind.

Oh, good Lord, that voice. She'd never heard a voice like that. It had a power all its own, like a fairy tale where the victim was lulled and bespelled, beguiled with words and charm. He was smiling, she knew it; she could hear the warmth of it within the words, hear the curve of his lips. With alarm, Alice discovered she was trembling, though her anxiety only grew as she realised it wasn't from fear. Not even a little bit.

"Why?" she forced the word out, determined to know.

"Because it's exciting, that you don't know who I am." The words were breathed rather than spoken, a soft susurration at the nape of her neck, standing all the tiny hairs on end. "You have no idea if we're acquainted, or if I'm a stranger."

"Oh, you're a stranger," she said with a huff of laughter, her words not nearly as steady as before.

"Oh?"

He moved closer, not that she saw him, not that he touched her, but she could feel him all the same, feel the heat of him at her back. It burned through her dress, warming her. The flush of it bloomed over her skin. "How can you be certain?"

Alice almost rolled her eyes. "Because I don't know any men like you."

That chuckle again, shivering over her skin, doing odd things to her already erratic heartbeat.

"We're here to complete a dare." He spoke close to her ear, softly, yet in the heightened atmosphere it felt as dramatic as if he'd put his hands on her.

Alice nodded. The dizzy sensation had returned, and she felt lightheaded with it. Was this how it felt to be inebriated: a dreamlike sense of unreality, the desire to take a foolish risk? To do something one would never normally do.

"I didn't hear your answer."

Mortified, she realised he would not allow her to hide behind passivity and nods of acknowledgement. Well, she'd wanted to prove her own courage.

"Yes," she said, wishing it had sounded a little less anxious but relieved it had been audible at least.

There was a low sound of approval and he shifted a little closer. "Tell me what it was. Tell me what dare you accepted."

Drat. He just had to ask.

"You know what it is," she said with more defiance than she'd thought she had, but rather that than say it out loud.

"I do," he agreed, sounding a little smug and pleased, though not in an unpleasant way, gently teasing her. "But I want to be certain you do. I need to be sure I keep my end of the bargain." His words were so intimate, suggestive in a manner that made anxiety and excitement shiver together. "I should hate to disappoint you."

Alice clutched at the railing in front of her a little harder. Why did his words sound so... so...? She didn't have a name for it, but she felt it in her toes, in the strange heat that seemed to unfurl deep in her belly with every word he spoke.

"Do you make a habit of disappointing women?" she asked lightly, trying to sound sophisticated, and then blushed scarlet as she realised that might not have been the kind of question she ought to ask.

"No," he said, with just a trace of arrogant amusement. "Which is why you'll tell me what the dare was, so I can be certain to complete it with the proper degree of diligence."

Alice's mouth fell open. It was the hardest thing not to turn and stare at him, but her cheeks were flaming now... and perhaps it was best to keep staring at the moon. The great white orb shone down on them, pristine and unblinking, unsurprised and certainly not shocked. Nothing Alice could do would shock it; the moon had seen it all before and still stared down, unchanged. Somehow that was comforting.

"To kiss a man in the moonlight," she said in a rush, the words tumbling out, each one tripping over the next.

"Ah, yes," he said, and she felt rather than saw his nod of agreement. "Well, then, you have the moonlight, and the man. What will you do with them?"

"*Me?*" Alice squeaked.

She almost turned around then, but stilled as his arms bracketed her, his large hands dwarfing hers as they grasped the railings on either side. Yet, still he didn't touch her, keeping a distance between them which was at once a relief and desperately frustrating.

"Who else is here, if not you?"

"You!" she exclaimed, rattled now. "You're here, that's the whole point."

"Ah, but it isn't. The dare is to *kiss a man* in the moonlight. Not... *be kissed*. This is all on you, Alice."

Alice's breathing hitched, but she wasn't sure if it was the realisation he was right or the sound of her name spoken by that wicked voice. What kind of man had a voice like that? It conjured up dark nights, and sin, and... and things she had absolutely no idea about, past the urgent desire to find out.

"Are you sure it's what you want?" he asked, gentler now, that caressing voice soothing her prickling nerves. "I can leave if it isn't."

"Is that what *you* want?" she blurted out, the sudden realisation that he might pray for her to give him a way out made her stomach twist with humiliation.

"Good God, no."

The reply was immediate, so much so that she couldn't help but believe it. Her heart sped up, which was a surprise; she'd not believed anything more could be expected of it. Perhaps it would give out altogether.

Please not before the kiss.

"I… I don't know if—"

"If you're brave enough?" he guessed.

Alice nodded, still staring at the moon. Would she still be able to see it for days to come? The dazzling light was already imprinted on her sight forever as a memory of this night.

"You're brave enough," he said, the words certain, certain of her though she had no idea why. Surely he knew why she needed this. "You're here, aren't you?"

The words were warm and reassuring, calming her.

"But… but I've never—"

"I know." He didn't mock her; there was no teasing tone as she might have expected. "Shall I help you?"

She nodded again and then scolded herself for it. "Yes," she said, forcing herself to sound decisive, to *be* decisive. "Yes, please."

"May I touch you?"

All the breath left her lungs in a rush.

"I won't unless you give me leave," he said. "And I'll stop the instant you ask me to."

Suddenly it was unbearable, having this wicked, beguiling man so close and yet not close enough.

"Yes," she repeated breathlessly. "Yes."

Once again for good measure, just in case he hadn't heard the first time.

Alice stilled, unsure of what to expect, and then jolted as the thumb of his right hand moved. Though his fist didn't shift from its position beside hers on the railing, his thumb stroked the back of her hand.

Alice thought her knees might buckle.

Good heavens. Don't be foolish, woman! He touched you with his thumb.

Just his thumb!

A bubble of hysterical laughter threatened to escape her, but then he moved closer and she felt his back press against hers as he leaned in and nuzzled at her ear.

"You smell like barley sugar," he murmured, as shivers erupted over her at the touch of his skin against hers.

"I've got some in my pocket," she said, and she could only blame her addled brain for saying something so bird-witted at such a moment.

"You do?" he asked, and she could hear the surprised laughter in his voice.

Alice closed her eyes and wished they were in the garden. Perhaps then she could dig a hole and bury herself in it.

"It's impossible to get a drink at affairs like this," she said, a touch defiantly. "Especially when you're my size. I get trampled in the rush. So I always bring some barley sugar, just in case. It's better than nothing...."

She trailed off, humiliation burning at her throat and cheeks, then gasped as he nipped at her earlobe.

"I disagree," he said, sounding perfectly serious. "I think it's better than anything. So... so sweet. I should like to taste it too."

For a moment, for a bare, heart-stopping moment she almost offered him a blasted sweet, and then her stomach did an odd little flip as she understood his words.

Gosh.

"Y-You would?"

His hands left the railing and covered hers, so warm, his touch sending heat coursing over her. She watched, mesmerised as they slid up her arms. Alice closed her eyes as they continued back down, but along a new path as they followed the contours of her ribcage, settling on her waist.

"Turn around, Alice."

Chapter 5

If only life could be like the stories you write, Prue. If only I could ask you to write a husband for me. Created to order. I would ask you for a man who was strong and kind and never treated me like a child.

A man with a devilish smile.

A man who was just the right amount of wicked.

—Excerpt of a letter from Miss Alice Dowding to Prunella Adolphus. Duchess of Bedwin.

Midnight. A moonlit balcony. 14th June 1814. The Ransoms' Ball, London.

Alice's breath caught in her throat, but she could no more have not turned around than she could have found the will to move away. She was alive with sensation, with anticipation. His hands remained in place as she turned within them, tightening a little as she faced him at last.

The moon cast his face into silver, and dark shadow, and Alice gasped.

Oh, thank you, thank you, Matilda.

He was… gorgeous.

It was hard to tell, but she thought his hair was blonde, certainly a light shade, glinting in the moonlight.

"Hello, Alice."

Alice shivered and a smile tugged at his mouth. It was a lovely mouth, with a full lower lip and a surprisingly feminine cupid's bow. It was the only soft thing about him. A square chin and firm jaw hinted at a stubborn nature, and his eyes... his eyes. Alice sighed. She couldn't help it. They glittered under the moon, dark and mysterious and full of promise. Yet she could not see what colour they were. She longed to know.

One of those big hands that had held her waist moved now, and he reached out, tugging at one of the loose curls that framed her face. It had been Matilda's idea. She said the severe style with tight little ringlets made Alice look like a child. Alice could believe it; that was how most people treated her.

She wasn't a child, though. She was two–and-twenty and soon to be married. Whether it was to be to the odious Mr Bindley or another man, a man of her choosing, a man like—

"Well, Alice? It's your move."

Alice blinked, shaken from her reverie by those words. Did he really expect *her* to kiss *him?* Judging by the sparkle of amusement in his eyes, he did.

"C-Couldn't you kiss me first?" she asked, hardly able to force the words out as she was breathing so hard. Here she was, Alice Dowding, alone on a balcony in the moonlight, with a strange man, begging to be kissed. The world had turned on its head, or perhaps she'd been dropped on hers. That might account for it. "Just to get used to the idea," she added hopefully. "*Then* I'll kiss you, b-but you go first."

He shook his head, a slow back and forth as his smile widened.

Alice sighed.

"That's not very gallant," she said with a little huff. "Are you sure you even want to kiss me?"

There was rather too much of a quaver in the question; her vulnerability was showing.

He touched her cheek with the back of his hand, so tenderly it made her heart ache with longing. If only he meant it. If only he wasn't just being kind to a timid wallflower.

"I'll kiss you back," he promised, with such a tenor to the vow her knees wobbled a little. She reached out and clutched at his lapels to keep herself upright. His grasp on her waist grew firmer and he tugged her closer, causing the air to rush from her lungs. "I'm looking forward to it," he added, that tempting mouth quirking a little. "More than you can imagine, but I can't if you don't kiss me first."

Drat it.

"I won't tell," Alice squeaked, and he laughed, a lovely, genuine sound that made her smile in response. "And surely you're too much of a gentleman to tattle on me?" she added, wanting to hear him do it again.

He did.

She'd made him laugh. She'd never made a man laugh before, at least not like that. He hadn't been laughing at her; she'd just amused him.

There had been plenty of times she'd been laughed at in her life, plenty of times men had chucked her under the chin or patted her head and laughed at the audacity of the little girl before them, pretending to be a grown up.

God, she was tired of being that little girl. She wanted to claim the woman inside her, the one fighting to get out.

Well, that's why you're here, Alice. Get on with it!

With a sudden rush of determination, she lifted her hands to his face, tugging his head down, and pressed her lips to his.

For a moment he seemed a little startled and he froze, stilling under the sudden advance. Alice wished he'd snap out of it, as she had the creeping suspicion there was more to kissing than pressing one mouth against another. She urgently needed a little guidance. Yet she was afraid, if she removed her lips from his, he might not keep his promise to kiss her back. She couldn't stand here all night with her lips glued to his. Not that it was unpleasant, but….

One hand framed her face, his palm, warm against her cheek as he drew back a little.

Oh.

Disappointment crashed through her. Except, barely a moment later, his lips returned, pressing against hers, softer than she'd done it. They retreated once more and brushed against hers again, and Alice sighed.

His hand slid from her face, cupping her neck whilst the other slid over her back, pulling her closer as his mouth continued the delicate press and brush of lips.

Alice shivered with pleasure and sighed again, and this time she felt the warmth of his tongue trace the opening of her parted mouth. He touched it to her upper lip and then nipped at the lower, making her gasp and shiver again, and his tongue dipped further into her mouth. This was not what she'd expected at all, but… but she wasn't complaining.

She'd wanted to feel confident after this; she'd wanted tonight to change her, to change her life, so she could live it instead of having others manage it for her. In this moment she was alive, more alive and aware than she'd ever been before. Why this man was here, she didn't know. What Matilda had done to get him here, she had no idea. She didn't want to know, but surely, *surely*, he couldn't kiss her like this if he found her completely unattractive.

He let out a low sound, akin to a growl, and Alice's breath caught as her heart skipped. That was for her. She'd drawn that sound from him. Emboldened, she slid one hand into his hair, and the next time that teasing tongue attempted to beguile her into opening further, she complied. Alice pressed her body closer, feeling dizzy as the kiss deepened. She slid her hand beneath his coat, wishing she could feel his skin beneath her fingertips instead of the warm silk of his waistcoat. Beneath that, however, she could feel the contours of a powerful body, the shift of muscles as his hand slid up and down her back.

Abruptly, he paused. She felt bereft.

"Don't stop."

The words were out before she could even think about them and his eyes widened with delight, a flash of a crooked grin making her heart skip.

"I wasn't about to. But I'm breaking my neck and I need you closer."

Alice frowned. It was true he was having to bend a great deal to reach her mouth. What did he intend to do about it, though? She watched, a little perplexed, as he moved away from her. On the far side of the balcony was a table and two chairs, and an elegant wrought iron footstool with a cushion atop. He cast the cushion aside and returned to her, his hands grasping her waist and lifting her as if she weighed nothing at all, and he proceeded to set her down to stand upon the stool.

"There," he said, sounding smug. "Much better."

It was, she realised, now that their faces were level.

"Do it again, Alice," he said, a challenge in his voice she couldn't mistake. "You've got your man in the moonlight. Make good use of him."

Your man.

The words rocked through her. He didn't mean them that way, of course. She wasn't a complete ninny. She knew that wasn't what he'd meant, but still, for now, for this moment, he was *hers*.

Alice stared at him.

You'll never get another chance, Alice, she told herself. *There will never be another night like this as long as you live. For heaven's sake—live this one to the full.*

With trembling hands, Alice reached out and touched his face, tracing the strong line of his jaw, the curve of his lower lip. He watched her, unmoving, his eyes intent as she catalogued all the elements that made up this handsome, intriguing man.

"Now with your lips," he said.

Alice's breath caught as desire lit something inside of her. *Yes,* she thought, yes, she wanted that. That and so much more.

She leaned in, trembling, though she was certain it was with excitement now, and with the need to do as he'd asked her. Tenderly she kissed his cheek, his jaw, and the corner of his mouth. She'd intended to creep up on that mouth, slowly, a little bit at a time as she gained confidence, but he turned his head, unwilling to wait and this time, when their mouths met, it was… stunning.

Whatever flame he'd lit before erupted now, in an inferno that blazed out of control. Alice sighed against him, her lips opening to him as he pulled her closer. She went, more than willing, pressing against him, revelling in his warmth, his heat, the sheer masculine weight and size of him against her small frame. He illustrated that masculinity all too clearly as one hand slid over her bottom, squeezing a little as he pressed her against him.

Innocent she might be, but Alice had friends who were better informed than she, and she never failed to make use of that. Prue, widely read and far bolder than Alice, had revealed a deal of information about the curiosities of the male form. Alice's ideas on exactly how things proceeded were a little hazy, but one thing she knew was that when a man was ready to… to… procreate, a particular part of him changed, lengthening and hardening.

The decidedly male body so intimately twined with hers was undoubtedly aroused, hard and impossible to misinterpret, pressed as it was against her softness. Intrigued, she pressed a little closer and he made a sound that reverberated through her, something akin to a growl, low and primitive and wildly exciting.

She'd done that, Alice thought, with a little surge of triumph.

At that moment he broke the kiss, staggering back a little, breathing hard.

"We need to stop," he said, his voice rough. "This wasn't what you wanted, what you needed. It was only supposed to be a kiss, nothing more. You've fulfilled your dare."

No. Oh, no, not yet, and who the devil was he, telling her what she wanted? Indignation and frustration rose in her chest. A lifetime of being told what it was she wanted and needed bubbled up and forced itself past any fears she had. It trampled down good sense, self-preservation and, God help her, any pretence at modesty.

"This *is* what I want, and what I need," she said, reaching for him. "And I don't want to stop." She grasped his lapel in one hand and put her hand to his neck with the other, tugging him closer, kissing him as she tangled her hand in his hair. He groaned and then his hands were on her again, one sliding up to cup her breast and squeeze.

"Oh, God," he murmured, kissing a path down her neck as Alice moaned and tilted her head back to allow him better access. "Oh, Alice, you're so sweet. I had no idea. I want... I want—"

"Tell me what you want," she breathed, knowing she'd give it to him, this nameless man who'd brought her such joy, such pleasure.

"Nate?"

He jolted away from her like he'd been struck as Matilda's voice whispered through the darkness. It was far away, perhaps from the doorway of the room they'd walked through to get to the balcony.

"Alice?" The soft voice sounded again, breaking the spell.

"Christ," he said, staggering back and staring at Alice in shock. His breath was ragged and he ran a hand through his hair, his eyes never leaving hers. He looked a little discomposed. "I... I must go," he rasped, sounding deeply unhappy about it.

Alice frowned with displeasure and frustration but knew he was right. Her little adventure was over, never to be repeated, but... oh, what an adventure it had been.

"Oh," she said, dejected and sighing with regret. "I wish you could stay longer, but... thank you, for everything."

His eyes widened a little and he gave an unsteady huff of laughter. "You are most welcome," he said. He held out his hand so she could step down from the stool, and Alice took it, wishing she could hold on tight and make him stay.

"Goodbye, Alice," he said, and then raised her hand to his mouth, kissing her fingers.

"Goodbye... Nate."

"*Nate!*" Matilda's voice came again, sounding cross now and suspicious.

Alice sighed as her moonlit lover squeezed her hand, smiling a little, and then hurried away.

Chapter 6

I hope I haven't made a dreadful mistake. Nate is acting so strangely. I'm certain something happened that night. Something he isn't telling me.

—Excerpt of a letter from Miss Matilda Hunt to Senorita Lucia de Feria.

The early hours of the 15th June 1814. Nathaniel Hunt's Carriage. Somewhere in London.

"*Nate!*"

Nate jolted as Matilda's voice pierced his brain.

"What?" he demanded, irritated and hoping to God he didn't look as guilty as he felt.

"What happened?" she pressed, leaning across the carriage towards him. Her lovely face lit up for a moment as moonlight slanted through the window, and then they were plunged back into gloom. "I've asked you three times and every time you evade me."

He threw up his hands in frustration. "Well, what do you think happened?"

"I don't know," she ground out, sounding as though her teeth were clenched. "That's why I'm asking."

Nate folded his arms and glowered. "I kissed her, or rather she kissed me. That was the point of the exercise, wasn't it?"

Somehow, he just knew she was narrowing her eyes at him, despite the shadowy interior where he could hardly make out his own hand when the moon disappeared. Thank God for that. His sister could read him far too well. Best to get this interrogation over now, under cover of darkness, or else she'd skin him alive.

"You were alone with her for an awfully long time, just for one kiss." The accusing observation hung in the air between them.

Nate closed his eyes as he remembered. *Oh, God.* It hadn't been a long time. Not nearly long enough. It had flown, delicious seconds speeding past him before he'd had time to fully appreciate them. How, in the name of everything holy, had that woman never been kissed? It was a crime of epic proportions. His body was still alive with the touch of her hands on him, with the feel of her under his own, with the taste of her on his lips.

Barley sugar.

He smiled.

"Well?"

Nate jolted again. *Damn it, keep your wits about you.* "Well, obviously. You roped me into the business because she's so bloody shy, didn't you? She needed a little time, a little... persuasion."

"*Persuasion?*" There was a sharp edge to his sister's voice now. "What kind of persuasion?"

"The kind you asked me for," he replied, exasperated now and a little offended. "You wanted me to charm her, to make her feel good, to give her confidence... didn't you?"

"Yes," Matilda replied, grudging but accepting. "Yes, I suppose I did. And... did you? Give her confidence, I mean."

Good God, if he'd given her any more confidence, he had no idea where they might have ended, the things they might have done. Desire pulsed through him, and he suppressed a groan. What wouldn't he give to be back on that balcony now? A tiny shiver of fear rolled over him as he realised he didn't much like the answer to that. He wondered if this was what opium addicts felt, this all-consuming need. How could he feel this way, be this affected by a kiss? It had been no ordinary kiss, though. He'd felt nothing like it in his life before.

It had been like putting a match to dry tinder, the tiny curling flame catching hold and setting a blaze capable of devastating a landscape. Just how much of herself had Alice kept hidden all these years? How had she suppressed all that... that fire? He felt changed by it, scorched and charred at the edges, and desperate for more.

He remembered her hair, the soft, thick coils that slid through his hands like silk. Even under the silvery light on the balcony he could tell it was red, red as flame, fierce as passion, heat, and sinful things that spelled danger in bright, bold letters.

Matilda had said Alice was meek and frightened and cowed, and at first, he'd believed her. Not now. Not for a moment. Matilda didn't know her. No one knew her, if that's what they thought. She was funny and beguiling, surprisingly bold with a little encouragement, and he'd wanted to stay with her so badly, to know her better. After her initial hesitation, she'd come alive in his arms and he'd been lost in hers. A few pretty words and a kiss, Matilda had said.

Just one kiss.

He'd been irritated when she'd said it. *It's never just one kiss,* he'd said. God, he'd not understood just how true that was. That *one* kiss had seared him to his very soul.

"Nate?"

Unwillingly, he dragged his thoughts back to his sister.

"You're in a very strange mood, Nate. Are you sure you're being honest with me?"

He folded his arms, feeling belligerent and aggravated. This was all Matilda's fault.

"Yes, I gave the requisite amount of confidence," he snapped, knowing he sounded like a sulky boy and quite unable to do a thing about it. "She ought to be more than capable of ensnaring herself a suitable man now."

The idea made him angry. Why the devil had he been put to work in such a way? He felt like a goddamn fool, something that had been used as a temporary measure until someone more worthwhile came along. God forbid anyone would think of him as worthwhile. No doubt Miss Dowding wanted better than him. A stab of pain and envy jabbed at his chest.

His thoughts ground to a halt. Good heavens. What the devil was the thinking? Miss Alice Dowding was in search of a husband, and there was no way that would ever be him. The very idea! He'd dreamed of such things once, a long time ago, but he'd been a different man then, a boy. Such foolish fancies had passed him by.

Hadn't they?

Nate went hot and cold in quick succession and sucked in a breath. The image came to him of a family home in Kent, one he'd known well once upon a time. The picture became clearer as he studied it, of the sunny room that overlooked the gardens, and waking to find Alice beside him in the morning, with a tumble of fiery curls on his pillow.

The sensation of something being profoundly changed in him was impossible to ignore. It left him shaken and unsettled, and he didn't like it one bit. One thing was for certain. That glorious blaze of red hair really did spell danger, and he must stay far, far away at *all* costs.

***

24th June 1814. Baker Street, London.

Alice lay in bed, one lazy finger trailing back and forth across her lips. It had been nine days since she'd seen him. Nine days since her life had changed.

Nine days since *she* had changed.

Her family thought she was acting a little out of character. Her mother said it was too many late nights making her brittle and short-tempered. At least they'd given her a reprieve from their constant arranging of her life and—except for a series of dress fittings—she'd only attended one event this week: a musicale where she'd spent the entire evening reliving every moment of that magical night.

Alice had kept to her room apart from that, agreeing with her mother that she was tired and out of sorts, and daydreaming about a man with golden hair and eyes that glittered with amusement and desire. Desire for her. At least that way she need not be in her parents' company and need not listen to them harping on about her upcoming betrothal. The betrothal she would fight tooth and nail. Perhaps her mother would think she needed more sleep when she told them that too. No doubt they'd think her hysterical with fear at the idea of being a married lady.

She snorted at that.

Little did they know. Though Mr Bindley could make her hysterical with fear, she supposed, Mr Bindley could also spur her on to do something bold—like meeting a man on a balcony, and feeling alive for the first time in her life—or like discovering she didn't have to be the wilting wallflower. Alice could be someone else; she could be herself, her own person. One she'd kept at bay for so long, but no longer. Not that she'd burst from her chrysalis and exploded upon the world as a tall, lovely goddess with the power to make men fall at her feet. Well, perhaps in her dreams, but not in real life.

In real life she was just testing the limits, pushing herself to speak up when someone assumed what she wanted; saying what she thought, when she thought it, rather than holding her tongue. It wasn't easy. It was easier to let them assume and take control, but that had got her nowhere and nothing. Nowhere and nothing were the path to misery, loneliness and, heaven help her, the Honourable Mr Edgar Bindley.

She shuddered.

Mr Bindley had repulsed her from the start. Now, with Nate's kisses still burning her lips over a week after that astonishing night, Mr Bindley made her heart cold with terror and fear. She would not let that be her fate. No matter how fanatical her parents' desire to climb in society, she would not be the rungs they trod upon to gain that lofty position.

With a sudden burst of energy, Alice sprang from the bed and called for her maid. It was the Eversley's' ball tonight. Mrs Eversley was not good *ton,* but her husband was one of the richest men in the country and everyone who was everyone would be in attendance. Not just the cream of the *ton,* but interesting people, writers and artists, poets and musicians. What a chance to meet a man she could actually fall in love with. A man who could even love her.

The image of the golden Adonis who had kissed her so tenderly on a moonlit balcony swam before her eyes and she sighed. Perhaps he would be there.

Stop it, she scolded. Matilda had arranged that. He was likely an actor himself, playing a part, pretending his desire for her. The thought put a little dent in her courage, and she forced it away. No. Nothing would spoil this, nothing would impede her newfound determination. She would not marry the odious Mr Bindley. She'd find a man of her own, no matter if it was a brilliant match or simply a good man with whom she could find happiness. Either way, the choice was hers to make and make it she would.

***

24th June 1814. Half Moon Street, London.

Nate walked into the parlour to find Matilda, dressed and ready for the Eversley's' ball.

"You're looking very handsome tonight," she commented as she looked up and saw him. "Where are you off to?"

"Why I'm going with you, of course," he said, as though that ought to be obvious.

"With me?" Matilda stared at him in astonishment.

"Yes," he replied, a little irritated. "You've been nagging me for weeks to attend this blasted party. Surely you haven't forgotten?"

Matilda pulled on one long evening glove, narrowing her eyes at him as she held out her wrist for him to fasten the buttons. "I haven't forgotten. Neither have I forgotten that you said you'd rather be roasted slowly over the fires of hell."

Nate winced and wished he'd been a little less vocal on the subject.

"A jest, sister dear. What could be more agreeable than chaperoning you for an evening?"

"Accompanying," she corrected tartly. "I have no need of a chaperone. Besides I have Mrs Bradford to see propriety is served."

"Of course you do," he said, as she offered her other wrist to him. "And Mrs Bradford is about as suitable a chaperone as ... well, as I am, but let us not argue the point."

Matilda snorted and gave him a suspicious look. Nate held her gaze, doing his utmost to look nonchalant, and not the least bit guilty. Not, at least, like a man who'd been dreaming about her friend Alice, the slender, red-haired temptress, every night for over a week. His sister's shy little friend, the one Matilda had insisted was the most fragile of wallflowers, had invaded his every waking moment too. Her kiss still seared his lips, and the touch of her small hands still lingered on his skin. It was intolerable.

He was losing his mind. There was no doubt about it. Every thought in his head revolved around her, about where she was, what she was doing now. Daydreams of a life he'd forgotten how to live invaded his heart, tempting him, beguiling him into wanting more. It scared him that it wasn't just desire that burned under his veins. He wanted to know her, to know everything about her, the sweet little redhead who carried barley sugar in her pocket and kissed like a fallen angel. He'd even caught himself considering things during the week, changes to his business, what colour waistcoat he should wear, would it rain today... and pondering, *what would Alice think?*

He was in deep trouble.

The only thing to be done, he'd reasoned, was to see her again. If he saw her in different circumstances, under the blaze of candlelight rather than the silvered light of the moon, perhaps he'd break the spell she'd cast upon him. Surely then he'd see she was just as Matilda had described her: a stammering little waif of a girl who wouldn't catch his eye under normal circumstances.

Problem solved.

Oh, God.

He had to see her again.

***

24th June 1814. The Eversley's' Ball, Regent's Park, London.

Nate surveyed the crush of people before him and sighed. Miss Alice Dowding had a great deal to answer for.

With Matilda on his arm, they braved the crowd. His sister was looking especially lovely tonight, and he glowered at many men who sent covetous glances in her direction. Bastards. They'd offer her insult but no proposals of marriage. All because of Montagu.

With all Nate's newfound wealth and power, he still couldn't touch the man. The breath of scandal fell far from his door; no one dared speak a word against Montagu. He was a dangerous man with a long reach and a longer memory, and he was known to annihilate those who threatened his family name, no matter how innocuous the slight.

Nate had tried to call him out for what he'd done, and devil had laughed in his face, as though Nate was beneath his notice. Which of course, he was. For now. With any other man perhaps there would have been the stigma of shame, an accusation of lack of honour or courage at not meeting the challenge.

No one in their right mind would level such an insult at Montagu.

Strangely, Nate accepted that the marquess did not lack honour either, in his own twisted manner. Only that his honour served himself and those bearing his name, no others.

Montagu would pay for the damage he'd done that night, though. Nate would make certain of that.

"Slow down," Matilda hissed, awaiting her chaperone, who was struggling to keep up.

Mrs Bradford was a no-nonsense, stocky woman of middling years, and the chaperone Matilda had taken on to attend to her on the occasions Nate refused to... which was most of them. How Tilda stood it, he didn't know. Why did she put herself through it, facing all these people who would rather gossip and shun her given half the chance?

Nate strongly suspected that Matilda usually installed Mrs Bradford in a comfortable chair with a glass and a companion to talk to, and never saw her again all evening, but it was none of his affair. Matilda had always been the sensible one, the one with her eye on propriety, which was half the reason that night had left such a ragged hole in his heart. Good God, Matilda at a men's club, alone, in the middle of the night! How desperate she must have been.

His heart clenched and, as he usually did with unpleasant things, he decided he didn't want to think about it.

"Oh, there's Lucia!"

Nate looked around as Matilda waved a gloved hand. Following the movement, his eyes fell upon a stunning woman. With golden skin and raven hair, she was creating quite a stir, and with good reason. Men fought and died for women like that, Nate thought. To his chagrin, however, it was just an observation. He didn't feel even a flicker of interest. What the hell was wrong with him? Why wasn't he salivating and demanding his sister introduce them at once?

A prickle of unease worked beneath his skin as he realised he didn't give a damn for the dark-eyed beauty. He was desperate for a glimpse of red hair. He wanted to know what colour her eyes were. Had they been green or blue? It had been impossible to tell, and the question plagued him. The need to know had attained vital importance. Bloody hell, just how ridiculous had he become?

Nate smiled and nodded through the introduction to Miss Lucia de Feria, his gaze sweeping across the assembled people, searching for that tell-tale glint of fiery locks.

"You are the proprietor of *Hunter's*, I believe, Mr Hunt?" The young woman asked him, and he forced his attention back to the conversation. Despite her foreign name, she spoke English as a native, without so much as the trace of an accent. He'd gathered she'd been raised here after being orphaned at a young age.

"I am," he said, smiling. "Do you enjoy gambling, Miss de Feria?" he asked, a teasing note to his voice. Of course, no young lady of quality could ever attend *Hunter's*.

"I do, as a matter of fact. Gambling everything on a solitary roll of the dice…." She paused, a rather enigmatic smile at her lovely mouth. "Yes, I think I like to gamble very much."

Nate frowned a little, aware that there was some secret meaning to the words he could not fathom. Under normal circumstances that would have piqued his interest. Tonight, he just wanted to find Alice. He craned his neck, scanning the far edges of the room and catching glimpses here and there of the young ladies who sat on the side lines. No sign of Alice, though.

"Are you looking for someone?"

Nate looked back to find both Matilda and Miss de Feria watching him with avid curiosity.

"No," he replied, perhaps a little too quickly, just a touch too defiant. "Just wondered if any of my cronies were in attendance," he added with a grin. "I need a drinking companion to get me through."

Matilda rolled her eyes and made a shooing motion with her hand.

"Away with you then, rogue. Don't forget you owe me a dance. Lucia too," she added, linking arms with the young woman beside her.

Nate regarded the two women with a dispassionate gaze. Good God, if there was any man with a pulse here tonight, the two of them ought to be danced off their feet.

Nonetheless, he bowed. "It would be a pleasure."

With relief he plunged into the fray, heading towards the ranks of the wallflowers. There was little point in kidding himself he was here for any other reason. He had to find Alice. Would she even recognise him, he wondered? The thought made him pause, a shiver of unease sliding down his spine as that thought led to another....

Would she want to?

He was supposed to have been a faceless, nameless creature, someone to give her a sweet little kiss and boost her confidence. Well, it hadn't been a sweet little kiss, and as for her confidence....

Perhaps she'd be annoyed to see him, or embarrassed? Regretful?

Nate's stomach twisted as he surveyed the rows of chairs where the less popular ladies spent their evenings. As his gaze passed over them, eyes widened, cheeks reddened, and lips parted in surprise. Men of his ilk did not hunt here, but then women like Alice ought not to be here either.

So, it ought not to surprise him that she wasn't.

With a dejected sigh, he resigned himself to searching the entire ballroom and turned around. As he did so, he heard a slight squeal of pain as his foot pressed down upon a delicate silk dancing slipper.

"Oh, I do beg your pardon," he began, and then the words died in his throat as he looked down, and there she was. Any sensible greeting, any acknowledgement of who she was, or their last meeting fled as he stared into eyes the blue of a summer sky. Well, there was his answer then. His heart gave an erratic thump in his chest, and he swallowed.

God help him. It hadn't been the moonlight.

The daydream of a life that was full and rich and filled with family and love and warmth hit him hard and fast, knocking the breath from his lungs. Hopes and desires Nate had thought lost and buried under years of sin and experience forced their bright tendrils out of the darkness he'd consigned them to, and lit the future with possibilities.

He watched as she stared up at him, an expression of pain and irritation chased away as her eyes widened and her porcelain skin blazed as red as that glorious tumble of russet curls. There were freckles on her nose, he noticed, the observation provoking a rush of tender feelings that exploded in his chest. Nate had seen nothing in his life so endearing, so lovely, so....

Hell's bells, it was worse than he'd realised.

"N-Nate," she stammered, blinking up at him.

He nodded, at a loss for anything to say. Better if he left it to her. After all, if she wanted to cut him—The thought that she might horrified him, cutting *him* to the quick.

She glanced around, and then back at him. He had no idea what she was thinking. Was she pleased to see him?

"Why?" she whispered, the word almost lost among the chattering crowds.

She said nothing more, but he knew what she was asking. Why was he here? Was it a coincidence, or was he here for her?

With anyone else he might have prevaricated, he ought to for sure. He knew that.

"I had to see you again," he said simply, and watched a smile dawn on that lovely mouth like a rising sun, lighting her face and making her eyes sparkle.

"Oh," she said, before looking around them and frowning. "Where…?"

She trailed off, her blush blazing brighter than ever, and Nate grinned.

Chapter 7

Dearest Prue,

*I wish you were here. Something extraordinary
has happened. I feel I could burst with
excitement at any moment. Matilda kept her
promise to me and with her help, I completed
the dare!*

Oh, Prue, everything has changed.

**—Excerpt of a letter from Miss Alice Dowding
to Prunella Adolphus. Duchess of Bedwin.**

**24th June 1814. A quiet corner, the Eversleys' Ball, Regent's
Park, London.**

"Where are we?" Alice asked, minutes after escaping the
crowds and running down shadowy corridors.

"I have no idea," he said, laughing.

He felt like a boy again, light-hearted and carefree, which was
utterly ridiculous. Nate had no business being here, let alone being
so blithe about it. He was Nathaniel Hunt, notorious proprietor of
London's most exclusive gambling club. A reputation as a charmer
and a libertine, whilst not strictly accurate, was nonetheless his to
own. He ought to be ashamed of himself for dragging sweet little
Alice Dowding into his shady world and into shadier rooms.

Instead, he was as giddy as a child with the promise of sweets
and a puppy.

Opening a door at random, Nate stuck his head around and reassured himself it was empty. Alice followed him in and lingered by the door as he hunted around for a tinder box and matches.

He only lit two candles, too impatient to do more, but he needed to see her. A quick fumble in the dark was, rather to his surprise, the last thing he wanted.

She stood against the door, petite and slender, with those rioting red curls tumbling about her face.

"You ought not be here," he said, with a rueful smile.

"N-Now you t-tell me," she said, sounding a little indignant.

To his delight, he realised she was teasing him, and he laughed, ever more charmed as she beamed at him. He moved back to her, noting how her breath hitched and the colour rose to her cheeks once again. God, she was lovely. Those dreams of home and family and things he'd not allowed himself to think about for so many years tumbled through his mind again, his heart, as he gazed at her.

Nate paused as the realisation that this was not a dalliance, that he ought not to have brought her here to this darkened room, made guilt flare in his chest. He could ruin her as Matilda had been ruined.

Except he couldn't.

Wouldn't.

If they were caught, he would marry her. He wasn't a man like Montagu, and this woman wasn't someone he was toying with. The realisation ought to have terrified him, but all it did was give him a sense of peace.

When he was close enough to touch her, he raised his hand, stroking her cheek with the back of one finger. "I can't stop thinking about you," he admitted, relieved to say it aloud at last. "About that night. You've haunted my every thought. I dream of you. I feel like I'm going mad."

"I know," she whispered, staring up at him.

He let out a breath, realising in that moment just how much he'd feared hearing anything other than that from her.

"May I kiss you again, Alice?" he asked, breathless with anticipation. Nothing had ever mattered more than the answer to this question.

She stared up at him and he waited, wondering what she saw, what decisions were being made behind those sky-blue eyes. When she nodded, Nate sighed with relief and reached for her, only to stop in his tracks as she pressed her hand to his chest, holding him back.

"Is...?" She swallowed, apparently needing a moment to gather her courage. "Is there a... a footstool?"

He grinned and moved away to search the room. It was sparsely furnished, unlike the rest of the rooms he'd seen tonight, which had been overstuffed and decorated to the hilt. No footstool was apparent, sadly, but as luck would have it, there was a mahogany sideboard. Gesturing for Alice to take his hand, he pulled her towards it and then picked her up by the waist and sat her atop it. She weighed nothing and he kept his hands at her tiny waist, pleased as she grasped his arms and didn't let go.

"There," he said, triumphant. "Up where you belong."

She said nothing, just stared at him, rather wide-eyed. He felt a pang of regret for the clandestine nature of this meeting. What the devil was he playing at?

"Second thoughts?" he guessed, his smile falling away. This woman ought to be courted in full view, with pride, not hurried into a shady corner. "I'll take you back. I ought never—"

"No!" she said at once, clutching harder at his arms and shaking her head. "No," she repeated, softer, yet firmer this time. "I'm just... gathering my courage

"I've been doing that all evening," he said, reaching out and taking hold of one of those tantalising curls, twisting the silky lock about his fingers.

"You have?"

She sounded so incredulous that he laughed.

"I have," he assured her, tugging a little on the curl. "I was afraid you might not recognise me or, if you did, that... that you might not be pleased to see me."

"Not pleased?" she echoed, staring at him. "Are you mad? I've thought of nothing but seeing you again."

Nate grinned, more delighted by this artless confession than he cared to consider.

Alice bit her lip and frowned. "I ought not say such things, I suppose. But it is true."

To his surprise, she reached for his hand, holding it between both of her own and studying it before lacing their fingers together.

"Nate?"

"Yes?"

"I don't know anything about you. Not even the rest of your name."

Nate raised her hand to his lips. "Nathaniel Hunt, Miss Dowding. *Enchantée.*"

"Hunt!" she exclaimed in shock. "B-But you're... Matilda's brother?"

He nodded, a little anxious. Had she believed him someone else, someone better? A nobleman, perhaps, or at least a gilded member of the *ton*? "Guilty as charged," he said, with a glibness he was far from feeling. "Do you mind?"

She let out a breath and shook her head. "Of course I don't mind," she exclaimed. "Only I can't believe I never realised.... My word, you even have the same eyes, the same colouring. How could I not have seen it?"

"It was dark," he murmured, turning her hand and undoing the buttons on her glove with deft fingers. He tugged it from her before putting her hand to his cheek and holding it there. "And we were rather preoccupied with other matters."

"We were," she agreed, rather breathless now. "So, you are the notorious Nathaniel Hunt, proprietor of *Hunter's*. My father has been trying to gain membership there for almost two years."

"Ah," Nate said awkwardly. Mr Dowding was an overbearing sort, loud and dull, and too ingratiating with those of higher rank. He got louder and duller the more he drank. He was wealthy, however. The last time the man had applied, the Earl of St Clair had told Nate in all seriousness that he'd give up his own membership if Dowding was accepted.

Alice just laughed. "Oh, don't look so mortified. Don't, I beg you, give him membership. We may be wealthy, but he is too easily led into extravagance. Mother worries about his gambling as it is. So, I don't care why you deny him, just continue to do so, or the poor woman will never sleep sound again. I promise you I am not the least bit affronted."

Nate gave a huff of amusement and turned his face into her palm, kissing it. "My sister told me you were a meek little thing, sweet and frightened of your own shadow. Why do I not see that when I look at you?"

She stared at him for a moment before she answered. "She's quite correct, I'm afraid. Much as I hate to admit it, and I can't really explain except... you make me brave," she said, before taking a deep breath and reaching for him.

Nate did not need asking twice. He moved closer beside her as her hand slid behind his neck.

"Kiss me... please," she asked, hesitant in her request, as if it were necessary to negotiate for his attention.

"No," he murmured, smiling to reassure her that he was only teasing. "I've spent the last ten days dreaming of a red-haired temptress who kissed me like no woman has ever done. You've ruined me, Alice and I long for the taste of you. Sweet as barley sugar. I want that. I want it again. You kiss me, Alice... *please.*"

There was too much emotion in his voice, too much raw need, but he was helpless to disguise it. There was no hiding from her.

And then she did. She kissed him. Oh, God in heaven, she did, and Nate was lost.

***

Alice clung to him as Nate's arms went around her. She was still in shock. Matilda's brother, of all people! She wondered if she should feel guilty about it, for meeting him here in such a way, when surely Matilda didn't know. Did she? She'd arranged the first kiss after all; no wonder she could assure Alice that he was someone she trusted.

Could Alice trust him, though? How well did Matilda know her brother?

She knew she ought not be here, she knew she was risking everything for this stolen moment of pleasure, and for what? Nate's reputation preceded him by a mile or more. Everyone had heard of the charming rogue, charismatic proprietor of the notorious gaming club that bore his own name. *Hunter's*, a place where fortunes were won and lost on the turn of a card, or the throw of a dice. The world knew him as the dashing young buck who'd sworn to never marry because it would be bad for business. Alice knew that, and surely she should run for the door right this minute. He would never marry her. This was likely only a game to him, a game of chance with her as the prize.

Was Alice gambling the only thing of value she owned with him now? Was this how his club had become so successful? He only need flash that charming smile, speak a few words in that honeyed, beguiling voice that sounded like sin and magic twined together, and the world fell at his feet, or into his arms.

It worked on her, that was the only thing she knew for sure. Well, that and that the act of kissing Nathaniel Hunt should to come with a warning attached. He was addictive in the best and worst possible ways.

She tried to press against him, to get closer as he kissed her, that sleek tongue exploring her mouth with deepening kisses. The angle was all wrong, though. He stood at her side and she had to twist, to angle herself towards him. Alice gave a frustrated little sigh and Nate drew back, wicked amusement in his eyes that made heat and desire uncoil inside her.

He moved to stand in front of her, holding her gaze, silently asking permission. Alice's breathing picked up. Surely, she couldn't be so brazen, but....

She opened her legs and he moved forward, into the space she'd made for him.

"Will you dance with me later?" he asked as he pressed closer, taking her in his arms once more.

The question surprised her, perhaps more than was reasonable. After all, they were doing this all back to front. The dance should have come first or, at the very least, before... before *this*.

Alice hesitated before smiling at him. "Yes, I'd like that."

His keen gaze studied her face. "But?"

She frowned at him, not understanding.

"You hesitated," he said, trailing a finger down her neck. "You don't want to be seen with me?"

There was hurt in his voice, a surprising show of vulnerability that made tenderness swell in her chest.

"Oh, no, that's not... not at all," she said in a rush, horrified that he should think such a thing.

He snorted and shook his head, a darker expression flickering in his eyes now. "I'd not be surprised, I assure you. I'm not good *ton.*"

There was a bitter, mocking tone to the words and she felt wretched for having put it there.

She reached for his hand and pressed it to her mouth. "I don't care for the *ton's* good opinion," she said firmly. "It's only—"

"Tell me," he said, removing his hand to slide it about her neck. The contact made her shiver.

"My parents," she said with regret. "They're the most frightful snobs."

"Of course they are," he said dully. "I can imagine the sight of their daughter in my arms would give them an apoplexy."

Alice imagined he was spot on but held her tongue.

"I don't care what they think, Nate," she said, feeling bold and like she could do anything if a man like this believed in her. "I would love to dance with you."

"You would?"

For a moment, Alice thought she heard doubt in his voice, but that was foolishness. She was making too much of this, of his attention. A man like Nathaniel Hunt was never anything less than confident and sure of himself. It was only silly creatures like Alice who dithered and prevaricated half their lives away before they woke up and realised what they'd missed.

"I can think of nothing I'd like more," she said, smiling at him, and then blushing a little as she realised that wasn't precisely true.

He chuckled and it felt like being caressed with a fur glove, the sleek touch gliding over her and making her shiver with pleasure.

"I think you've just thought of something else you'd like more than that dance, Miss Dowding," he said, a teasing note to his voice.

She dared to hold his gaze. "I... I have," she admitted, reminding herself she would speak her mind from now on.

"Shall I show you what it is?" he asked, the question low and heavy with the promise of pleasure and wickedness.

"Yes, please."

His hands fell to her ankles, the warmth of his palms encircling them and sliding up the back of her legs.

"Tell me stop, Alice, and I'll stop," he said, never breaking her gaze. "Just say the word."

Alice nodded, though she doubted her ability to breathe in the near future, let alone form actual words.

She closed her eyes as he moved closer, his hands sliding over her thighs now, pushing her dress higher and higher. Those strong hands grasped her hips and tugged her to the edge of the sideboard.

The movement forced her against him, and Alice gasped.

"Alice," he whispered, kissing his way up her throat, as his hips pressed against her again, so close, so intimate. He pressed closer still, a slow rocking movement that chased away thought and the ability to breathe, just as she'd feared. "Alice, what have you done to me?"

She closed her eyes and surrendered to the moment, to the pleasure of his strength and his heat and his wonderful, wicked mouth as it sought hers again.

If she had a shred of sense left to her, she ought to ask him what his intentions were. Even though she already knew he wasn't offering her anything, she should ask. Perhaps hearing the answer would wake her from this trance, this decadent dream. Only she didn't want confirmation of that fact, not yet. She could wait a little bit longer.

Please let it last a little bit longer before the bubble bursts.

Chapter 8

Oh, Lucia,

What have I done?

**—Excerpt of a letter from Miss Matilda Hunt
to Senorita Lucia de Feria.**

**24th June 1814. Somewhere lost at the Eversley's' Ball,
Regent's Park, London.**

"Damn you, Nate," Matilda raged as she stared down a never-ending corridor that lay to both her left and her right. "Damn and blast, you wretched man."

It had only been a glimpse out of the corner of her eye, but Nate's tall blond figure was unmistakable, and a glimpse of Alice's red hair was all she required to know who his companion was.

How could he?

She'd hoped that her brother and her friend would hit it off, it was true, and she'd believed that there might be a match to be made there, but how could he do such a thing? What manner of madness would possess him to lead Alice away from the ball?

Good God. If they were discovered….

Matilda felt a wave of icy cold shiver over her as her stomach pitched.

Which way might they have gone? There were dozens of doors, not to mention other corridors and staircases. The Eversley's' were among the minority who could keep such a huge behemoth of a house in town. Most of the *ton* preferred a snug little town house, saving such grandeur for their country estates.

Of course, most of the *ton* could not afford to keep such a grand house in town and in the country, not any longer. That pleasure was left to the merchant class with more money than breeding, and the *ton* enjoyed laughing behind their hands about it, and pretending they didn't care.

Matilda hesitated and then took the left-hand corridor. She'd barely gone ten steps when movement from a staircase to her right caught her attention.

Oh, no. It simply couldn't be.

She froze in place, pierced by cold, grey eyes, like a butterfly impaled with a pin through its gut.

"Well, well, Miss Hunt. We meet again."

God, his voice unnerved her. It was precise and cold, sharp enough to cut through rock.

"Oh," she said, hoping she looked disgusted and not as though fear was sliding down her back in a sickening wave. "It's you."

"It's you, *my lord*," he corrected, his cruel mouth twitching just a little. He looked amused by her intentional rudeness which surprised her somewhat, almost as if he enjoyed it. Perhaps it was the novelty. She doubted anyone dared treat him with anything less than deference.

"Go to Hell," she replied, telling herself to turn around and move the other way, but just like the blasted butterfly she could not, held as she was by his gaze. She'd never known a man to exude power like the marquess could. He was frightening and compelling all at once.

"Oh, give it time," he said, eyes the colour of storm clouds glinting as he watched her, making her feel ever more like a scientific specimen. "I'm a relatively young man yet."

"What do you want?" she ground out, folding her arms, in part to hide the fact her hands were trembling.

He frowned at that, his head tilting a little to one side as he considered the question.

"Want?" he repeated, like she'd spoken in some foreign tongue. "Of *you*?"

Matilda felt fury rise within her. Well, naturally, a man like the Marquess of Montagu wouldn't touch her with a ten-foot pole, she thought savagely. He wanted none of her, that much was abundantly clear, and thank God for it.

"You should have a care, walking around a place like this alone," she said, sneering at him. "You never know what dangerous single females are lying in wait for you, poor unsuspecting creature that you are."

He shrugged, dismissing this attack. "I have a fool proof method for dealing with such presumptuous jades."

Matilda flinched, just a little, but never let her gaze fall from his. *He can't hurt you,* she reminded herself. *They're just words. He's done his worst already.*

"What on earth are you doing at such a disreputable affair in any case?" she demanded. "The Eversleys are hardly worthy of your distinguished presence. They let in any old riffraff," she added, sweeping a gesture towards herself.

His keen gaze followed the movement, returning to look her in the eyes. "I was... bored."

The answer surprised her, more so by the realisation he was surprised at having admitted as much.

"Well, there's nothing to see here," she said, putting up her chin. "So, go away," she added, waving her hand up and down the corridor, indicating he should take his pick of destinations.

Not so much as a flicker of anger or irritation crossed his austere face. "I am unaccustomed to being given orders," he replied, his tone as indifferent and emotionless as ever. Did he ever get angry? She had the sudden urge to make him lose his temper, to fluster that unshakeable calm.

Matilda wondered how he was with a lover. Was he even capable of pleasure? His reputation certainly suggested so, one of wickedness and depravity, of the kind of pleasures no good girl would ever understand, even a married one. She'd heard the whispers as women talked. He rarely took lovers, which perhaps increased his appeal. The arrogant air of unattainability was a lure of its own, and because of rather than despite his cruelty, by all accounts. Matilda couldn't understand that in the least. She tried to imagine how he might act in the throes of ecstasy and couldn't. Then she blushed furiously as she wondered with horror why on earth she'd even considered the matter.

To her dismay, his eyebrows drew together as that unnerving, icy stare hit her again, no doubt taking in her heightened colour.

"What?" he asked, and for the first time he looked something other than proud or aloof as curiosity glinted in the grey.

"Nothing," Matilda said, turning on her heel and leaving him where he stood. She hurried away, not looking back.

***

Still the night of the 24th June 1814. An inadvisable rendezvous, the Eversley's' Ball, Regent's Park, London.

Nate was beyond sanity. Drugged, bespelled, caught in Alice's lovely snare.

She had seduced him with her sweet barley sugar kisses and her freckles, and her soft, teasing words.

A voice in his head kept urging him to take her back, now, this instant. He should heed it; he knew he should. Alice was not for the likes of him, he knew that. No doubt her parents would marry her off to some titled fool, and then he remembered Mr Bindley. She was practically engaged, Matilda said.

Something in his chest lurched. It was the strangest sensation, akin to fear, panic even. He drew back from the kiss, breathing hard. Alice sighed and looked up at him. Her eyes were dark with desire, her lips reddened from his kisses. She smiled up at him, hazy, as if she'd just woken from a lovely dream. There it went again, that sensation in his chest, urging him to do something, say something, anything, to make sure this woman couldn't leave him. He had to make sure she was his. Losing her to another man was not an option.

"What is it?" she asked, reaching up a hand to stroke his face.

Nate sighed and turned his face into it, kissing her palm.

"Alice," he said, his heart thudding as the enormity of what he was about to do hit home.

Once he'd mourned the loss of his dreams, but he'd spent so long telling himself he was a lucky dog—that every man in the country envied him—that he'd begun to believe it. He'd sworn this would never happen to him, sworn he would never, ever lose his freedom, but he'd risk losing everything else in the world before he lost Alice.

It was insanity after such a short acquaintance, he knew that. He knew it and he didn't care. This was real, this was honest, and he'd find no one else like her if he lived to be a hundred. "Alice," he said again, breathless now. "I…."

Alice jolted in his arms as the sound of the door opening stopped the question before he could voice it. Instead another voice asked a question of its own.

"W-Well, well, A-Alice. Who w-would have thought it?"

***

Matilda was frantic. Picking up her skirts she broke into a run, and as she recognised the figure walking ahead of her, she knew her fears were well founded.

"Wait!" she called, trying to still the hand that reached for the doorknob. "Wait a moment."

The man just turned and smirked at her, before pushing the door open.

No. No. No.

Matilda prayed, prayed he'd got the wrong door, prayed it wasn't Nate behind that door, that it wasn't Alice in his arms.

The familiar stammering voice was filled with self-satisfied contempt and confirmed her worst fears.

"W-Well, well, A-Alice. Who w-would have thought it?"

She wanted to weep as she hurried into the room after him. Nate had obviously leapt away from Alice, putting distance between them, but it was evident what they had interrupted. Alice looked thoroughly kissed. Her skin was flushed, her hair coming loose, lips red and swollen. She'd never looked lovelier. Matilda's heart lurched. *Oh, God. No.*

"And with your b-b-brother, Miss Hunt." Mr Bindley turned to smile at her, a reptilian smile that set every sense on alert. "I can s-see where you get it from."

"You take that back, you bastard," Nate growled, taking a step towards Bindley.

"Never mind that, Nate," Matilda snapped, giving him a look that promised retribution. She turned instead to Bindley. "What do you want?"

A man like Bindley always wanted something, and Matilda knew what it was.

A little gossiping this evening had put her in possession of a deal of information. Mr Edgar Bindley might be the son of the Earl of Ulceby, but he was up to his neck in the River Tick. The entire family was. Everything that wasn't entailed was mortgaged to the hilt, and the family owed vast sums of money. Alice's generous dowry and sweet nature would make her perfect for a man like Bindley. No doubt he'd been spying on her, waiting for an opportunity to have something over her, and Nate had all but gifted him leverage.

"W-Why, I want Miss Dowding to stop playing c-coy and agree to m-marry me," he said, a smile on his lips that made Matilda shudder. "If she does it right away, I m-might consider forgetting the fact my b-betrothed is a slut."

Both women gasped as Nate closed the distance between himself and Bindley. He grasped Bindley by the cravat and hauled him up, so his toes barely touched the floor.

"I'll kill you for that," he said, the fury in his voice suggesting he wasn't paying lip service to the words. He meant it. "You'll not lay a hand on her, or look at her, or speak of her, to anyone. She's marrying me."

Matilda let out a breath of relief. Thank God. She ought to have known her brother was too honourable for anything less than that. After what had happened to Matilda, he'd never allow another to suffer what the marquess had done to his sister.

"Her parents will n-never allow it," Bindley sneered, clutching at his cravat and trying to get free. "I'm an earl's son, and you're... N-Nathaniel Hunt." He said the name as though there was some insult imbued within it, and Nate reacted.

Matilda shrieked as he drew his fist back but, before she could do anything, Alice had laid her hand on Nate's arm.

"Stop," she said, her small hand clinging to him. "Stop this."

Nate threw Bindley away from him with a look of utter disgust.

"Alice, darling. I'm so sorry. Can you forgive me?" he said, and Matilda was startled by the sincerity in his voice, the look in his eyes, as he turned to Alice. "There's no need to worry. We'll be married at once. I'll arrange everything. We'll do it before there's even a breath of scandal—"

"No."

Nate froze. They all did. Alice took a deep breath and repeated that unlikely word.

"No," she said again. "I won't marry you, and I certainly won't marry him."

Matilda blinked, a little startled at Alice's vehemence. Half the time you had to listen closely when conversing with Alice, as she was so softly spoken it was impossible to hear her if there was any background noise. That was not a problem now.

"Alice," Matilda said, moving closer to her and taking her hand. As she did so, she realised Alice was trembling. "Alice, darling, Nate is right. That odious man will tell the world what happened here. I applaud you for not marrying him, I think you'd regret it for the rest of your days if you did, but you must marry Nate. You simply must."

To Matilda's consternation, Alice shook her head.

"I won't."

Matilda looked at her brother, shocked at the raw emotion she saw in his eyes. As he saw her watching his expression shuttered up. His jaw tightened, but she'd seen it.

"You s-see," Bindley said, triumph in his voice. "Even the s-slut knows you're not worth marrying."

Nate spun around, fist raised, as Alice and Matilda cried out and Bindley gave a muffled squawk of terror.

"Stop."

Silence filled the room.

Oh, God, no. Fear prickled down Matilda's spine. She'd thought this evening could not possibly get any worse, but it just had. The Marquess of Montagu stood in the doorway, proud and implacable. The severe lines of his face made him look harsher than ever in the dim candlelight.

Stop, he'd said, and they had stopped. The man hadn't even raised his bloody voice over the din of screams and shouts, he just stood there and told them stop, and they'd all frozen in place as if God himself had given the order. What was it about this man that commanded such authority?

"This is none of your affair," Nate said savagely as he stared at the marquess.

A terrible situation had just become a great deal more combustible; Nate hated this man more than anyone else in the world.

"I should think not," Montagu said, looking revolted at the idea. "However, it seems the children are up past their bedtimes and need an adult to supervise them."

Nate opened his mouth, no doubt with some stinging reply on his tongue, but the marquess just quelled him with a look.

"Miss Dowding," he said, still staring at Nate, daring him to speak. "Am I to understand you have refused both offers of marriage?"

Oh, no. Matilda's heart plummeted. The wretched man must have followed her and heard it all.

"Y-Yes," Alice stammered, whatever bravery had fuelled her moment's ago dissolving in Montagu's presence.

Matilda couldn't blame her. For a moment, she hoped the marquess would bully Alice into accepting one of them, but he didn't. He just nodded his understanding.

"And you realise you will be ruined, when word of this gets out?" He turned to give Bindley a look which made the man blanch. "And it *will* get out. Our loquacious friend here will see to that."

Alice nodded and Matilda pulled her into her arms. The girl was ashen now, trembling, and Matilda hugged her tight.

"I'm here, love," she said, for all the good it would do. "I won't leave you."

"You won't like being ruined, Miss Dowding," Montagu continued, the words hard and unvarnished. "You'll be talked about, laughed at, disparaged. Acquaintances will cut you; friends will no longer be available when you call. I'm afraid you do not have the force of character to withstand that in the manner Miss Hunt does. It will crush you."

"Any friend that would cut her is no friend worth having," Matilda said, wanting to cover Alice's ears to save her from the cruel words, and shake her too, to make her understand it was true, all of it. She knew that to her cost.

"A pretty enough sentiment," Montagu replied, unmoved. "But it won't change the outcome, as you well know, *Mademoiselle la Chasseuse.*"

Matilda flinched at the sound of one of the names people whispered behind her back. *The Huntress*, or *Mademoiselle la Chasseuse.*

"Shut your mouth, you bastard," Nate growled, looking as if he was on the verge of committing murder. "You did that. *You.*"

"No," Montagu said, utterly emotionless. "*You* did that, and *you* did this. I merely deal with the consequences." He turned his back on Nate and gave Alice his attention. "I imagine you have reasons for your decision. This one at least," he said, inclining his head to regard Bindley with an expression of mild distaste, "needs no explanation. However, bearing in mind you came here alone with Mr Hunt…."

Alice blushed scarlet. The colour was so intense Matilda could feel the heat of it against her as she held Alice in her arms.

"That's enough," Matilda said angrily. "Do you have a point to make, or are you simply enjoying playing with our lives? We're not here for your amusement, you know."

Montagu turned his attention to Matilda, and she suppressed a shiver. "Well, if you were, I'd be bound to say you're making a lamentable job of it, as I am far from amused. And yes, there is a point."

"Then get to it," she snapped, unnerved as always by the intensity of his gaze.

His eyes were almost silver in this light, the pale irises rimmed in black. She'd never seen eyes like his before, so cold and unmoved by everything, yet capable of instilling fear with such ferocity. His hair, such a startling blond, looked white against the shadows, giving him an inhuman, unearthly beauty. Like some mythical creature drawn from the shadows.

"The point is that your friend here is reacting with emotion. She is not troubling to think the matter through. A foolish trait, but far from unusual. Therefore, I suggest both gentlemen hold their tongues and give the lady the space of three weeks to consider their suits. During this time, no one in this room will breathe a word of the events of this night."

Matilda stared at the marquess in shock. Had... had he *actually* done something to help?

It seemed so unlikely that she kept considering the matter from all angles, certain he must have some ulterior motive, but she could find nothing.

"Why the d-devil should I hold my tongue?" Bindley objected, standing a little taller now, as if he believed the marquess could stop Nate from tearing him limb from limb, the bloody fool.

The marquess' presence had surprised Nate into inaction the first time, but Matilda doubted it would work a second.

Bindley looked rather less sanguine as the marquess turned on him.

"Edgar Bindley," Montagu said, his lip curling a little as though it sullied him to even speak the name. "The youngest son of the Earl of Ulceby. Ah, yes, you're hoping to marry for money. Though even Miss Dowding's dowry won't stem the tide, will it? Not for long. Are you hoping her father will keep bailing you out?" He snorted, such a contemptuous sound that Bindley flushed a dull red. "The earl is teetering on the edge of bankruptcy," he said, taking a step closer to Bindley who physically recoiled, as if in proximity to something venomous and liable to strike. He wasn't wrong. "I need only breathe in his direction," Montagu said, his voice so soft the words were chilling, "and he'll take such a fall there will be no coming back from it. Not for any of you."

"Y-You're threatening me," Bindley said, aghast, but the marquess just regarded him with an implacable expression.

"I never threaten," he said simply. He turned back to Matilda and met her eyes, inclining his head just a little. "Miss Hunt. I bid you a good evening."

Matilda watched, stunned and quite beyond speech as the marquess left as silently as he'd arrived.

Chapter 9

Dear Alice,

For the love of God, marry Nate. This life is not for you, darling girl. The world is cruel and cold and lonely.

—Excerpt of a letter from Miss Matilda Hunt to Miss Alice Dowding… never sent.

The early hours of the 25ᵗʰ June 1814. The Eversley's' Ball, Regent's Park, London.

Once the marquess had gone, Bindley went to open his mouth, but Nate advanced on him with such a look in his eyes the man wisely changed his mind and headed for the door.

"You'd be a f-fool to refuse me, Alice," Bindley said, once he was far enough away from Nate to make a run for it. "Your p-parents will disown you if you m-marry that scoundrel."

The vile creature hurried through the door before Nate could thump him, but Matilda had seen that remark hit home and knew it had hurt. Was that why Alice had refused? Nate believed it, she could see the pain of it in his eyes.

Nate turned, staring at Alice.

"I'm so sorry, Alice," he said. "I…."

Matilda shook her head. Alice had begun to cry, and for once she thought the marquess was right. There was too much emotion here for a sensible decision. She must discover why Alice had rejected Nate and see if she could address the problem.

"I'm going to take Alice home, Nate," she said, smiling a little at her brother. "I'm sure you can speak to her again once she's had a good night's sleep. Go home now, it's late and we're all tired."

Her brother stared at her, and she could see the turmoil in his eyes, the desire to make the problem go away, to beg her pardon too.

"Matilda," he began, his voice breaking with emotion.

"I know," she said softly, not needing to hear him say the words to understand. "We can talk when I get home."

Nate swallowed, his eyes over bright and full of emotion, still watching Alice, and then he gave a slight nod, and left the room.

Matilda let out a breath.

"It's all right, darling. They're all gone now," she said.

"Oh, Matilda," Alice sobbed.

Matilda held her closer as she wept.

***

By the time Matilda had seen Alice home and returned to Half Moon Street, she was exhausted. She hadn't questioned Alice about her decision yet. The girl was too miserable to speak with her, and Matilda hoped a good night's sleep would give her perspective.

Perhaps Nate's reputation was rather colourful, but he was a good man, a kind one, and Matilda felt sure he cared for Alice. Judging on what she'd seen to date, she believed he cared a great deal. She had to admit to surprise at the discovery. To her knowledge, Nate had had nothing but brief affairs. He never dallied with women liable to expect marriage or commitments. That he'd done so with Alice of all people... he was serious about her, he had to be.

So, perhaps in the morning Alice would come to see that, and realise he was her best option, even if her parents disliked the idea.

It had to be better than marrying Bindley. Everything about him set Matilda's teeth on edge.

Matilda climbed the stairs with what remained of her energy and went to the front parlour to find Nate standing by the window, glass in hand. He turned to stare at her as she came in.

"Tilda," he said, his voice rough. "I—"

"Don't you dare tell me you're sorry," she warned him, squaring her shoulders. "And give me one of those. I think I've earned it."

Nate raised his eyebrows. "Cognac?"

Matilda glared at him and he said nothing more, just poured her a small measure.

"Thank you," she said, easing off her satin dancing slippers with a sigh of relief before reaching for the glass. "Now then," she said, gesturing for Nate to sit down with her. "Explain what the devil you were playing at tonight?"

For the first time since he was a very young man, Matilda saw a tinge of colour at his cheeks, but he held her gaze. "I wasn't playing, Tilda. Not this time. I *want* to marry her. I intended to ask her, anyway, and then that cretin poked his nose in."

Matilda gaped at him. She'd suspected he had feelings for Alice, but... he'd been going to propose? So soon? Her incredulity must have shown on her face, for Nate gave a bitter laugh.

"I know. I wasn't expecting it either," he said with a wry smile. "I thought love was something that crept up on a fellow slowly, in increments, and that you could avoid it if you kept your eyes open, but it wasn't like that, Tilda. Not for me. I feel like I've been run down by the blasted mail coach."

"Oh, Nate," she said, seeing the truth in his eyes. "Why didn't you tell me? I would have helped you."

She watched as he rubbed a weary hand over his face, hearing the scratch of stubble beneath his fingers. "I know that, only I didn't realise myself until tonight. I kept telling myself it was just that night, the moonlight, the romance of it. I thought if I saw her again, it would put everything in perspective."

"But it didn't?" Matilda guessed, feeling her heart ache at the look in his eyes.

"Oh, it did," he replied, surprising her again. "It put everything in perspective. How bloody empty and shallow my life is, for one, and how it always will be, unless there is someone to share it with, someone I…."

He shook his head.

"Someone you love," she finished for him.

Nate shrugged, but she knew her brother. On reflection, he was always like this. It was rare for him to feel passionately about anything, but when he did, that was it. If he'd truly fallen for Alice, he'd not betray her, never be unfaithful. It was the reason he'd refused to contemplate anything more serious with any other woman, knowing that when he fell, he'd fall hard.

And Alice had refused him.

"Did she… did she talk to you, say anything…?" he asked, his voice halting, and for a moment Matilda wished she had pressed Alice to speak with her.

"No, Nate. The poor girl was so shocked and upset, I couldn't. I had to tell her maid she'd been taken ill, and the woman had no trouble believing it. She was shaking like a leaf."

Nate groaned and slumped in his seat, the picture of misery. "This is all my fault."

"Yes, it is," Matilda agreed, seeing no point in evading the issue. "If you cared for her that much you should have thought of her, not your own desire." She sighed, relenting a little in the face of his obvious distress. It was like kicking a puppy. "I'm sure she'll come around, Nate. It's clear she desires you, at least."

He snorted at that. "Did you hear her when she refused me, Tilda? I've never heard a woman say no with such certainty. I was just a bit of fun, an exciting dalliance that got out of hand. It wasn't anything more than that for her."

Matilda frowned and shook her head. "I don't believe that," she said. "Alice wouldn't use you like that. She wouldn't have gone with you, left the ballroom... not just for that."

With a weary sigh, Matilda hauled herself to her feet and crossed over to him, ruffling his hair a little with exasperated affection. "Don't worry so. I'll speak to her tomorrow, find out what's on her mind. It will be all right, you'll see."

Nate shook his head, too gloomy to look on the bright side. "She doesn't feel the same. It's clear enough. If she'd rather ruin herself than marry me...." He gave a mirthless huff of laughter. "I knew I wasn't exactly the catch of the season, but I had no idea it was that bad."

"It isn't that bad," Matilda said, frustrated now. "And I'm sure there's more to it than that. Now, go to bed for heaven's sake. Everything will look much brighter in the morning."

She watched as he swallowed the last of his drink and pushed to his feet. "I'm going to the club," he said, setting his glass down and heading for the door.

"Oh, no, not now," she exclaimed, hurrying after him. "It's nearly two in the morning. For heaven's sake, Nate!"

But she knew she may as well save her breath. By this time, he was downstairs and, a moment later, the front door opened and then slammed shut.

Matilda sighed. Good heavens. What a night.

***

89

The morning of the 25th June 1814. Baker Street, London.

Alice stared down at the hastily scrawled message from Matilda, asking her to come for tea this afternoon. She would be at the meeting for the Peculiar Ladies this morning, the note went on, but she obviously assumed Alice would not be there.

Alice couldn't blame her for it. Going on past experience, Matilda would think she would lie low, cowering from the world.

The old Alice would have, too mortified to show her face, even if no one knew her shame.

This Alice was different, though. If she was bold enough to follow a man into the darkness and kiss him like... well, like she had, then she was bold enough to deal with the consequences.

Even if they broke her heart.

When that vile, odious man had caught them, Alice had been horrified, but that had been nothing compared to hearing Nate propose to her. The poor man. Caught like a rat in a trap. At least he hadn't accused her of arranging it on purpose. Not that she had. How could she have? Until last night it hadn't even occurred to her that he'd spared her a second thought since he'd left her on the balcony. That she'd been wrong had been a revelation, a wonderful, joyous revelation.

She did not believe for one moment, however, that any one of those thoughts had contained a marriage proposal. That *The Hunter* himself should propose to Alice Dowding, of all people? No. He'd done it for Matilda. Alice knew Nate blamed himself for what had happened with his sister. Though she'd only alluded to it once or twice in passing, Matilda had given her reason to believe it, and that must be why he'd proposed. Because he had to. Because he couldn't ruin Matilda's friend as the marquess had ruined Matilda.

When the Marquess of Montagu had turned up, the whole thing had seemed like some preposterous nightmare. What had he been doing there? He was an intimidating presence and even

Alice's newfound determination to be brave and speak her mind had shrivelled up and died before such a man.

Now, however, it was a new day and it was time Alice took hold of her own life. She'd allowed her parents to move her this way and that, and had always done her best to be a dutiful daughter. Now, however, the rest of her life was at stake. She'd never marry Mr Bindley, not for any reason. After his behaviour last night, she was all too aware of his true nature, and such a man would only make her life a misery.

Yet, Alice would rather die than marry a man who was wedding her against his wishes, no matter if she wanted him with all her heart. So, thanks to Montagu's influence she had three weeks before her life imploded. Three weeks before they shunted her off to some forgotten corner of the countryside in shame, never to be heard of again.

"Well then, Alice," she said to her own reflection, straightening her spine as she regarded the pale young woman in the looking glass. "You'd better make the most of it."

***

25th June 1814. Meeting of The Peculiar Ladies Book Club, Upper Walpole Street, London.

Matilda sipped at her tea, rather distracted and not paying much attention to the conversation. Harriet, the most serious of all the Peculiar Ladies, had of late been reading *A Vindication of the Rights of Women,* and was expounding on the theme.

"As Wollstonecraft says, if natural rights are given by God, then it is a sin for one segment of society to withhold them from the other."

"Aye, a sin it is," Bonnie said, nodding her head as she reached for a cream bun. Ruth was a wonderful hostess and always supplied the most marvellous tea and cakes for them all. "Why, my brother and my blasted cousin got to learn the most interesting things while I had to sit at home and learn to sew," she said in disgust before taking a large bite of the cake. "It's not fair," she added, once she'd swallowed the mouthful down. "I could ride and fire a pistol just as well as they could, but I still can't embroider to save my life. So why couldn't I learn maths or the sciences? It makes no sense at all."

There was a chorus of agreement around the room.

"I'll tell you why," Lucia said, leaning forward with a conspiratorial air. "Because men are devious, deceitful, and power hungry. They know if they give us an inch, they'll discover we're every bit as intelligent and capable as they are, and it scares them to death. So, they subjugate us and keep us where we can do them no harm, cause them no trouble… and it starts with education. A stupid woman is a good deal easier to control than an educated one."

Everyone blinked, a little taken aback by the vitriol of that statement.

"Well," Ruth said, looking a little doubtful. "I have to say at this point that my father gave me the best education available. Including maths and science, and I'm ashamed to say I loathed it, though I think I did a fair job all the same, but, as for men being devious and deceitful," she added, a frown furrowing her brow. "I think that is a little harsh. Perhaps it is true of some men, but not all men are the same."

"Exactly," Minerva piped up. Minerva Butler was Prue's cousin, and new to their group, but she had fit in right away. "Like Bedwin. He's a lamb, despite what everyone thought of him."

Everyone murmured their agreement on this score, but Lucia snorted and sat back, folding her arms, clearly unconvinced. Matilda watched her with interest. She'd spent time with Lucia of late and liked her a great deal, but the woman was a ball of barely repressed energy. She seemed restless, and always on the edge of some outburst, whether anger or a sudden urge to go somewhere and do something. Her words now made Matilda wonder if there wasn't a man at the bottom of it, someone who had hurt her?

Any further thoughts on the matter were put aside, however, as the butler entered and announced, "Miss Dowding."

"Alice!"

Everyone exclaimed at once, having heard that Alice had indeed completed her dare. Sadly, Ruth had been ill the previous week, and their usual meeting had been postponed, so this was the first time she'd seen everyone together. Matilda scrutinised her friend, frowning a little.

She'd expected to encounter a weeping Alice this afternoon, yet the young woman before her appeared calm and composed, if a little pale.

"Tell us everything," Kitty demanded, pushing Bonnie and Harriet further up the settee to make enough space for Alice to sit beside her. "Was it terribly romantic?"

Alice blushed and avoided Matilda's eye. "Yes, indeed, it was. Terribly romantic."

Matilda watched as Alice tried to answer the barrage of questions.

Was he handsome? How did he kiss? Did he put his arms around you? What did he say?

Who was he?

"Oh," Alice said to this last question, and Matilda listened with interest as she stammered a little. "I c-can't tell you that. It's a secret."

Kitty tried in vain to prise more information from Alice, but none was forthcoming, so the conversation moved on.

"Well, then," Kitty said, grinning. "Time for the next round of dares, I think."

The young woman leapt from her seat, dark curls bouncing around her face as she sought the top hat which Ruth had put away in the sideboard. She passed it to Bonnie, who looked at her in surprise.

"It's your hat," she said. "Don't you want to do it?"

"Not this time," Kitty said, breathless with eagerness. "I want to take a dare."

A murmured *oooh* of excitement shivered over the group as Kitty looked round at them expectantly. "Who else is going to dare?"

There was a tense silence and then Lucia reached out and stuck her hand into the hat, pulling out a thin slip of paper. "There," she said, her beautiful face flushed and strangely defiant.

Kitty crowed with delight. "Hurrah! Now my turn."

Her dark eyes were alight with excitement as Bonnie made a show of stirring the hat.

"Very well then, Kitty. Fate awaits you!" Bonnie said with a thrilling tone. Of all the girls, she had something of a flair for melodrama.

"Eeek!" Kitty said, before plunging her hand into the hat and rustling about for a bit. She withdrew a slip of her own, and everyone held their breath.

"You go first," she said, as she turned to Lucia.

They watched with avid attention as Lucia unfolded the slip of paper. Matilda noticed her fingers tremble a little as she did so.

"Oh, come on!" Bonnie exclaimed, sitting on the edge of the settee. "Don't keep us in suspense."

Lucia read the words of her dare, the corners of her mouth twitching a little. "Smoke a cigar and drink cognac in a man's study."

There were murmurs and gasps as everyone considered this.

"Drat," Kitty said, scowling a little. "I would have liked that one."

"Read yours, Kitty," Ruth urged as everyone's attention turned to the girl.

Kitty stared at the piece of paper in her hands and took a deep breath as everyone waited. She read the dare and a frown of consternation wrinkled her forehead.

"That makes no sense," she said, looking up at everyone.

"Read it out loud," Lucia suggested as everyone leaned in, eager to hear what challenge awaited Kitty. The girl had been rather vocal on the idea of these dares, so she was in no position to back out.

"Dress the Earl of St Clair's bear in evening attire."

Everyone gaped at her and then burst out laughing.

"His bear?" Harriet asked, wrinkling her nose. "I do hope that's not a euphemism." This was said with the utmost sincerity but caused the rest of the group to dissolve into giggles. Harriet looked nonplussed. "What? I don't think it's funny. That's a good way to get yourself ruined."

"Oh, oh," Minerva said, clutching at her sides and struggling to speak through her laughter. "B-But it does make sense, and it isn't a euphemism. He really does have a bear."

"He does?" Kitty stared at her, aghast.

"Not a real one," Minerva said in a rush. "At least, it was real, but it's dead. Stuffed."

Kitty heaved a sigh of relief. "Oh! Thank goodness." She grinned at Minerva. "I had visions of wrestling a grizzly bear and trying to tie a cravat around its neck."

Minerva shook her head. "No, it's in the library at Holbrooke House."

"That's close to our home in Sussex. It's huge, an Elizabethan behemoth," Harriet said, pushing her spectacles up her nose. "It's a fascinating place, said to be haunted. Apparently, St Clair's great-great-grandfather rebuilt the west wing and put a kitchen over the original chapel. He's punished for it by being forced to walk the corridors on stormy nights."

"Good heavens." Ruth looked amused and sceptical at this idea. "Surely you don't believe it?"

Harriet shrugged. "No. But it hasn't been disproven and many people believe they have seen it. I would love to understand what causes the apparition, and what it really is. For it can't be a ghost, of course." She frowned, turning her teacup on the saucer. "I haven't been there since last year, but I certainly don't remember a bear. It must be new."

"Anyway," Minerva said, returning the conversation to the point. "Every summer, they hold a grand party. Everyone who's anyone will be there."

Kitty scowled and folded her arms. "Well, that's torn it. I'm no one. I won't be invited."

"Oh," Harriet said, "I will be. They're our neighbours you see, and my brother is the earl's best friend. You can come along, as my guest. That is...." Harriet hesitated.

She was a serious girl and the only one who had yet made no close friendships in the group. Matilda watched with interest. Shy, studious Harriet and brash, energetic Kitty seemed an unlikely pairing, but perhaps one that would do them both good.

"That is, if you would like to," Harriet added, sounding unsure.

Matilda looked between the two young women.

Harriet seemed diffident now, waiting to be rejected, and Kitty was wary, sensing charity.

"Don't you need to ask your parents?" Kitty asked, sceptical.

"Oh, no," Harriet said, sitting up a little straighter. "To be honest, they'll be so thrilled to see me with a real live friend they'll probably try to adopt you."

Kitty snorted and returned a dark look. "Oh, give it a day or two. They'll have had enough of me by then."

"You'll come then?" Harriet said, and Matilda felt a little glow of pleasure at the excitement in Harriet's eyes.

This was what the group was about: friendship and support. Seeing it in action was rather wonderful.

"Won't it bother them, though?" Kitty said, folding her arms, her face hard all at once.

"What?" Harriet looked from Kitty to the others in the group, nonplussed.

Kitty rolled her eyes. "That I'm Irish."

There was defiance in her tone, suggesting she'd flatten anyone who agreed it was a problem. It made Matilda's heart ache.

"Oh!" Harriet said, as if this hadn't occurred to her. "No. I shouldn't think so. Why would it?"

Kitty snorted, as if this ought to be patently obvious, which it perhaps was, to anyone but Harriet who was oblivious to such mores of society. "Because it does."

Harriet stared at Kitty. "You're very welcome, Kitty," she said decisively. "And I know they will say the same."

Kitty stared at her for a long moment and then gave a nod and held out her hand. "In that case, I will. Thank you, Harriet."

Chapter 10

I won't live like this any longer. It's my life and I must make the best of it. I made a foolish error and I must pay for that, but from now on, all decisions will be mine, whatever the outcome.

—Excerpt of a letter from Miss Alice Dowding to Prunella Adolphus, Duchess of Bedwin.

25th June 1814. Meeting of The Peculiar Ladies Book Club, Upper Walpole Street, London.

After the meeting, as the ladies went in search of hats and pelisses, Matilda sought out Alice.

Alice had known she would, of course. Indeed, she knew they must speak, but there was someone else she wanted to speak with more. She must see Nate and thank him for his kind offer. It had been churlish of her to refuse him so harshly, especially in front of Bindley of all people. She'd been in such a state in that moment though, she had hardly been able to think at all. The only thing she'd known was that she could not marry a man she was in danger of falling deeply in love with, when he was only offering for her to save her from ruin.

Everyone knew *The Hunter* had sworn to never marry. She'd not be the woman to catch him. Especially when everyone would know the truth, that he was only doing the honourable thing. He'd be pitied and she'd… well, she'd rather not think on that.

"Hello, Alice. How are you?" Matilda's voice was gentle as they moved a little away from the other women.

"I'll live," Alice said, doing her best to return a bright smile.

"Will you come back with me, then? We can talk."

Alice bit her lip, considering.

"Will Nate be there?"

Matilda shook her head. "He stayed at the club last night and sent a note saying not to expect him until this evening."

Alice nodded. No doubt he was counting his blessings. No, that was unfair. He'd feel wretched, she knew that. He was a good man and wanted to do the right thing. She just wanted to explain to him that it wasn't necessary.

Matilda moved closer to her and laid a hand on her arm. "Have you changed your mind, Alice?" she asked in an undertone.

Alice shook her hand, tugging on her gloves and wriggling her fingers until each one was snug. "No."

She heard a sigh and looked up to find Matilda staring at her in frustration.

"But why, love? He's a good man and we would be sisters. Don't you like him at all?"

That made her laugh a little. She didn't think there was a woman with a pulse who wouldn't like Nathaniel Hunt; he was inherently likable.

"I do like him," she admitted, turning to smile at Matilda. "Too much to trap him into marriage."

Matilda gaped at her. "Oh, Alice! Is that what you think? You goose. The poor man was in pieces last night. I don't know what you've done, but he said meeting you was like being hit by the mail coach."

Alice stared at her, uncomprehending.

In pieces? Nate? Hit by the mail coach?

"What are you talking about?" Alice asked, blinking in confusion. "You make it sound like I broke your brother."

Matilda threw up her hands. "You did, Alice. His heart at least." She lowered her voice to a whisper and tugged Alice closer. "He's in love with you. He was going to ask you to marry him last night, *before* Bindley came into the room."

Alice opened her mouth and closed it again. "That's… that's not—"

"Don't you tell me it's not possible or true, or whatever words were about to come out of your mouth," Matilda warned, sounding rather stern. "I know my brother. I saw him when I got home. He means it, Alice. He loves you, and the way you turned him down made him think you don't care a straw for him."

"Oh!" Alice said, feeling a little giddy as her heartbeat gathered speed. "But that's not true, I do care a straw. Lots of straws. Stacks of them, or is it stooks?" she said, knowing she was gibbering but not entirely certain how to stop.

Matilda took her hands and squeezed them. "I'm so relieved, Alice. I felt certain it was a misunderstanding."

Alice nodded and then frowned a little. "Only—"

"Only?" Matilda repeated, her smile reassuring.

"Only he doesn't know me at all, not really. It's all very sudden, isn't it? Two meetings, Matilda?" she added, knowing this was nothing short of folly. The man must be deranged, or at least… *ill*. Perhaps he'd hallucinated her into something more… well, *more*. Did he have a temperature? She should at least check. "Maybe, when he knows me…."

She trailed off, anxiety plucking at her heart with sharp little claws.

"When he does, he'll love you all the more, I'm certain."

Matilda *did* sound as if she was certain, which was reassuring, but....

"He needs to be sure. We both do," Alice said, feeling breathless. "But we have three weeks, don't we? We can meet and take that time... to be certain."

Matilda took her arm as they headed for the front door, pausing a moment to say goodbye to Ruth and the other ladies.

"Nate is already certain, Alice," she said, tugging Alice out onto the street. "And you *must* marry. There is no choice in the matter, but I don't think spending time with him is a bad idea if it reassures you."

Alice was still feeling rather dazed, and suspected it would take a good deal longer than three weeks to convince her that a man like Nathaniel Hunt loved her and wasn't either experiencing some manner of fevered phantasm, or simply an excess of chivalrous sentiments. Still, she kept such opinions to herself.

"Mr Bindley was right about one thing," she said, lowering her voice and feeling wretched about having to say it at all, but she had to warn Matilda. "My parents...." she said, mortified and not knowing how to say that they would never consent to a marriage between her and Nate. "They really are the most dreadful snobs," she said, wanting to curl up and die.

How did you tell your friend that your parents though her brother was beneath contempt?

"They'd been hoping I'd catch the eye of an earl, or at the very least a viscount, but when it became apparent it would never happen, they were forced to consider Mr Bindley when he expressed his interest. He's at least an *Honourable*, for what that's worth," she added bitterly. "Though they're dreadfully disappointed that it's the best I can do."

Matilda nodded, her expression grave. "I know, Alice. I know just what they will think, though you know we were respectable once."

She gave a heavy sigh and Alice felt even more wretched for making Matilda feel bad.

"Oh, but, Matilda…. You mustn't think I give a brass farthing for such things. I don't, I assure you."

Matilda laughed and shook her head. "I know that, Alice. I don't think you've ever thought badly of anyone in your life."

Alice returned a sceptical look. "Then you think I'm a deal nicer than I am, is all I can say. Are you sure you want me as your sister?"

"Above all things." Matilda grinned. "Listen, instead of coming this afternoon, come for dinner tonight. Then you and Nate can spend time together. I'll make myself scarce, I promise," she added with a wink.

Alice bit her lip. It was a tantalising prospect, and she longed to see Nate again, especially in the light of Matilda's revelation. Getting away would be nigh on impossible, though. Her parents had already commented upon her friendship with Matilda and had been aghast to learn she'd visited the house. They believed the association would tarnish her.

"I'm not sure I can," she said, with a sigh of impatience. "But… I'll try, I promise."

***

Alice sat back against the plush interior of the carriage as it manoeuvred through the heavy London traffic. Many interesting scenes passed her by, the kind which she usually found absorbing, but nothing could hold her interest today. Nothing except the unlikely revelation that Nathaniel Hunt, the notorious rogue and charismatic club owner, was madly in love with her. The more she thought about it, the more preposterous it seemed.

Even she couldn't put her hand on her heart and say she loved him, and he *was* Nathaniel Hunt, notorious rogue and charismatic club owner! She'd been dazzled by him, intrigued, beguiled, and blinded with desire and curiosity.

Did she long for him?

Yes.

Did she ache for his kisses and burn to see him again?

Yes.

Did she want to know him better?

Oh, yes.

Did thoughts of him plague her from morning to night, and did he invade her dreams?

Yes, and yes.

Love, however?

That was something she knew she *could* feel, without any doubt and with a scandalously short acquaintance, but how could such a man fall in love with mousy Alice Dowding in the space of two evenings? Two extraordinarily magical evenings, it was true... but still.

She was struck with the urgent desire to see him again. Well, yes, she'd had the urgent desire to see him for days now as she'd just established, but this time... she would do something about it.

With her heart beating in her throat, Alice got the driver's attention and gave him the address of number eleven, Henrietta Street. Being rather new to the art of deception, she rather over-complicated matters by explaining she'd just remembered she simply must buy some new lace to trim a hat which she'd discovered was very unbecoming. Nowhere else was there to be had such a variety and quantity of lace than Layton and Shear's, and so she'd be most obliged if he would convey her there at once.

Thankfully, the driver looked unimpressed by this surfeit of information, but agreed to the change in destination without so much as a murmur. Alice sat back, feeling exhilarated and dreadfully wicked.

Henrietta Street, was, after all, in Covent Garden.

As was *Hunter's*.

Henrietta Street was a busy thoroughfare. So busy that the driver readily agreed to wait a little further down the street while Alice made her purchases.

Not wanting to allow her story to trip her up, Alice hurried in and bought a deal of lace she had no need for and stuffed the little bundle in her reticule. This done in record time, she crossed Henrietta Street and headed into the Garden.

Here, her senses were assaulted on all sides. The morning market was almost over now, with many of the stallholders moving to pack up goods and load them onto handcarts. Throngs of people still filled the area, though, buyers and sellers of such a variety of goods that Alice was quite stunned.

Although she'd visited Layton and Shear's frequently with her mother, she had never permitted Alice to walk into Covent Garden proper, and now she could see why.

It was marvellous.

Scents beckoned her on all sides, teasing and intriguing. Flower stalls, their gaudy blooms arrayed like jewels, infused the air with such perfume it made her head spin. Fruit stalls flanked her on both sides, with exotic wares like pineapples and juicy melons cut in two, their succulent flesh bared to the slavering onlookers.

Jostled on all sides, Alice held tight to her reticule, remembering stories of cutpurses and thieves in this enticing place. She glimpsed snatches of another world as she walked, a world she'd been sheltered from and guided past without being given so much as a peek. Now, though, she drank it in.

Down the side streets, old ladies lined the buildings in rows, shelling peas and gossiping as they sat on upturned baskets. From the apothecary shops drifted both the strange and familiar smells of herbs and spices and concoctions for gout, pastilles for putrid sore throats, creams and ointments, and possets and infusions. The coppery tang of meat and the stench of livestock reeked in the poultry market where fowl of every variety hung with their heads arrowing down. Glassy eyed ducks and geese swung gently in the breeze as it ruffled feathers no longer fit for flight. Here and there, dogs snuffled and snarled, growling over a discarded scrap and scenting the air with hopeful noses.

The fishmongers made her nose wrinkle as she stared at creatures so large, she couldn't imagine how they'd ever been caught at all. Alice marvelled at the lobsters with their blue shells, having only ever seen them pink and cracked open on a plate. Daring to reach out and touch one vicious looking claw she leapt back with a shriek as an antenna flicked, the movement making her realise the creatures were not yet dead.

Drawing a roar of laughter from the owner of the stall, Alice flushed the colour of the boiled variety of his wares and hurried on her way.

Despite enduring a few leering stares and some very lewd comments shouted in her direction, Alice was entranced and wished she could investigate further. Perhaps Nate would show her around, she thought. That would be a very pleasant way to spend the afternoon. Though she supposed much of the market would be gone soon.

At last, *Hunter's* came into view. Once the site of an old theatre, Nate had relocated here two years ago when *Hunter's* had finally gained its reputation as *the* place to be for those who could afford to frequent it.

During daylight hours it appeared shut up and sleepy, and Alice rapped upon the main doors to no avail. Refusing to give up now, she worked her way around the side of the building and discovered a back door. Here, she was more successful. After a solid minute and a half of pounding her small fist against the glossy black paintwork, sounds of movement reached her ears.

The sliding back of bolts accompanied a deal of muffled muttering and cursing and the turning of a key, and finally the door swung open. A man stood in the entrance. Not Nate, sadly, but still, it was a start, if an intimidating one.

The fellow glared at her from under thick, bushy, black eyebrows. Alice stared at them in consternation. Eyebrows were not usually so disconcerting but these, paired with a head as smooth and shiny as an egg, were rather remarkable.

"Yes?" the fellow said, giving Alice a look of deep suspicion.

Possibly a hard expression to avoid with eyebrows like that, Alice supposed, deciding she'd not hold it against him.

"I have an appointment with Mr Nathaniel Hunt," she said, wondering from where she was dredging up this ability to lie through her teeth. She hadn't even stuttered.

The suspicious look deepened.

"Oh, aye?" The doorman, or… whatever he was, looked her up and down in a manner Alice took exception to. "He never said he had a woman calling today, and he told me nothing about no appointment."

For a moment, she quailed. The old Alice would stammer and flush and turn tail now, an urge which was tugging at her right this minute.

No.

She took a deep breath.

"Well, I'm very sorry about that, but he did tell me," Alice said, standing as tall as she was able and doing her best to smile sweetly, a little discomforted as the extraordinary eyebrows drew further together and met in the middle. It looked as if a large, furry insect was travelling across his forehead.

"And who might you be?" he demanded.

With difficulty, she tore her gaze from the fascinating spectacle on the man's face and met his gaze. Alice's stomach pitched as she forced the words out.

"His fiancée."

Chapter 11

I seem to have bought three yards of the ugliest lace I've ever seen in my life. I haven't the first idea what to do with it.

—Excerpt of a letter from Miss Alice Dowding to Miss Jemima Fernside.

Noon. 25th June 1814. *Hunter's*, Covent Garden, London.

Nate sighed, and then cursed himself for sitting about sighing. He should get up and do something. Anything. Except he didn't know what.

Surely there were a dozen or more things needing his attention? He knew damn well there were, there always were. Yet he couldn't summon the energy to discover them, or to care. The place could burn down around his ears and he suspected he'd find himself too apathetic to go to the bother of saving his own skin.

What was the point?

There was no point. There had been no point for much of his existence. Only, for the last six years, he'd lived in blissful ignorance of that fact. Now, however, his mind had been focused, his thoughts marshalled and herded—protesting as they went—and forced to come to the point.

Only to discover… there wasn't one.

He sighed, and then swore again for having done so.

Pitiful. That's what it was. Nathaniel Hunt flat on his back, prostrate, like a fighter being counted out while his opponent celebrated and raised his fists in victory....

Flattened by love.

He'd told Tilda it was like being run down by the mail coach and that had been no exaggeration. In those brief, glorious, heady moments with Alice in his arms, he'd glimpsed a world he'd forgotten existed. He'd made himself forget. He'd made himself despise the idea because he'd thought it lost to him.

Domestic bliss was something that caught you like a noose about the neck, and once caught your pleasure was as cooked as your goose, not to mention other vital parts of the male anatomy.

Except it hadn't felt like being caught. It had felt liberating, as if at last he might be free to be himself. With Alice he'd thought he'd found someone in whom he could put his trust, someone who wouldn't expect him to always be the charismatic scoundrel everyone knew him to be. He hadn't really meant to become that man, except that after his father had lost everything and tossed him and Matilda into the gutter, what choice had he had?

His pride—the fierce pride of a young man too aware of his own failings—had been crushed. His friends pitied him; some cut him dead, others were kind. Nate had never been sure which was worse. So, he'd fixed a careless smile to his face and adopted a cynical air, and lived up, or perhaps down, to the reputation his father had gifted him: that of a dissolute gambler and libertine. The only difference being, Nate was good at it. Winning needed the luck of the devil, and Nate seemed to have that in spades.

Or he'd thought so, until it had run out last night.

Hunter's was all the rage, frequented by the famous and infamous; a place where dukes rubbed shoulders with self-made men, if their pockets were deep enough. That was something Nate always took a great deal of trouble to investigate. No one got membership to *Hunter's* if there was a risk it would ruin them to do so. Nate refused to bear the burden of that guilt. Yet, that gave the club an exclusivity that made men fall over themselves to gain membership. It had become a badge worn by the elite, and only those who could lose a fortune and not blink needed to apply.

So, Nate was a vastly wealthy man, and yet his reputation was besmirched, his sister ruined, and any chance of anything decent long gone, or so he'd believed. Alice had opened his eyes to the possibility that maybe, just maybe the right woman might see past the persona of *The Hunter*. Just maybe, she might realise there was someone else waiting in the shadows of that reputation. He'd believed it. For the space of those moments they'd shared, he'd been fool enough to lose his heart for it.

Hearing her reject him so summarily, without so much as a moment's hesitation, and in front of Edgar Bindley... he'd been that awkward young man all over again, with his pride in tatters.

Nate sighed.

A knock at his office door had him scowling. He'd expressly forbidden anyone to disturb him. At least here he'd expected to mope in peace. Hopkins was on duty, and he should have more sense.

"Go away," he yelled, folding his arms and staring up at the ceiling.

"Can't," yelled back an indignant voice. Yes, that was Hopkins. "There's some fancy bit here to see you."

Oh, good lord, the last thing he wanted now was some sordid dalliance. It wasn't unheard of for married ladies to seek him out here, in the hopes of excitement and the illicit brand of pleasure he could provide. Today the idea made him sick. He was tired of being some woman or other's dirty secret. He'd had a glimpse of another life and the longing for it consumed him.

"Tell whoever it was I'm not here," he shouted, before inspiration hit. "Better yet, tell them I've got syphilis." That ought to cool their ardour, he thought with a grim smile.

"No need," Hopkins replied, sounding amused. "She heard that. Besides, the chit reckons she's your fiancée."

Nate froze, his heart pitching in his chest.

Fiancée?

He scrambled to move so fast that he fell off the settee and bashed his knee on the floor. Cursing, he hurried to his feet and struggled to smooth down his hair, before realising he was wrecked and there was little he could do about it now. If that was Alice... if she'd come here....

Nate snatched the door open. Hopkins's burly figure filled the doorway.

"Where is she?" he demanded.

Hopkins moved a little to one side, and there she was. Petite and lovely, dressed in a light, sprigged muslin gown, a summer green spencer and matching bonnet, with her fiery curls framing her face, she took his breath away. Nate felt suddenly giddy and then told himself to stop being such a bloody fool; there might be any number of reasons she was here... not that he could think of a single one.

"Hello, Nate," she said, her cheeks scarlet as she twisted the handle of her reticule all out of shape. She was nervous. "M-May I come in, p-please?"

For a moment Nate just stared at her, too stunned to do anything as intelligent as reply to her.

"Well?" Hopkins demanded, staring between them both. "Do you want to see 'er or shall I put her back outside?"

That woke Nate up.

"Lay a hand on her and lose it," he said succinctly, before guiding Alice into his office and closing the door.

His heart thudded, hope bursting in his chest no matter how hard he forced it down. Why was she here?

"Was there something I can do for you, Miss Dowding?" he asked, hating himself for sounding so polite and distant, but not daring anything more intimate. He wanted to pull her into his arms and never let go, but she had burned his pride enough for the time being.

The colour in her cheeks mounted.

"Miss D-Dowding," she repeated, and he hated that stammer. Not because of the way it sounded, but because it meant she was unsure, nervous in his presence, but perhaps that was for the best. "I was Alice last night."

"And I was the man whose proposal you rejected. So, Miss Dowding, how may I be of service?"

She stared at him and something in her eyes made him look away, unable to hold her gaze.

"I assume you came with some purpose in mind. If anyone saw you in a place like this—"

"I'd be ruined," she said, speaking over him before he could finish. "I think that horse has bolted, don't you?"

It was Nate's turn to blush. His fault. It had been all his fault. He never ought to have taken her from the ballroom, he'd known it, but... but he'd been so full of hope, so eager to discover if this feeling bursting in his chest was filling her too.

"If you want my apology, you have it. I—"

"I don't want your apology." Her words were firm, her gaze intent. Whatever had made her stammer and blush, it had gone. Now she was in charge of herself—and him, if she only knew it.

"What then?" he asked, the words raw as he held his hands open to her. He knew how he looked. He'd not shaved, and his coat and waistcoat had long been discarded, along with his cravat. His shirt was rumpled, and he'd drunk too much and slept not at all. No doubt he looked like what he was: a reprobate, a good for nothing rascal, and now he'd no chance to be anything else.

"I spoke to Matilda," she said, holding Nate's gaze as his heart dropped to the floor.

Oh, God. No. Not that. Surely, his sister hadn't betrayed his confidence. His pride was in the gutter already, surely she'd not humiliate him further by telling Alice—

Without realising it his breathing had picked up, the scald at his cheeks growing hotter.

"She said—"

Nate turned away as Alice spoke. He couldn't look at her, not now.

"What did she say?" he demanded, the words vicious and angry. "That I was a bloody fool?"

There was a long silence, and then he started as Alice's hand slipped into his. She curled her fingers about his. Despite his best intentions, he looked down at her, and was at once caught in eyes of such blue he felt he would drown.

"Nate, why did you propose to me?" She was staring up at him, her voice soft and intimate.

"Why do you think?" he said, gruff and ungentlemanly. Damned if he would lay his heart before her a second time. She'd ground her heel into it quite adequately enough the first time.

"I thought it was because you had to," she said as her other hand joined the first, both clasped around his, the warmth of her gloved fingers sinking into his skin. "I thought it was because you had no choice. You blame yourself already for Matilda's situation and you're too honourable to allow her friend to be ruined too, when you could stop it. I thought you had no choice but to ask me."

Nate frowned, turning to face her.

"You believed I didn't wish to marry you?" he asked, too stunned by the idiocy of that idea not to sound sceptical.

"Of course," she retorted. "No one else has ever wished to."

"Bindley seems keen enough," he said, his tone dark.

She snorted and gave him a fierce look. "He wants my money, not me."

Nate felt jealousy rise in his chest. "That's not all he wants, I assure you."

"What do *you* want, Nate?" she asked, her voice little more than a whisper. "That's why I'm here. That's why I risked coming here to you. I won't marry a man who doesn't want me, who doesn't even want to marry at all, let alone be forced into it, but...."

She trailed off and Nate wanted to shake her for it. What a moment to stop talking.

"But?" he echoed, holding his breath with anticipation.

"But... if I thought for a moment that... that you'd wanted me—"

"Wanted you?" he exclaimed, stupefied. "If I'd *wanted* you? Good God, Alice, were you not there last night?" He took hold of her by the arms, staring at her. "I was out of my mind with wanting you, which was why we ended up where we were. If I'd been thinking clearly, I would never have put you at such risk but I ... I was mad with wanting you."

Alice smiled a little at that, her expression shy and hesitant, making his poor heart ache with longing. "Yes, but... but that kind of wanting doesn't always mean a man wants to marry you."

Nate couldn't help but smile at her being the worldly one and trying to explain the facts of life to him.

"No," he said gently as he lifted his hand to touch her cheek. "No, you're right, it doesn't, but it did last night. For me it did."

His words hit her hard. He could see it. It was as if whatever courage had brought her here to this place—a place she would never have dared set foot in before now under any circumstances—fell away in the rush of relief. She gave a sob, her eyes glittering as one hand flew to her mouth.

"Alice, Alice, darling, forgive me." He swept her up, lifting her into his arms as he carried her back to the settee and sat down with her on his lap, holding her close to him. "I thought you didn't want me," he said, tugging at the ribbons of her bonnet, keen to cast the impossible thing aside so he could kiss her before his heart gave out. "I thought I wasn't good enough."

She shook her head as he dealt with the bonnet, laughing and crying all at once.

"I would… n-never… n-never," she stammered, wiping her face. "Never would I think that," she said, staring at him, such sincerity in her eyes that his breath caught in his throat.

"I love you," he said, daring to expose his tenderest feelings once more, knowing there would be no coming back from it if she crushed him now.

She didn't, just stared at him in wonder and lifted her hand to his face. Soft, kid gloves touched his cheek and he longed for the feel of her skin against his. Taking her hand, he undid the tiny button at her wrist and tugged the glove from her, raising her hand to his mouth and kissing her palm.

"I love you, Alice," he said again, fiercer now.

"You hardly know me," she said, though there was no reproof in her words, only confusion. "I don't see how—"

"Neither do I," he admitted, smiling at her. He knew it was unlikely and probably unreasonable. If a friend of his had declared himself in love after such a short acquaintance he'd have questioned the man's sanity. Perhaps he was mad, perhaps love at first sight was a myth, but his heart told him otherwise. "I only know how I feel."

"What if it isn't real?" she asked, and he could see the doubt, the fear, in her expression. "What if we marry and you realise it was all a mistake, and when you do know me—"

"Marrying you could never be a mistake."

She smiled at that and he could resist no longer. He leaned in, pressing his mouth to hers. She was as warm and sweet and soft as he remembered, and she opened to him at once, twining her arms around his neck and shifting closer. Desire rose like a tide and he forced himself to move back. He'd do this right from now on. She was a lady and deserved to be treated like one.

"Does this mean you've reconsidered?" he asked, fear stalked him, a cold weight in his chest at having to ask her again, despite everything that had been said.

She hesitated, and his heart plummeted again. Dear God, he didn't think the wretched thing could endure much more of this.

"I want you to court me," she said at length.

Nate's eyebrows rose in surprise.

"Alice, you must marry me, or you'll be ruined."

She frowned at that and shook her head. "Matilda has managed; so shall I. I would rather be ruined than make a mistake."

"And I would be a mistake," he guessed, withdrawing from her embrace, but she just tightened her hold on him.

"Good heavens, I thought women were supposed to be the flighty, over sensitive ones?" she said, a scolding note to her voice. "I never said that and, if you will keep putting words in my mouth, then I'd best make this clear. I *want* to marry you."

He let out a breath he thought he might have been holding since the moment she'd stepped into his office.

"You do?"

She smiled then, a sweet, soul-stealing smile that made him feel about ten feet tall.

"I do," she said shyly.

That deserved a kiss, he decided, and he refused to allow her to speak for several more minutes. When he released her, she was flushed, dishevelled and utterly lovely.

"You want me to court you," he repeated, understanding a little better now.

She nodded and leaned into him, laying her head on his shoulder. "I want us both to be sure, Nate, or at least as sure as we can be in such a short time. I just want to know you a little better, and for you to know me, to be certain of me."

He sighed and refrained from pointing out that he was certain. He'd said it before, but she refused to believe it. Not that he could blame her, and there was no harm in doing as she asked... except that they risked discovery.

"I can't call on you, Alice," he said, feeling wretched at the admission, though she must know it well enough. "I can't bring you flowers or take you for walks in the park. From what you've told me, your parents would never allow it."

"I know that," she said, so solemn it broke his heart. "They would never agree to our marriage, so we must do this in secret."

Nate balked at that as he realised what it meant. "No," he said, knowing how badly this would reflect on her. "I don't want it to be that way. We can contrive to meet each other easily enough if Matilda helps us, but I won't make this more clandestine that it must be. Once you are certain, I shall ask for your father's approval."

"Oh, Nate, no!" she said, clutching at his shirt. "There's no point. He'll be dreadful to you, and he'll never allow it. He'll just make it impossible to see you again."

"He wants membership to my club, doesn't he?"

Alice hesitated, and then shook her head. "It might tempt him, it's true, but marrying into nobility, being accepted among the higher ranks of the *ton,* that's what he craves most."

Nate shrugged, a strange sense of belligerence forcing him to cling to the idea. He wanted this done properly, for Alice's sake. He'd started things badly, he knew that much, but could he not make amends by doing the right thing now? He wanted everything to be perfect for her, with no hint of shame. "Perhaps. But I have to try, Alice."

"Why?" she demanded, not understanding why he would willingly beat his head against a brick wall and suffer the humiliation of being refused to boot.

"Because," he said, pressing a soft kiss to her mouth, "you are worth doing everything right. If I fail, then I'll put you over my shoulder and carry you to Gretna Green if it comes to it, but I must try to be honourable in this. You deserve that. Good Lord, Alice, you deserve a far better man than me, but I swear, if you'll give me a chance, I'll never give you cause to regret it."

Chapter 12

Dearest Prue,

How I wish you were here with me. I need your advice. How did you know you loved Bedwin? When were you sure he was the one, and that he loved you?

—Excerpt of a letter from Miss Alice Dowding to Prunella Adolphus, Duchess of Bedwin.

Noon. 25th June 1814. *Hunter's*, Covent Garden, London.

"Good Lord, Alice, you deserve a far better man than me, but I swear, if you'll give me a chance, I'll never give you cause to regret it."

Alice stared at Nate. It was hard to breathe and look at him at the same time. When she'd walked into the room and seen him just in his shirt, with the sleeves rolled up to show powerful arms… it had been the most extraordinary thing. She'd gone hot and then cold, her knees had felt uncertain, and her mouth had gone dry. He'd been devastating enough dressed like a gentleman, but dishevelled and unshaven with a roguish, rumpled appearance, he was positively lethal.

All she could hope was that Matilda hadn't got it all horribly wrong, for if so, she was in a great deal of trouble. Except Matilda hadn't been wrong at all. Nate loved her.

He didn't, of course. Alice might have dreamed of love at first sight and handsome princes as a girl, but at the ripe old age of two and twenty, she did not believe a man could fall for her in the space of two evenings. Especially not an extraordinary specimen like Nathaniel Hunt. She believed he desired her, however, and that he liked her, so far at least. Surely, love could come? It was more than many marriages began with.

"I don't think that's true," she said, rousing herself to answer. "That there *is* a better man," she added in a rush, before he could take her meaning all wrong. She'd never realised men were so easily hurt and offended. His pride seemed a fragile beast that would need careful handling. "And I believe you will make me happy, Nate, only... let us do as I ask, and get to know each other."

He nuzzled into her neck, making her sigh. "I have no argument against spending time with you, darling. I never want to be anywhere else."

She chuckled and shook her head. "You say that now. I'll no doubt be consigned to the rank of nagging wife in short order if we do marry."

"*When* we marry," he said, his tone brooking no argument. "And I swear that won't happen."

"How can you possibly swear?" she demanded, tart now, though a smile tugged at her lips. "I might play the part of a shy little nobody when really I'm a dreadful harridan."

"Then," he said, nipping at her earlobe, "you may command me to love and obey you and I'll follow behind, meek as a lamb."

Alice gave an incredulous and very unladylike guffaw of laughter at that. The very idea of Nathaniel Hunt, meek as a lamb, was preposterous.

"Meek as a lion with a thorn in his paw, maybe," she replied with great scepticism.

Nate grinned, turning her face towards him. "Perhaps," he conceded. "So, come and kiss my wound better." He kissed her again, deep and tender, one hand cupping her cheek as the other drew her closer.

"That's not your paw," she said, amused as she drew back a little, gasping for air.

"We'll get there," he chuckled, a wicked sound that made her heart skip about in the most peculiar fashion. "When do you need to be home, love? Will anyone have missed you?"

She shook her head. "I was with the Peculiar Ladies this morning—"

"The what?" he asked, laughing.

Alice pursed her lips, putting up her chin and pretending to look affronted. "The Peculiar Ladies Book Club. Surely Matilda has mentioned it?"

He gave another bark of laughter, for which she returned a reproving look.

"She did mention a book club," he admitted. "But I can see why she left that detail out. Why on earth the *Peculiar* Ladies?"

Alice shrugged, thinking that ought to be patently obvious. "Because we are," she said simply. "We are the misfits and the rejects, the ones there is no place for, so we made one of our own."

"You never belonged there, Alice," he said, growing serious now. "And I have the perfect place for you." He took her hand and guided it to his chest, covering his heart. The steady thud beneath her fingers made Alice feel rather breathless. "Right here," he said.

Alice's breathing hitched and she looked away from him, the moment too intense. Good Lord, but he was…. She sighed.

"And th-then," she stammered, trying to get the conversation back on track, "I was going to Matilda's for the afternoon. So, my parents won't expect me before five. Only Matilda changed it and said I should come for dinner so I could speak with you."

Nate smiled at that. "She did? That was good of her."

"Only I couldn't wait that long," she admitted.

Alice reached out and dared to trail a finger down his cheek, entranced by the rasp of whiskers beneath her touch. To her surprise he shivered, his eyes growing dark.

"I'm glad," he said, as she replaced her finger with her palm, stroking his cheek, captivated by the feel of him, rough and soft all at once. "I was in despair. I'd have been nothing more than a puddle of misery by this evening."

"I'm so sorry, Nate," she whispered, hanging her head. "Your sister was rather cross with me too, for hurting you," she said, meeting his eyes. "Forgive me."

Nate shook his head, smiling. "There's nothing to forgive. It doesn't matter now."

Alice looked away from him, a little overwhelmed by the look in his eyes. Instead, she turned her attention to the room. She'd not taken stock of her surroundings before, too consumed with seeing Nate. Now, she did.

It was a sumptuous room. Thick rugs covered the floor and huge gilt framed paintings dominated the walls. The subject matter was rather risqué, but she supposed that was to be expected in such a place. Scantily clothed beauties dallied with angels, who appeared to be taking liberties, but rather than shocking her, the paintings only made her smile. A large desk took pride of place, heavy with ledgers and stacks of receipts. Nate had sat her on his lap, his long limbs sprawled on a comfortable and capacious settee. She suspected he'd slept on it. Two sturdy, masculine leather chairs flanked an ornate fireplace.

"So, this is your office," she said, smiling a little. "Will you show me the rest of it?"

"Would you like to see?" he asked, surprised.

"Of course!" Alice shook her head at him. "I've never seen such a place in my life. I'm dying to know what it's like."

He grinned at her and then his smile faltered, an anxious look entering his eyes.

"Alice, what I said earlier. Before... before you came in."

Alice raised an eyebrow at him. "About having syphilis?" She'd known from his tone when he'd said it that he was making it up for some reason, though why she couldn't fathom. It had shocked her all the same.

He nodded, looking rather mortified, which was the most adorable thing she'd ever seen in her life.

"It wasn't true," he said in a rush. "I know my reputation is... is... not good," he added, rubbing the back of his neck. "But at least half of it is nonsense, and I only said that because I thought you... were someone else."

"Who?" Alice asked, a little alarmed by the spark of jealousy that lit in her heart.

"Oh, no one in particular," he said at once. "That is, I wasn't expecting anyone," he said, looking increasingly ill at ease. "But sometimes women... turn up."

Alice raised her eyebrows once more. "And you didn't want to see them?"

He shook his head. "I was heartsick for you, Alice. I didn't want anyone else."

Alice digested this and then considered everything she knew about this charming man, everything his reputation suggested. She stared down at him, knowing he would be only too easy to fall in love with. Who was she fooling? She was more than half in love with him now, it would only get worse. As would that spark of jealousy. It would consume her if he betrayed her.

"And what happens if we marry? What happens then when a lady turns up here, seeking your company?" she asked, feeling that spark ignite into something hot and hateful.

"Nothing," he said, never wavering as he looked back at her. "I'd never betray your trust, Alice. If you do me the honour of marrying me, I'd never dishonour you in such a way."

He meant it. She could see it in his eyes and hear it in the solemnity of his vow.

"Well then," she said, letting go of a breath of relief. "You'd best show me around your kingdom."

***

It was strange, seeing *Hunter's* through her eyes. Nate could tell Alice was awestruck, both by the scale and the lavish nature of the place. As a theatre it had an inevitable grandeur of style and decoration. Whilst he'd sunk a small fortune into remodelling the place for his requirements, he'd carefully preserved the building's origins. This was a temple to gambling, after all, and the theatrics of the surroundings suited the immoderate lifestyle it was a part of.

Everything was the best money could buy, from the crystal glasses to the dozens of massive, glinting chandeliers. He employed two of the finest French chefs in the country to feed the members in an opulent dining area. Throughout the vast building there were carpets so thick your boots sank an inch deep into the pile. The best brandy and liquor of every variety, Champagne and wine, cigars and sweetmeats, all were available at the snap of the fingers… whatever a gentleman desired.

In the Garden any exotic fare from the far reaches of the globe was available, for a price, and so it was at *Hunter's*.

There were girls too, naturally, though Nate did not employ them directly. They were hand-picked, of course, his manager saw to that. Only the most beautiful gained entry, Hunter's was exclusive in all ways, but they came of their own accord. They were well treated, protected from harm and they made their own bargains, kept all their earnings. He'd had no desire to be a procurer of flesh of any description.

"It's remarkable, Nate," Alice said, trailing her hand across the smooth green baize of a Faro table. "I'd never dreamed of anything so... impressive."

Nate shrugged. "Impressive, perhaps," he agreed, giving her a crooked smile. "But a very long way from respectable."

"Respectability is overrated," she said with a prim sniff, and it delighted him she would tease him so as he saw the laughter in her eyes. Yet, he grew serious, knowing this was not at all the case.

"Darling," he said, taking her hand and drawing her close again. "You might lose a deal of your friends in choosing me. You do understand that? Your parents may wash their hands of you. People may cut you in the street. I... I know I've left you little option in the matter, but... you must prepare yourself for some unpleasantness."

He felt his heart clench at the idea she should suffer a moment's unhappiness because of him, but there was little point in denying the obvious.

"Matilda is far braver than I, you know," he said, sliding an arm about her waist. "There are enough who knew her before Montagu's refusal to marry her, who know and believe her story. The Earl of St Clair and his mother have been wonderful in showing their support, as have a handful of others. Thank God, Matilda was well liked before the scandal, so that has saved her from complete ruin, but there are many who have been cruel, more who closed doors on her and laughed in her face. Yet still, she stands tall and dares them to do their worst. She's never hidden herself away or acted as though she has something to be ashamed of. She meets everyone's eye, and people respect her for that."

"You admire her," Alice said, smiling.

He nodded. "I admire her enormously. She has more strength than anyone I've ever known. When times were dark, she kept me going. I owe her a great deal, and I've given her little reason to thank me."

"I'm sure that's not true."

He laughed at that. "I'm afraid it is, but that's Matilda's story to tell if she wishes to. I'm afraid you'll not think well of me once the story is done."

She leaned into him. "I know the story, Nate, and Matilda has long forgiven you, as you well know. You were at your wits' end, sick with grief and worry. It was just a dreadful stroke of luck; she knows that as well as I do. Of all the men to encounter, though, Montagu had to be the vilest."

Nate nodded, his jaw clenching. He'd give no argument on that score. "He'll get his comeuppance eventually."

Nate smiled, not wanting to think about that, not wanting to think about anything but Alice, and the fact she was really considering becoming his wife. It seemed too extraordinary. He'd told himself he didn't want the life most men had. Marriage, a home, children… of course not. Nathaniel Hunt didn't crave such dull, commonplace aspirations. Except he had, he'd craved them so badly he couldn't even acknowledge the desire, for knowing he'd never have it might destroy any peace of mind left to him.

And then he'd met Alice.

"I can't believe you're here," he said, tracing a fingertip down her jawline. "Promise I'm not dreaming."

She blushed a little and smiled, looking pleased at his words. "I think you'd conjure something a little more impressive if it were a dream," she said, and he saw again the doubt flickering in her eyes, the uncertainty she was worth such a compliment.

Nate caught her chin, making her meet his gaze. "You're all I dream of, Alice. Never doubt it."

She blinked up at him and then gave a slight shrug. "I'll try."

"You must promise me something else, though, darling," he said, trying not to consider all the horrors that could have befallen her in Covent Garden among the cutpurses and scoundrels. It made his blood run cold even thinking of it. "You must never come here again."

Her face fell in such dramatic fashion he couldn't help but laugh, and he pressed a kiss to her nose by way of apology.

"I only mean before we are married. *When* we're married," he said, softening the blow a little. "I can accompany you, but never, ever come here by yourself again. It's too dangerous for a woman alone. Promise me?"

To his amusement she glowered a little before huffing out words of acknowledgement.

"Very well."

"Thank you," he said, so adding, "My heart can't stand that kind of worry, love. Be gentle with it."

Once the tour was done, Nate smuggled Alice out of the club and into her waiting carriage.

"Go straight to the house. I'll follow on in a little while and join you for dinner."

Alice nodded and gave him a little wave. Nate smiled and closed the door on her, turning to give the driver the address. He watched as the carriage threaded through the bustling streets and tried to breathe. She'd come to him. Shy little Alice Dowding had faced her family's rage and heaven alone knew what risks to come and find him at his club. Alone. The enormity of that wasn't lost on him. Whoever had said she lacked courage? Besides his sister, he suspected she was the bravest person he knew.

Chapter 13

The strangest thing happened this morning. I was out shopping with Mama, and I swear I saw Alice walking alone through Covent Garden. Of course, it couldn't have been. Can you imagine, dear little Alice alone in the big city? How absurd. I don't know what I was thinking.

—Excerpt of a letter from Miss Ruth Stone to Miss Harriet Stanhope.

The evening of the 25th June 1814. Half Moon Street. London.

"Alice!" Matilda beamed at her as she was shown into their elegant parlour. The young woman had the most exquisite taste, Alice thought, as she looked around the room. "How lovely to have your company. Have you had a restful afternoon?"

Alice bit her lip and was quite unable to hold back the fierce blush that scalded her cheeks. Matilda looked at her in surprise and they waited until the footman who'd shown her in closed the door on them.

"Why, Alice, whatever have you been up to?" she asked with a mixture of amusement and alarm as she crossed the room to take Alice's hands. "You look thoroughly guilt-ridden," she added, looking her up and down with a frown of consternation.

"I…." Alice began, wondering if it would shock Matilda. "I went to *Hunter's*. To see Nate."

For a moment Matilda just gaped at her, her hand covering her heart in shock. "You... went to *Hunter's*. Alone?"

Alice nodded. "I did. I spoke to Nate. He said to tell you he'd be along presently."

Matilda gestured for Alice to sit and did so herself, apparently too surprised to speak. Alice busied herself with taking off her gloves and avoided Matilda's scrutiny.

"Why didn't you ask me to accompany you?" Matilda said, once she'd found her voice again. "You ought never to have gone alone."

Alice bit back a sigh. She knew that, obviously, but it rankled a little that everyone was so utterly dumbfounded, even though she didn't know why it bothered her so. Apart from meeting a strange man on a moonlit balcony, it *was* the most daring thing she'd done in her life. That night had changed her, she realised. She didn't want to be meek little Alice any longer. She wanted to know who she really was, and what she was capable of.

"I'm quite all right, Matilda," she said, smiling at her friend. "And I didn't plan it. I was on my way home and suddenly I... I just had to see him. I can't explain it. I imagine you think me foolish, when it was only a few hours before he'd be here."

"No," Matilda said, shaking her head. Her voice was quiet, and she returned a look of understanding. "No, I don't think you foolish, but I do think you must take a great deal more care, darling." She sat forward then, fixing Alice with her gaze. "So, you saw Nate?"

Alice nodded.

"And?"

"And...." Alice shrugged, not entirely sure what to say. "And I asked him to court me, so that I may get to know him a little better before—"

"Before?" Matilda squeaked, sitting up a little straighter.

Alice smiled, knowing there was one person in the world who would be delighted. "Before I accept his proposal."

There was a shriek of joy and Matilda crossed the distance between them, tugging Alice to her feet and throwing her arms about her. "We're going to be sisters!"

Alice laughed with her, wondering at how easy this was. She'd always longed for a sister, for a family where hugs, warmth, and laughter were easy and natural, unlike her own parents, stiff with formality and the terror of putting a foot wrong in society. They didn't touch. Her mother's idea of affection was a pat on the hand. She might allow Alice to kiss her cheek if she were in particularly good spirits. Such a display of happiness as this would have been considered vulgar indeed in the Dowding household. The idea made Alice quail inside, and she pushed it down. She had a few weeks before they would discover the truth.

Once the euphoria had died down, the two women sat huddled together on the settee, all formality cast aside. Matilda had kicked off her shoes and drawn her legs up under her skirts, and feeling terribly daring, Alice had copied her. Such unpretentiousness was new to her and seemed wonderfully freeing.

"Tell me about him, Tilda," Alice said, leaning her head on the back of the settee and watching her friend.

"What do you want to know?"

"Everything," Alice said, grinning.

Matilda pulled a face and then laughed. "Good heavens, now I've no idea what to tell you. Let me see." She tapped a finger against her chin, considering. "Well, he's not at all like his reputation, for starters."

She must have caught Alice's sceptical expression as she pressed on.

"Oh, I'm not saying he's an angel. There's no smoke without fire, I know, and yes, you'll have heard of his opera singers and dancers, I've no doubt. He's been a devil in the past, but it's not who he is. After father died...." Matilda sighed and shook her head. "They were so close when he was a boy. Nate adored him; we both did. Such a charming and funny man. Only we didn't realise then how irresponsible he was. Nate has inherited his charm, but he's matured and takes his responsibilities seriously. That was a trick papa never learned."

"It must have been a dreadful shock to you," Alice said, feeling her heart clench as Matilda laughed. She tried to make light of it, but her regret was all too clear.

"We never mixed in the most illustrious of circles, but our name was a good one. We were accepted to nearly all the best events and I had everything I could possibly want. Pretty dresses, jewels; my father never denied me anything I wanted, and I never questioned it. We were wealthy, so why shouldn't I have those things? We had a smart town house and yes, our country home needed a little work perhaps, but it wasn't so shabby. In fact, I rather loved the rough edges. It was home."

Alice nodded and reached out, taking Matilda's hand, sensing this was hard for her to relate.

"It was all so sudden," she said, her voice growing quiet. "Father had been in a strange mood for weeks. Quiet and sullen one moment, and then losing his temper for no reason at all. Whenever we asked him what was wrong, he'd smile and beg our forgiveness and tell us there was nothing wrong, nothing for us to worry about. I remember those exact words. *There's nothing for you to worry about, Tilda, darling.*"

Matilda snorted and shook her head. "He fell ill and took to his bed, and so we sent for the doctor. Nothing seemed to help him, and he grew feverish. That's when we suspected that there was something wrong. He rambled in his sleep about money and... and we felt a little uneasy, but Father liked to gamble. We knew that. We just assumed he'd played rather too deep and it was on his mind."

Alice squeezed Matilda's fingers and watched her friend smile, but it didn't reach her eyes.

"The first bailiff arrived the next day. I was so frightened. Nate sent him away with a flea in his ear. It had to be a mistake, just a bill that had gone astray. Then Father called Nate to his room and explained he'd made a few bad investments and he'd been gambling to make up the money he'd lost. He was so rueful and apologetic; we never guessed how serious it was. Nate comforted him and told him not to worry, he'd sort it all out. So, he went to see Papa's man of business and…." Matilda drew in a deep breath. "Everything was gone. The houses, the jewels… we couldn't even pay the staff. Men came into the house and took our things away."

She pressed the back of her hand to her mouth and stifled a sob.

"Oh, Tilda, I'm so sorry." Alice shuffled closer and put her arms about her. "You must have been so frightened."

Matilda nodded. "We had to move into a horrible little house. It was damp and dirty, but it was all we could afford. Of course, the damp made Father worse, too, and he was hardly ever in his right mind. He rambled and got cross with us, he didn't understand why he wasn't at home in his own bed. Nate took it hard, but he swore he'd get it all back. He promised me it would only be for a little while. Thank God, he had a little money of his own put away and he invested it in a gambling club. He knew the fellow who owned it well and knew he could make the place more than it was, so he bought into the partnership. He said if there were bloody fools out there who would beggar their families over the throw of a dice, he was only ever going to be on the other side of the table from now on."

"So, *Hunter's* was born?" Alice said, smiling a little, but Matilda shook her head.

"Not then. It took months, and all the time Father's doctor's bills ate most of what Nate brought home. Nate despised him for that. He couldn't bear to look at him."

Alice couldn't wonder at it. What must have it been like, to have lived a life of privilege only to have it stripped away from you in a matter of hours? To discover the man who ought to have protected your interests had squandered and gambled with your futures?

"You know what happened when Father died," Matilda said with a sigh. "But you don't know how hard Nate worked. He barely slept. He was drowning in guilt. Guilt for leaving me in a position where my reputation was left in tatters, guilt for the fact I had no pretty clothes, no hopes for the future. He swore he'd make it right, that I'd be so wealthy I'd never have to worry again." She smiled then and swept her hand around them to illustrate the luxury of their surroundings. "*Et voila*," she said with a chuckle. "He kept his word."

"He did," Alice agreed, smiling.

"The only thing he could never fix was our name," she said with a shrug. "*Hunter's* is now synonymous with luxury and vice, and so are we."

"That's not true, Tilda." Alice frowned. "You wouldn't be invited to so many events if it were the case."

Matilda gave her a pitying look, not unkind but implying that Alice was far more an innocent than she. Which was true, she supposed. Smoothing out the heavy swathes of her gorgeous blue silk gown, Matilda spoke in a low, measured voice. "Nate has powerful friends, darling. The kind of people who owe him favours, and Nate collects by ensuring I get entry to all the best events. However, that does not mean they accept me. I will never get a marriage proposal and make the match I might once have done," she said with a twisted smile. "Though I'm not short of other kinds of propositions."

Alice gasped in shock. "You don't mean—?"

Matilda reached out and tugged one of Alice's red curls. "Yes, I do mean. If I want a position as a rich man's mistress, I've offers aplenty. Why, even a duke has vied for my company."

"Oh, Tilda, no." Alice stared at her, not knowing what to say but Matilda just laughed.

"Oh, don't look so mortified. Nate has made me a wealthy woman in my own right. I'm independent, and maybe I'll find some nice, penniless gentleman who will overlook my tarnished past and fall in love with me. It's all I really want you know, to love and be loved in return. Well, anyway, hope springs eternal."

Alice stared at her, knowing—as if she hadn't always known—why Nate admired his sister so. A lesser woman might have hidden herself away in shame and let the world win. Alice would have been that woman such a short time ago. Not any longer. Matilda had inspired her too, with her bravery. Perhaps Alice had made mistakes in trying to break out of her shell, but they were her mistakes to own, and to fix. If she was to marry Nate she'd not do so out of desperation, but because she wanted to, and because he wanted her.

As if she'd conjured him with the thought, the door opened, and Nate walked in.

"My two favourite ladies," he said, grinning at them. "Is dinner ready? I'm half-starved."

He looked different from earlier. Washed, shaved, and immaculately turned out: every inch the gentleman. Perversely, Alice rather regretted it. She'd enjoyed seeing him a little less than perfect. It had made him seem a little less godlike. Not much, but a little.

"I imagine so," Matilda said, smiling at him as she stood. "Let me go and see."

She gave Alice a sly wink and left the room, leaving the two of them alone.

"Hello," he said, staring at her in a way that made her breath catch.

He moved closer and took her hands, pulling her to her feet. He raised first one and then the other hand to his lips, kissing her fingers.

"I missed you," he said, placing both hands upon his chest and holding them there beneath his.

"It's only been a couple of hours at most," she said, laughing. "I can't believe you missed me in that time."

He made a pained sound and winced a little. "So, I see you didn't miss me in the least then. My poor heart."

"Foolish man," she scolded, laughing and moved away from him as there was a discreet knock before Matilda entered the room.

"Dinner is served," she announced, imitating the sound of a snooty butler.

Nate laughed and offered each of them an arm apiece, before leading them into dinner.

***

26th June 1814. Baker Street, London.

"Oh, but Papa, we have to go," Alice said, wondering at her rotten luck. "It's all arranged."

They'd all been due to attend the Vauxhall Gardens this evening in company with several other families of their acquaintance. Lucia and Bonnie and many of the others would be there too, as well as Matilda and Nate. Alice had hoped to meet with her friends and to find an opportunity to slip away in the crowds and spend time with Nate in private.

"I do think it's too bad of you, Mr Dowding," her mother said with a sniff, "to spoil our enjoyment at this late hour. How is Alice supposed to get herself suitably betrothed if we spend our evenings at home?"

Alice looked between them. Her mother had been a handsome woman in her youth, and still had a slender figure, her red hair now faded to a pale apricot which was most becoming. However, there was an air of dissatisfaction that always hung about her. It made her features appear more severe than they perhaps might, drawing her mouth into a line of displeasure in repose. Her father, by contrast, was a large ruddy face man, currently flushed with irritation.

"Dash it all, one night will hardly ruin her chances. Besides which, young Bindley is good and hooked. It doesn't matter what happens now, we've all but made the arrangements."

"Papa!" Alice replied, the colour leaching from her face in horror.

"Yes, really, sir," her mother reproached him. "That was not well done of you, to speak of such things before your daughter." She turned back with what Alice assumed was supposed to be a reassuring smile. "Don't you worry your head about it, Alice. Papa will deal with all the vulgar financial details."

Alice felt her heart beating in her throat and, for once in her life, couldn't hold her tongue. "But mother, I don't—"

"I know you don't want to consider it," her mother said, speaking over her and waving a hand to silence any further exclamation. "But you will be a married lady soon enough, with a grand household of your own. Just think, an earl's son," she said with a happy sigh, before adding brightly, "and if anything happened to his brother—"

"Mother!" Alice exclaimed, shocked and horrified.

Mrs Dowding did at least have the grace to blush a little. "Well, one doesn't like to think of it, naturally, but accidents happen, and his brother *is* some ten years older *and* still unmarried. Once his father has passed… well, you might yet become a countess one day, and any son you bore would be the next earl."

Mrs Dowding gave a wistful sigh and even her father returned to the conversation and looked quite animated.

"My grandson, the earl," he said, shaking his head and looking proud as punch. "Now, that would be something."

Alice's stomach churned with the strong desire to lose her lunch. Never mind the fact her parents were blithely killing off the rest of the family, begetting an heir with Edgar Bindley? Please, God, no. Anything but that. She'd long since decided one thing: ruination was far more attractive than a life with Mr Bindley.

"Perhaps he'll be there tonight," she said in a rush, too desperate to get out of the house and away from this appalling conversation to consider the fact she was manipulating their ambitions to her own ends. Any chance of seeing Mr Bindley again was to be avoided at all costs in her opinion, but they didn't know that. They were too caught up in their own daydreams and ambitions to consider for a moment she might not be of the same mind.

"She does have a point," her mother said, casting Alice a sly smile of approval that made her stomach turn over again. "If he's there and she's not, he might find another young lady to fix his interest with."

This argument seemed to weigh on her father's mind and he heaved a heavy sigh. "Oh, very well, then. Never let it be said I stood in the way of my daughter's dreams."

Alice almost gaped at the man. *Her dreams*? When had he ever asked her what her dreams were? When had he ever asked if she liked or esteemed Mr Bindley, let alone if she felt any desire to spend the rest of her days with him? Nonetheless, she had achieved her aim and so she swallowed down the bitterness in her mouth and forced something resembling a smile to her face.

"Thank you, Papa," she said, and hurried away to get ready.

Chapter 14

I'm so looking forward to Vauxhall Gardens. Mama has bought me a lovely new gown in a splendid bronze colour, and I am to accompany Bedwin's sister, Lady Helena. She's such a comical thing, and not a bit high in the instep as you might imagine of a duke's sister.

—Excerpt of a letter from Miss Minerva Butler to Miss Kitty Connolly.

The evening of the 26th June 1814. Vauxhall Gardens, Lambeth.

A great deal of screeching and shrill cries of distress rent the air as the Dowding family's hired boat and a half dozen others approached the shallower waters at the edge of the Thames. The boats knocked together in their bid to reach the shore as watermen leapt forward, grabbing hold of the wherries and hauling them towards the banks. Ladies squealed and grabbed at their hats as the boats pitched and lurched. Alice gasped and took hold of the boat itself as the filthy water of the Thames lapped high up the sides. It had been rather lovely during the crossing on a beautiful summer's evening, but less so when one considered being tipped in head first. Still, they were here, thank goodness.

Alice picked up the skirts of her dress and stepped carefully from the wherry as it swayed beneath her. Duck boards covered the filth and reek at the banks of the Thames, and she stepped with care on the slippery wood, picking her way in her satin slippers. It was a relief to be on solid ground again. The boat had seemed a slender thing to her eye, and low in the water once loaded with her well-sprung father, her mother, and several other guests. The watermen seemed blithely unconcerned, however, and so she'd tried to trust in their confidence and enjoy the experience.

Indeed, it was a lovely evening, the sun just setting and glinting in coral colours upon the dark waters of the Thames. The huge façade of the proprietor's house greeted them, belonging to the urbane and compelling Mr Jonathan Tyers. Flaming torches lined the path from the water gate to the entrance. On exiting the building on the far side, it was like stepping into the colourful environs of a dream.

Vauxhall was lit up, a romantic and exotic setting, akin to entering the land of the fae.

Music was audible, drifting on the warm evening air, and Alice experienced a little shiver of excitement. She would see Nate tonight. This was what lovers did, arranged illicit rendezvous and used any excuse to meet in secret. That she had a lover seemed extraordinary and improbable, and only added to the dreamlike feel of the evening.

The gardens themselves were vast and Alice felt her fist twinge of anxiety at seeing just how expansive they were. Thank heavens she'd planned to meet Matilda and Nate by the cascade, for there would be little chance of stumbling upon them by accident.

There were a variety of walks to take around the gardens, all of them brilliantly lit by variegated coloured lamps. This gave the walks and gardens themselves an enchanting sweep of stained glass-like shadows that delicately painted all of those who walked beneath them.

They first made their way in the direction of the music, and the incredible sight that greeted her delighted Alice: a building of such fanciful design it looked like the sugar icing on a bride cake. It took the form of a temple, built on several levels and decorated with colourful paint and ornate spires. There were balconies where the orchestra sat in semicircles to face the audience. On the largest balcony was a huge organ, the silver pipes glinting in the lamplight. Ladies and gentlemen in all their finery stood before them, listening to the music and chatting, milling about and greeting acquaintances.

"Alice!"

Alice turned and beamed with delight to see Harriet and Kitty hurrying towards her. Greeting her friends, she was pleased to see that the two women seemed to have decided to further their friendship before their trip to the St Clair estate later in the summer.

"Isn't it enchanting?" Kitty said, staring about her wide-eyed. "I've never seen anything like it."

"Have you never been here before?" Alice asked in surprise.

Kitty shook her head. "Never. Harriet asked me to come and I nearly snapped her hand off," she said, grinning.

Alice smiled at her enthusiasm, more so as she could see that Harriet was enjoying Kitty's excitement too.

"Harry, aren't you going to introduce me?"

They turned as a man approached and Harriet nodded. "Of course," she said as the man stood at her side, grinning.

It was apparent at once that this must be her brother. They were alike and yet quite obviously different. Harriet, who was always a rather serious and even stern presence, was the opposite of the man beside her. He beamed at Alice, hazel eyes alight with good humour and mischief as Harriet presented him.

"Alice this is my brother, Henry Stanhope. Henry, my friend, Miss Alice Dowding."

"Charmed," Henry said, beaming at her.

"Pleased to meet you, Mr Stanhope," Alice said, quite unable not to return his smile. He had the look of a cheeky schoolboy despite being almost in his twenties. A scattering of freckles over his nose and cheeks did little to dispel the impression.

"I'm playing chaperone tonight, Miss Dowding," he said, offering her his arm. "Would you like to accompany us?"

Harriet snorted. "You? Chaperone?" she said, sounding incredulous. "What an idea. You couldn't chaperone a sponge cake." She rolled her eyes, ignoring Henry's exclamation of protest. "My Aunt Nell is with us too, Alice, if you do wish to accompany us."

"For what that's worth," Henry said, giving his sister a reproachful look. "I'm a deal more effective than she is."

"Yes," Harriet agreed. "Until you get sidetracked by a pretty girl or a game of chance. Aunt Nell is, at least, perfectly respectable."

Henry blushed a little but held his tongue, so Alice assumed Harriet had the right of it.

Once she had introduced Harriet, Henry, and Aunt Nell to her parents, Alice gained permission to go with her friends. She would return to her parents for supper, later in the evening. With a light heart and a deal of anticipation, Alice took Kitty's arm and they set off to explore.

Chattering happily the group made their way along the Grand South walk, admiring the splendid Triumphal Arches as they passed beneath. Alice was enraptured. Although she had visited Vauxhall in previous years, never had she been so captivated. Perhaps it was the warmth of the evening, or the company of her friends, or perhaps it was the anticipation of seeing Nate, but the evening had a magical air impossible to resist. Not that she had any desire to do so. She felt alive and full of hope, and just a little reckless.

The gardens seemed vast indeed as darkness fell, despite the illumination from the thousands of lamps. The many gravelled walks were bounded by high hedges and trees, interspersed with ever more extraordinary delights. Pavilions, lodges, and groves, temples, porticoes, and colonnades; at every turn there was something new to attract the senses, and at every interval music from a variety of bands and orchestras. The people themselves were no less entrancing, everyone bedecked in their finery and laughing and gossiping with such animation.

"Oh, what time is it, Henry?" Harriet asked as they moved along the Dark Walk. "We mustn't miss the cascade."

Alice's heart skipped a little as this was where she would meet Nate. She held her breath as Henry took out his pocket watch. "Good heavens," he said, surprised. "It's almost ten o'clock."

With a cry of dismay Harriet glared at her brother. "You were supposed to tell us when it was a quarter to," she said, shaking her head. "Well, there's nothing for it, we shall have to run."

Grasping hold of Alice's hand, Harriet took off. With a shriek of surprise, Alice had little option but to run after her.

The scandalised calls of Harriet's Aunt Nell followed them. But, if Alice was intent on seeing Nate, Harriet was just as passionate to see the cascade, which was said to be a miracle of modern engineering. Kitty ran beside them, one hand holding her bonnet in place as she laughed with delight.

As they ran, the bell sounding the commencement of the spectacle clamoured through the gardens, and the girls shrieked and laughed harder as they scurried down the paths, their dainty satin shoes sliding and slipping on the gravelled surface.

"This way!" Henry called, turning left onto a wide path that led into woodland. He seemed to have the right of it as they joined dozens of other people, all hurrying and jostling in their eagerness to reach the cascade.

Flushed and breathless, finally they reached their destination and Henry redeemed himself in his sister's eyes by elbowing and forcing his way forward and making a path until they reached the front. Before them was a huge, heavy dark curtain, and the crowd murmured with excitement to see what lay behind the thick swathes of material.

Alice, by contrast, was scanning the crowd, straining her neck in a most unladylike fashion which would have gained her a dreadful scolding had her mother witnessed it.

"Looking for something?"

Nearly leaping out of her skin, Alice drew in a sharp breath at the sound of the familiar voice close behind her.

"Don't look round," he whispered, his lips so close to her ear that Alice shivered with pleasure from the warmth of his voice against her skin. To her shock, one large hand moved to her waist, the warmth of his palm burning through the soft muslin of her gown, resting beneath her spencer.

With a guilty glance to her side, Alice wondered if anyone had noticed his audacity or her blushes, but Kitty and Harriet were introducing Matilda to Henry and Aunt Nell and the rest of the crowd were intent on the spectacle before them.

"Do you mind?" he asked, his voice low and eliciting another round of shivering. "I'm a wretched fellow for such liberties, and I shall stop at once if you prefer, but I've missed you so much. I'll go mad if I can't touch you."

Alice's heart pounded as a delighted smile curved over her mouth. Perhaps she should scold him, but she didn't want to. She wanted to lean into him, to press her body against his and feel the heat and weight of him at her back. The desire to do so was an ache beneath her skin.

"I don't mind," she whispered breathlessly.

"I want to kiss you," he said, his thumb stroking her side in slow, insistent sweeps.

Her colour rose higher and Alice was glad of the darkness, but before she could consider an answer, the curtain drew back, and the crowd gasped in awe.

Before them was a rural scene painted in extraordinary detail. So skilful had the painter been that Alice felt she could walk into the design and find herself in the depths of the countryside. A miller's house and a water mill set the scene, but the most striking feature—and the one that drew murmurs of wonder from the crowd—was the cascade itself. The water seemed to be moving, rising up with foam at the bottom and gliding away again and the sound of rushing water was loud enough to make it necessary to speak a deal louder to make oneself heard.

"It's mechanical," Harriet exclaimed, looking more excited and exuberant than Alice had ever seen her. "The water is made of sheets of tin on large belts. The mechanism is moved by a team of men."

"Dash it all, Harry, don't spoil the spectacle by explaining it!" her brother protested, shaking her head at her.

"How can the explanation spoil it?" Harriet demanded, genuinely perplexed. "I think it's marvellous."

Henry rolled his eyes and turned his attention back to the cascade.

"Come with me," Nate whispered, the hand on her waist guiding her away from her friends. Alice hardly dared breathe as they moved away from the cascade, away from the crowds and into the darkness of the surrounding woodland.

Once out of sight and in the privacy afforded by a huge oak tree, Nate pulled her into his arms.

"May I kiss you?" he asked, his voice rough with desire.

By way of answer, Alice reached up and tugged at his neck, wishing there were a handy footstool to be had. Nate's lips were soft and warm, his mouth urgent upon hers as they kissed.

This, she thought as all the worries and stresses of the day fell from her shoulders, *anything is worth this.*

Nate drew back, his face only dimly visible as a little moonlight filtered through the canopy overhead.

"Matilda will invite you and some of the others for a walk at Kensington Gardens tomorrow," he said, one large hand cupping her cheek. "Can you come?"

Alice bit her lip. "Mother has told me I'm not to visit with her again," she said, feeling wretched. "But if I go with one of the other girls... maybe?"

Nate sighed and pressed his forehead to hers. "Do you hate me for having to lie and plot in such an underhand manner?"

"Never," she said, sliding her arms around him and pressing close. "I hate my parents for their snobbery. It's them that force me to lie. You're a good man, a kind one, one who would make me happy. They're just too blind to see it, or to care what I want."

"Do I make you happy?" he asked, a thread of anxiety in his voice. "I think I must cause you a deal of worry."

"Yes, you silly creature," she said, marvelling that he could doubt it. "You do make me happy, but I'll be happier still if you kiss me again. We can't be gone long; the spectacle must be almost over."

He chuckled at that but instead of kissing her he turned away.

"What are you...?" she began, and then smothered a squeal of surprise as he swung her up into his arms.

"Here," he said, moving sure-footed in the darkness. "A tree stump should suffice."

He set her down and Alice beamed at him as she discovered they were now level.

"Oh, yes," she said, sighing with pleasure. "That's much better."

Nate stared at her, smiling, and Alice blushed a little at the look in his eyes. He looked as if he wanted to devour her. It was rather thrilling.

"Aren't you going to kiss me, then?" she asked, feeling a little of her shyness return, which seemed odd as she'd thrown caution to the wind already tonight.

Nate shook his head, his smile widening to include a glimpse of white teeth. Like the smiling jaws of a tiger. Alice experienced a visceral thrill of anticipation.

"No," he said. "I did already. It's your turn."

He stared at her and she became aware of the rapid rise and fall of his chest, the desire darkening his eyes.

"I'm all yours," he said, his voice rough. "Do with me what you will."

The words set sparks in her blood, blazing to life like a match to brandy. It was heady, that invitation, giving her power and permission to do as she pleased.

Alice reached out, cupping his face between her hands. She stroked his cheeks and frowned a little at the neatly tied cravat. "I preferred you without the cravat, and coat, and waistcoat," she said with a sigh.

"You mean to tell me I'm wearing too many clothes?" he asked with a wicked chuckle that might have made her blush once again, but Alice raised her chin.

"Yes," she said with a touch of defiance. "I rather think you are."

"Touch me then," he said, sounding breathless. "Put your hands on my skin."

Alice gasped, but the idea was too tantalising to resist. "How?" she asked, frowning. "There are too many layers."

He moved at once, unbuttoning his waistcoat and tugging his shirt free of his waistband. "Here," he said, taking her hands and guiding them beneath his shirt. If Alice felt the shock of his skin, hot against her cool hands, it was nothing to his gasp as she put her palms to his sides.

"Oh, God," he murmured, ducking his head and nuzzling her neck. "I've done nothing but dream of this, of you," he said, pressing kisses to her skin. "Of your hands on me."

Alice sighed with pleasure, overwhelmed by the softness of his mouth at her neck, of the heat and power of the big body beneath her hands. Feeling wanton and adventurous, she slid her hands higher, delighted at the shivers that ran over him as she moved. Her fingers revelled in the feel of him, soft skin and the tantalising rasp of coarse hair. She slid over muscle, over the ridges of his abdomen, to lay her fingers upon his chest. His heart was a fast, heavy thud beneath her palm, making her own race in acknowledgement of his desire. Smoothing her hands over the broad expanse, her thumb found the tiny nub of a male nipple, pebbled and hard beneath her touch.

Nate shivered and groaned, and Alice felt a surge of power the like of which she'd never known. That this strong body should quiver at the touch of her fingers seemed unlikely, but the knowledge made her bold. Her thumb slid back and forth over the tiny peak as Nate covered her mouth and kissed her again, a desperate sound torn from his throat as he pulled her closer.

"I can't bear this, Alice," he said, when he finally let her up for air. "We must marry, please, love. Tell me you want it too?"

Before she could answer he kissed her again and she was relieved for the reprieve. Her head was spinning. Desire was telling her to say yes, *yes please,* as soon as may be. Yet what remained of her cautious soul pleaded with her to have a care. Could she really keep a man like this happy? Would he always want her like this? Or once the novelty had worn off would he seek diversions away from home? She just needed a little longer, a little more time to be sure.

"I'll be so good to you," he said, covering her neck with open-mouthed kisses. Alice inclined her neck as his hand sought the buttons of her spencer, exposing more of her collarbone as the low neck of her gown was revealed. "I'll give you everything you desire, I swear it. I'll make you happy."

It was overwhelming and wonderful, her blood surging in her veins as her hands still explored beneath his shirt, yet dimly she became aware that the sound of the waterfall had stopped, and voices were filling the clearing once again.

"Nate," she said, regretful for forcing them back to reality as her hands slid up his back and clutched at heavy shoulders. "Nate, the spectacle is over. We'll be missed."

Nate cursed and leaned his forehead to hers, breathing hard. "Alice," he whispered. "Tell me you're as insane as I am? Tell me you feel it too?"

"I do," she said, drawing back to meet his eyes. "I do and... and it frightens me a little."

"Me too," he said with a rueful smile. "My life is in your hands. Such power you have over me, love."

There was indeed trepidation in his eyes, but Alice did not feel power at his confession, only a wave of tenderness. She pressed a kiss to his mouth, sweet and loving, and he sighed, closing his eyes.

"Come," he said with obvious reluctance. "We'd best join the others." With deft hands he returned his shirt to rights, but allowed Alice to button his waistcoat, smiling fondly at her.

"There," she said, smoothing her hands over the warm silk that covered his chest. "Good as new."

Nate gave a wistful sigh and guided her out of the trees, slipping them expertly into the crowds with none the wiser.

"Matilda is just there," he said, bending to speak into her ear. "I'll rejoin you in a moment."

Alice nodded and hurried back to her friends. Matilda turned to give her a knowing smile before sliding her arm though Alice's and returning to her conversation with Henry. From the look in the young man's eyes, he was smitten. Alice smiled and couldn't fault him. Matilda, as ever, looked exquisite. Her dress was a rather daring shade of violet which a lesser beauty could never have carried off but, matched as it was with a white satin spencer and a charming hat trimmed with ostrich feathers, she was quite startlingly lovely.

Alice started as she looked across the crowds, seeking Nate, and found instead the unemotional, intent gaze of the Marquess of Montagu.

"Tilda," she whispered, once a lull in the conversation allowed her to draw Matilda's attention.

"What is it?" Matilda asked, alerted by the tone of Alice's voice.

"Do *not* look to your right, but Montagu is here, and he's been staring at you this past minute or more."

What Matilda felt or thought of this information, Alice was none the wiser, for neither her expression nor her posture changed in the least. To her chagrin, however, Matilda did not heed her advice, but turned and looked directly at the marquess.

Alice held her breath. How Matilda could dare to hold the gaze of such a cold and powerful man she could not fathom, yet hold it she did, staring back at him as though she were the Queen and he an impudent pleb. It was like being caught between wolves, one circling the other, and all the tiny hairs on the back of Alice's neck stood on end.

After what seemed an eternity, the marquess inclined his head, such an infinitesimal gesture it would have been missed on any other man. From him, it seemed vastly significant.

They watched as the party he was with gained his attention, a beautiful brunette moving closer and clinging to his arm. For just a second, Alice thought she saw irritation flash across his granite features, but a moment later he had turned away and she could no longer be sure.

"My word," she said, letting out a breath she'd not realised she was holding. "What was that about?"

Matilda shrugged, moving away as the rest of the crowd dispersed now the show was over. "He likes to remind me I am nothing to him," she said, the words spoken lightly though Alice thought her voice trembled a little. "And I like to prove to him he's less than nothing, the dirt beneath my heel."

Privately, Alice thought there'd been a great deal more than nothing exchanged or proven in the space of those fraught seconds, but she kept such opinions to herself. There was something between the marquess and Matilda, some strange connection that drew them together. Alice decided to speak to Nate about it, to warn him that the marquess was not done with his sister. Though what the man had in mind she didn't dare consider.

They walked in silence for a little. She thought perhaps Matilda needed a moment to compose herself, and Alice was more than content to remember the moments she'd just shared with Nate, and the illicit thrill of his hot skin beneath her hands. Her fingers still burned with the memory. She could see him now, walking a little ahead of them with Henry, his broad shoulders filling the dark blue coat he wore like a hand in a glove.

Alice sighed.

"Did you enjoy the cascade, my dear?" Matilda asked, sounding altogether too innocent.

Alice looked up to see amusement glimmering in her friend's eyes and blushed furiously.

"It was most... diverting," she said with dignity, putting her chin in the air. Then she caught Matilda's eye again and could do nothing but dissolve into giggles as Matilda joined her. Nate turned and looked at them, raising one eyebrow, and the two of them only laughed harder, drawing stares of reproach from disapproving matrons on all sides.

Alice felt a rush of happiness. Not only was Nate hers, desperate to wed her and make her his own, but Matilda was by her side too. She would have a sister, a family who were warm and loving and so different from her own it was hard to credit.

She felt a pang at the idea her parents might disown her if she followed this path to its natural conclusion. Though their selfishness hurt her, their ambitions were for her as much as for themselves. They simply didn't understand why such things were not of importance to her too. That happiness should come before status was something that would be as foreign a concept to them as the reverse was to Alice. Would they ever forgive her? The likelihood that they would not was one she could not ignore.

If she married Nate, they would believe she'd brought shame upon their family. Indeed, she knew in the eyes of the *ton,* it would be true.

If she loved Nate, however—and she was rushing towards that inevitable conclusion at a terrifying rate—she wouldn't care a straw for the *ton,* or for their opinions. Alice smiled as she realised, that was already true. She didn't care what they thought. For her whole life the idea of doing something that would incur the censure of the ton had terrified her. No longer. She didn't care what they thought of Nate, nor or Matilda, she knew what *she* thought, who *she* cared for, and that was all that mattered.

Chapter 15

Did you see St Clair at Vauxhall? I don't know why everyone insists on sighing and mooning over him. Even Henry idolises him. Well, I certainly do not. He's nothing but a conceited coxcomb.

—Excerpt of a letter from Miss Harriet Stanhope to Miss Bonnie Campbell.

The evening of the 26th June 1814. The Supper Rooms, Vauxhall Gardens, Lambeth.

Alice bid Matilda goodbye with regret, sharing a last lingering look with Nate as he touched a finger to his hat and gave her a secret smile. Tomorrow, she would see him again, she promised herself, a flutter of anticipation filling her chest.

"Are you enjoying yourself, Alice?"

"Oh, yes, indeed," she replied, turning as Kitty took her arm. "It's all been wonderful. Have you?"

"How could I not?" Kitty exclaimed, looking as though she might burst. "It's been marvellous, but where did you get to during the cascade? One moment you were there, and the next...."

Alice fought the blush that rose at her cheeks and cursed her pale complexion. Before she could even consider a lie to cover her blushes—which she really ought to have thought of before now—Kitty grasped her arm.

"Alice!" she exclaimed, lowering her voice to a thrilled whisper. "Who is he?"

"Whatever do you mean?"

Kitty returned a blank look. "That blush was a dead giveaway," she replied, looking unimpressed with Alice's attempt at deflection.

"Well, w-who says there's a *he* at all?" Alice said with a huff, glancing around to ensure no one overheard them.

"The colour of your cheeks says so," Kitty said, snorting with delight. "Oh, Alice, you look like a boiled lobster."

"How kind of you to observe it," she said, rather mortified.

"Oh, don't be like that," Kitty pressed, and then took Alice's hand, holding it between hers. "There *is* someone, isn't there?" she asked, a wistful look in her eyes that gave Alice pause. Kitty gave a heavy sigh. "You lucky thing. Is he very handsome?"

Alice smiled despite herself and nodded. "He is rather, yes."

Kitty gave a delighted squeal and threaded her arm though Alice's once more.

"Do you love him?"

Alice caught her breath, allowing herself to think about the question once more, not that she'd thought of much else of late. A smile curved over her mouth as she remembered Nate, his soft kisses and desperate promises for the future, his plea to her to marry him.

"Oh," Kitty said, sighing. "You do, don't you?"

Alice blinked, inexplicably finding her eyes filling. "Yes," she said, a little unsteadily. "I rather think I do."

"Being in love is so... lovely," Kitty said with a sigh. "Until it isn't," she added, frowning and looking away from Alice.

"Whatever do you mean?" Alice asked, a little startled by the comment. "Have you been in love, Kitty?"

Kitty nodded and Alice squeezed her arm as she realised her friend's eyes were too bright and filled with sorrow.

"Oh, I'm so sorry," she said, wondering what had happened. Kitty had never indicated that there had been someone in her life.

"It's all right," Kitty said, laughing a little as she wiped her eyes. "It's not like I regret it. Not a moment of it," she added, with such longing Alice's heart twisted. "It was the happiest time of my life."

"But what happened?" Alice asked, lowering her voice.

She waited, wondering if perhaps she ought not pry, but Kitty answered her.

"I don't know," she said, giving Alice a rueful smile. "One day he was there and everything was perfect and the next...." She frowned as though she was looking at something far in the distant past.

Alice watched in consternation, wanting to ask more, but Harriet tugged at her sleeve.

"Alice, is that your mother waving at us?" she asked, interrupting their sudden intimacy as she moved back to them.

Alice looked around and nodded. "It is," she said, casting Kitty a look of frustration at not being able to continue their conversation. "I suppose we are late for supper and Papa will getting tetchy."

The group moved towards Mr and Mrs Dowding where her father was, indeed, looking rather morose despite the convivial atmosphere. No doubt he was now lamenting his decision to come out this evening.

"Well, at last," her mother said, giving Alice the benefit of an impatient look. "We have been waiting for you to take our place. You know you father hates tardiness."

"Sorry, Mother," Alice replied, smiling and feeling quite unrepentant.

"Goodbye, Harriet, Mr Stanhope. Goodbye, Kitty dear."

Kitty winked at her and gave her an impulsive hug. "Goodbye, Alice. I did enjoy it. Enjoy the rest of your evening."

As Kitty spoke, Alice caught the look of undisguised horror in her mother's eyes and her heart sank. Before she could do anything, her mother had grasped her arm and was towing her away.

"Really, Alice. If it's not bad enough I had to put a stop to your association with that scandalous Huntress chit, now an Irish girl? Whatever has come over you? As if I haven't raised you better than that."

Alice snatched her arm away, mortified, as her mother has spoken loud enough for everyone to hear, Kitty included.

"Mother!" Alice said, furious with her as she turned and saw a brittle, cold expression slide across Kitty's face. Without saying a word, Harriet rushed forward and took Kitty's hand.

"Come along, dear. Henry has found us somewhere to sit and have something to eat," she said, her voice soothing as she hurried Kitty away.

"How could you?" Alice cried. "How could you say such a thing? If you must be so insulting, could you not at least keep your voice down? Kitty is my friend and you've hurt her with your attitude."

"That girl is no fit friend for you," her mother said, gripping Alice's arm once more, her fingers biting into her flesh. Alice struggled a little, wanting to get free, to escape, but perhaps her desire to flee was written on her face, for her mother only grasped her harder. "Don't you dare make a scene," she added in an undertone, fury in her eyes.

"Me, make a scene?" Alice cried in outrage. "You were the one shouting like a fishwife and disparaging my friends at the top of your voice."

Her mother gasped in shock and even Alice felt a pang of anxiety at her words, though she could not regret them. She only wanted to return to Kitty and beg her a thousand apologies.

"You will not speak to your mother like that."

Alice turned to stare at her father, a little daunted to see real anger in his eyes. He rarely bothered dealing with Alice at all, leaving such things to his wife, but now he looked to gravely offended.

"I can't believe you'd take the feelings of some low bogtrotter over your own mother."

Alice gaped at him, believing she perhaps saw her father for the first time. She'd always known him for an ambitious man, and one who would not scruple to use his daughter to further his own ends, but this….

Her mother's grasp on her arm had slackened and Alice didn't waste the opportunity. Snatching it free once again, she backed away, staring at her parents with undisguised horror. With her heart beating too hard, she turned and fled.

It didn't take Alice long to realise she'd been a little rash. There was no sign of either Kitty or Harriet. The crowds were thick and impenetrable, especially around the supper booths, and many of the revellers were becoming rowdy as the drink flowed. Jostled and elbowed on all sides, Alice searched in vain for her friends, or anyone of her acquaintance. Surely, in this crush of people, there must be someone she knew.

Sadly, she was correct.

As an all too familiar hand slid around her waist and pulled her tight, Alice yelped and swung around to confront the devil who had taken such liberties.

"G-Good evening, s-sweet Alice. All alone? N-Now, that won't do, w-will it?"

Alice's skin prickled, some sixth sense telling her in no uncertain terms that she would regret being alone in Edgar Bindley's company.

"Unhand me, sir!" she exclaimed, struggling to get free as Edgar just chuckled and pulled her closer. She could smell strong spirits on his breath and realised with dismay he was more than a little foxed.

"N-No, I don't think I shall," he said, a threatening tone to his voice. "I think I shall take you s-somewhere quiet and teach you how t-to be nice to me. You didn't seem to mind being n-nice to Mr H-Hunt after all, did you, you little s-slut?"

He propelled her through the crush, pushing and shoving as Alice struggled harder. As the crowd thinned, Edgar moved her towards the dark of the gardens where private walks and shadowy nooks and corners abounded. Fear turned to terror as she realised she could not allow him to drag her into the darkness and she filled her lungs, ready to scream, when Edgar stopped in his tracks.

She looked up at him, wondering what had happened, to see his flushed countenance pale in a dramatic sweep of white. Alice followed his gaze and gasped. Never in her life had she believed she would welcome the sight of the Marquess of Montagu, but at that moment she could have embraced him.

"Put the girl down, Edgar," Montagu said, looking bored in the extreme. "I think she is not enjoying your attention."

"Oh, sh-she'll enjoy it well enough," Edgar said, obviously foxed enough to dare brazening it out. "And what do you care for her? She's n-nobody."

"I don't care a damn for her," the marquess said, without as much as a flicker of interest. His features may as well have been carved from marble for all the emotion visible in his expression. "Less so for you," he added with a sigh that seemed to indicate his distaste for this unpleasant interlude. "However, I cannot abide displays of vulgarity, and you, sir, are vulgar in the extreme. Now unhand the young woman, or I shall do it for you."

Alice held her breath. The marquess had spoken softly, never raising his voice, so quietly in fact they had to still to hear his words. The devil of it was, they *had*, because there was menace in that soft-spoken voice; the precise, cool way of speaking hid none of the implicit threat. The lack of any show of emotion or anger only seemed to highlight the danger, rather than dispel it.

Edgar was scowling now; the sulky fury of a spoilt boy refused a treat.

"This is n-none of your concern," he said, and Alice almost expected him to add, *it's not fair,* so petulant were the words.

"No," said the marquess, inspecting his impeccable grey gloves with a frown of irritation. "And you weary me with your continuous stating of the obvious. Unhand Miss Dowding, or I rather think I shall make you regret it."

"Why?" Edgar demanded, taking a step back as Montagu settled his grey gaze upon him.

"Am I required to explain my motivation... to *you*?" The marquess' gaze swept him from head to toe and Alice couldn't blame Edgar for the flush of mortification that coloured his face.

To Alice's immense relief, the hands that had gripped her fell away and Edgar gave her a hard shove, almost sending her to her knees. Before she could tumble, the marquess reached out and grasped her upper arm, steadying her for just a moment before releasing her once more. She had the distinct impression he couldn't let go fast enough.

159

Turning his attention back to Edgar, the marquess made a dismissive shooing motion, and to her immense satisfaction, Edgar stalked away.

"My lord," Alice said, breathless with relief. "I don't know how I can ever—"

"Enough," Montagu said, silencing her with a look of cold contempt. "I have no desire for your thanks, nor small talk. I will return you to your friends. I suggest you stay close to them in the future, you foolish child."

Alice's cheeks burned with humiliation, but she held her tongue as he escorted her back to the supper booths. To add to her discomfort, the marquess located Harriet and Kitty with ease.

The two young women and Henry all looked shocked and stunned as Montagu accompanied her to their table.

"Miss Dowding," said the marquess, barely looking at her as he gave her a brief nod and left her beside their table.

"Alice!" Harriet exclaimed, getting to her feet. "Whatever happened?"

Alice was so shocked that she was trembling, and Henry ordered her a glass of rack punch and ordered her to drink it to settle her nerves. Once she'd given them her sorry tale, Henry looked furious.

"That white-livered cur," he said, smacking the flat of his hand on the table. "I never did like him, always trying to ingratiate himself with St Clair, though the earl won't give him the time of day either... but trying to haul you off like that? It won't do."

"Henry," Harriet said, a warning note to her voice. "Don't you dare. You know what father said would happen if he found you'd been fighting again."

"Oh!" Alice exclaimed, horrified. "Oh, no indeed, Mr Stanhope. I beg you will not trouble yourself. I ought not to have run off alone like that, and I assure you I won't again, so he'll not have another opportunity, but I could not bear for you to be hurt or at odds with your father on my account."

"Well, someone ought to do something," Henry muttered, folding his arms and looking mutinous.

Alice turned as Kitty laid a hand on her arm. The girl had been silent since Alice arrived, and Alice had yet to muster courage enough to beg her pardon. Heaven alone knew what Kitty thought of her.

"You argued with your parents, Alice?" she said quietly. "Over me?"

Alice swallowed and reached to take Kitty's hand. "Kitty, I've never been more mortified in my life. They had no right... I would never have believed...."

Kitty gave a little huff of laughter that had little humour to it. "It's far from an unusual reaction, Alice, don't worry. My uncle would have me rid myself of my accent, but...." She paused, two high spots of colour burning on her cheeks. "Why should I?" she demanded, defiant as she stared back at Alice. "I'm no different from you, or Harriet. Why should I change?"

"You shouldn't have to," Alice replied, her voice firm. "You're lovely and clever and full of life and I'm proud to have you as my friend, Kitty. That is... if you can forgive me for—"

"Forgive you?" Kitty exclaimed, looking at her with wide eyes. "Alice, you confronted your parents, argued with them to defend me. No one has ever...." She stopped as her voice broke and Alice gasped as Kitty flung her arms about her neck. "Thank you," she whispered.

Feeling rather exhausted by the events of this extraordinary evening, Alice could do no more than hug her in return. "Of course, Kitty. That's what friends are for."

Harriet insisted that Alice eat something before they returned her to her mother and father. Once the meal was done, however, they left Aunt Nell with Kitty and Harriet, and Henry escorted Alice back to find her parents.

***

For the entirety of the journey back home, Alice was soundly scolded for her behaviour. She was a disappointment and they were shocked and saddened by her bold tongue. Alice endured it all until her father spoke.

"I think you have proven to us that the sooner we get you married to Mr Bindley the better it will be for all concerned. Perhaps he can instil some degree of good behaviour into you, as everything we have taught you seem to have come to naught."

Alice's heart stuttered in her chest.

"I shall never marry Mr Bindley," she said, her voice faint but firm. "In fact, I shall tell you a little about Mr Bindley, Father. When I was looking for my friends, he discovered me and he... he hurt me. He manhandled me in the most lewd and disrespectful manner and, if not for the intervention of the Marquess of Montagu, he would have dragged me into some quiet part of the garden and...." Her voice faltered, but she forced the words out, determined that her parents should know what their choice of husband would have done to her. "And his intentions were certainly not honourable."

"That's what you get for going off alone," her mother said, shaking her head in disgust. "Of course he thought you were open to his advances. You are soon to be engaged and he discovered you alone, what else was he to think?"

Alice gasped, staring at her mother in shock. "B-But Mother, this was not some romantic interlude! He grabbed hold of me, handled me with violence and impropriety and said vile, disgusting things."

"For heavens' sake, Alice," her father said impatiently. "A young man of Mr Bindley's age will no doubt be enthusiastic in his advances. It is to be expected, and a gently bred young lady would no doubt be shocked by it, but there is no point in being so missish about the affair. You'll be married soon enough."

Alice stared between her parents in bewildered horror, her heart thudding so hard she felt nauseous and light-headed. There was no reason to be had here, she realised. If she protested, they would only accuse her of becoming hysterical. Her parents would not shield her from a man like Bindley; indeed, the sooner they could hand her into his keeping, the better they would like it.

Memories of Nate, of his tenderness and his passion filled her memory. He said he was insane with desire and love for her, yet he had never kissed her or touched her without asking her permission, and he had stopped the moment she showed the slightest indication of being unsure. He had always treated her with respect and never hurt her, never made her afraid. He would do anything to keep her safe, she knew that instinctively. She trusted him, she realised. She trusted him with her safety, with her happiness.

With a numb acceptance, she endured the rest of the journey home, listening to her parents' plan when Father would speak with Mr Bindley to accept his suit so he could begin calling on Alice. A short engagement would suit everybody, by all accounts.

Panic lingered just beneath her skin, and she knew that it would take little to send her into hysterics, but she held on tightly to an outward show of calm. She would see Nate tomorrow. Everything would be fine. They would find a way forward.

Somehow, she held her tongue until they got home. As they climbed the stairs to bed, Alice turned to her mother.

"I'll be going out with Miss Stanhope tomorrow, Mother. She and her aunt and her brother are going for a walk in Kensington Gardens."

Her mother frowned a little. "Her brother is Henry Stanhope?" she queried. "He's a good friend of the Earl of St Clair, isn't he?"

Alice nodded, her hopes sparking that perhaps her mother's ambitions might allow her to get out of the house. "Indeed, I understand the earl will accompany us, as well as Miss Minerva Butler. She's the Duchess of Bedwin's cousin."

"Yes, in that case you may attend," her mother said with a gracious smile that set Alice's teeth on edge. "However, I do hope you will comport yourself with more grace and dignity than you have managed this evening."

"Yes, Mother," Alice said, tamping down a barrage of unhelpful emotions as she turned and hurried to her bedchamber before the woman could change her mind.

Chapter 16

But Harry, how can you speak so of St Clair?
He's so charming and positively swoon-worthy.
You're lucky to have a brother with such
eligible friends.

—Excerpt of a letter from Miss Bonnie
Campbell to Miss Harriet Stanhope.

The 27th June En route to Kensington Gardens.
1814.

"Do stop tugging at your cravat, Nate, dear," Matilda said with a sigh. "It was perfect when we left, but you will spoil it if you keep on."

Nate sighed and returned his attention to his horses as the curricle bowled along at a brisk pace. He didn't know what had got into him of late, or at least he knew full well, but he couldn't seem to do anything about it.

"Are you actually nervous?" his sister said, sitting forward to better look at him.

He could hear the amusement in her voice, but found nothing the least bit funny in the situation.

"Yes, damn it," he said. "And there's no use in telling me I'm acting like a lovesick schoolboy; I know I am. I... I can't seem to stop."

He expected to hear a burst of laughter at the admission but, when it didn't come, he turned his head to find Matilda staring at him with sparkling eyes. She reached out and laid her hand on his arm.

"Oh, Nate, I'm so happy. Alice is such a sweet girl. I know she'll make you happy."

He let out a breath and laughed. "If she'll have me," he said, trying to sound offhand, but the anxiety in his voice was audible enough.

"She's not accepted you yet?"

Nate shook his head and swallowed down the lump which seemed to have settled in his throat the night he'd been discovered with Alice. He knew there would be no getting rid of it until she'd agreed to marry him.

"No," he admitted. "And I feel like I'm going mad. Matilda, what the devil is wrong with me? I can't sleep, I can't stop thinking about her. I'm not a green boy, for all I'm acting the part. I've had affairs, too many to count. Why is this so… so intense?"

"Because it's what you've always wanted, Nate," Matilda said, her voice soft. "Before Papa ruined everything, I always knew you weren't the sort to carry on and hold on to your freedom until you were forced to marry. You *wanted* a home, a family, security. You never made a secret of it, but then Papa stole that future away and you had to become Nathaniel Hunt, proprietor of the most exclusive gaming club in the city. I watched you change, outwardly at least, but I knew it wasn't really you."

Matilda watched him in silence for a moment, but Nate's throat was too tight to speak.

"Do you ever think of Glebe House?" she asked.

Nate swallowed. Before their father had gambled their future away, they'd had several properties, including a snug little house in Kent. It had been promised to him when he married, and Nate had dreamed and planned of all the things he would do, the improvements he would make. How strange that he'd not thought of that in so long.

"No. Not for years," he admitted.

"Why not?" she asked.

He drew in a breath. "Do you ever think about marrying that dashing Lord Dawlish, who you spend weeks mooning over, or about having a family and children?"

"No," she said, turning away from him.

"Then you understand," he said, his voice hard. "Those dreams were lost to us, and to think on them only brought misery. I let them go, Tilda."

Matilda took a deep breath and turned back to him. "But your dreams are not lost, Nate. I think Alice loves you, or at least she's halfway to being in love with you. Don't let her go. Hold tight to your dreams this time."

Nate reached out and took his sister's hand, giving her fingers a brief squeeze. "I won't, though it pains me to know that her parents will likely disown her."

"What, and risk never being a member of *Hunter's*?" she said with a smirk. "Oh, I think you may have some power there, Nate. Over her father at least."

"I'm not so sure." Nate paused to negotiate a tight corner and weave around a hackney carriage on a narrow stretch of road. The horses' hooves clattered smartly over the cobbles, the tack jingling as the shiny metal fastenings glinted in the afternoon sun. "They would marry their only daughter to a vile piece of work like Bindley just to get close to an earldom. Marrying such a scandalous character as myself will be a deep disappointment to them."

"Stuff," Matilda said with clear annoyance. "Our mother was the daughter of viscount, and father's great-uncle was an earl.

We're not badly bred, for all our apparent shame, and don't you forget it. Mr and Mrs Dowding are wealthy but not much better than gentry. There's not a noble drop of blood in their veins. They're on the fringes of the *ton* and well they know it. They should consider themselves privileged to have you as a son-in-law."

Nate turned to smile at his sister, touched and a little surprised by her defence of his character.

"Thank you, Tilda," he said quietly. "And don't think I have forgotten your dreams either. We shall make them come true. Once I'm married, I will be better placed, with Alice's help. With your beauty and dowry, we'll find an eligible man for you."

Tilda snorted at that. "That's sweet, Nate, and don't think I don't appreciate it, but we've seen the kind of men that generous dowry attracts. Honestly, I don't care a straw about catching a title or finding a wealthy man, or even a handsome one. I don't care if he's nobility or gentry, or a banker or a merchant. I just want a good man, an honest one. I want someone who will be kind. Someone warm and loving and loyal. Is that too much to ask?"

Nate felt his heart contract at the pain in his sister's voice and, once again, the guilt of his part in her ruination weighed heavy on his soul. Somehow, he would make it right. He would see Matilda happy.

"No, Tilda," he said with a smile. "It's not too much, and I'll do everything in my power to see you find him."

***

27ʰ June 1814. Kensington Gardens.

"Thank you," Alice said as Henry handed her down from the carriage at Hyde Park Corner. Turning, she smiled as she caught sight of Ruth and Lucia making their way towards them.

"Oh look, there's Kitty too, and Bonnie," Harriet said as she stepped down behind Alice. "What a merry party we shall be this afternoon."

Alice watched Harriet's expression cool, however, as a glorious looking blond man moved to greet her brother.

"Afternoon, Henry," the exquisite fellow said, clapping Henry on the back and grinning.

Despite herself, Alice felt her breath catch a little. Nate was a handsome man, but with a slightly rough edge to him that Alice found very appealing. This fellow bore refinement and grace in every line of his being. He looked like a pagan god in human form, his blond hair shining gold in the sunlight, everything about him screamed of privilege and wealth and the knowledge of exactly who he was and where he belonged.

"Jasper!" Henry said, beaming. "Good to see you, old man. Oh, let me introduce you to Miss Alice Dowding. Miss Dowding, the Earl of St Clair, and you know my sister of course."

"Miss Dowding, charmed," he said, turning a pair of quite startling indigo eyes in Alice's direction before moving to Harriet. Alice thought there was something of a mischievous glint to his eyes as he addressed her. "Miss Stanhope, a pleasure as always."

"St Clair," Harriet replied, her voice and expression stony before turning away from him.

Alice was a little surprised at the frosty reception, but the earl seemed to take it in good heart.

Once everyone had gathered, they moved off down the path through the gardens. There were many such groups enjoying the afternoon sunshine and making the most of the fashionable hour to see and be seen.

Alice tried to enjoy the warm sun on her face and the company of her friends, and not to think too hard about the events of yesterday, and especially last night.

"Oh, look," Kitty said, hurrying to take Alice's arm. "There's Matilda and her brother. He's very dashing, isn't he, Alice? I only spoke to him a little last night, but he was very polite, not at all the libertine one expects him to be."

Alice hid her smile and tried to remain unmoved as Matilda and Nate drew closer and exchanged greetings with everyone. St Clair and Nate appeared to be well acquainted and, once the introductions were done, the two men strolled together and chatted. Alice did her best to keep her gaze from Nate, and failed dismally. To her relief, Nate seemed to find the task as hard as she did. Several times when her eyes inexorably drifted to rest on his figure, splendid in a dark blue coat and polished black boots, she found him watching her in return.

Forcing her attention away from him once again, she smiled as she saw Henry offer his arm to Lucia as the young woman stumbled a little. She gave him a dazzling smile that even made Alice catch her breath, and seemed to knock the air from Henry's lungs altogether, judging by the flush on his cheeks and the rather awed expression he wore. Kitty chuckled beside her, having witnessed the little scene too.

"Oh, to be born beautiful," she said wistfully.

Alice tutted and looked to Kitty. "Are you fishing for compliments, young lady? For you know you are perfectly lovely."

Kitty gave a low chuckle of laughter. "Ah, I'm easy enough on the eye, but that kind of beauty, that's power, that is. That's the power to bring a man to his knees and keep him there."

Alice's eyebrows rose a little. "And should you like to have such power?" she asked in alarm, watching as Kitty considered the question.

"Not especially, I suppose," she admitted, wrinkling her nose. "I'm not sure I'd like a man I could command at a whim, but I should like to be noticed for once, for something other than my heritage, that is," she added with a twisted grin.

"And who would you like to notice you?" Alice asked, teasing her a little.

Kitty's dark eyes glinted as she turned to look at her. "Ah, and who is this young fellow who haunts *your* dreams, Miss Alice?" she demanded, raising one eyebrow in challenge.

Alice opened her mouth and closed it again.

"For shame," Kitty lamented. "And I thought you might trust me with your secret, but I shan't give you mine unless you give me yours first. Fair's fair."

Feeling amused and rather pleased at their growing friendship, Alice stuck her tongue out at her, and Kitty laughed and stopped sharply as they'd nearly walked into Minerva, who had ground to a halt and was staring at the floor.

"Oh, what a pretty butterfly," Minerva said, bending to inspect the lovely thing as it alighted briefly on the ground.

Harriet moved closer to look herself and crouched beside it. "A small tortoiseshell," she declared, squinting a little as she pushed her spectacles up her nose. "*Aglais urticae. Urtica* is of course, from the Latin for stinging nettle, *urtica dioica*."

"*Of course,*" St Clair remarked mildly, his lips twitching a little.

Harriet looked up and glared at him, her jaw growing tight. "The small tortoiseshell lays its eggs on stinging nettles, which is why it's significant, and Aglaia was one of the three Graces, a daughter of Zeus admired for her beauty," she added, sounding almost defiant as she stood once more and stared at the earl with undisguised hostility.

"My, my, the things you know, Miss Stanhope," the earl said, holding her gaze.

Alice looked between them, there had been a teasing note to his words that suggested he knew Harriet and was deliberately baiting her. Harriet, for her part, clearly disliked him intensely for her response was immediate and cutting.

"Yes, books are an immense source of knowledge, my lord, if one troubles to read one on occasion rather than just keeping them as a vanity collection or merely to gather dust."

"Well, naturally I'd know nothing about that," St Clair replied, his voice as easy and urbane as before, yet Alice felt there was an edge to it now.

"Lord no," Henry said, chuckling to himself. "St Clair wouldn't sit still for long enough to read a book. Always in the basket for it at Harrow with the masters, weren't you, Jasper?" he said, grinning.

The earl smiled, though it was a tight expression which didn't quite reach his eyes.

"Quite so, Henry," he said softly.

Alice frowned, wondering what she was missing and why Harriet was so brittle with the man when he was so clearly a good friend of her brother's. Perhaps he led Henry into bad behaviour? The earl was a wealthy man and known to have a wild and rather extravagant reputation. No doubt Henry could ill afford to keep up with such illustrious company. He'd easily find himself in debt if he tried, that was for certain.

The mystery did not hold her attention for long, however, as she found her gaze drifting back to Nate. He gave her a sly wink, and she blushed and turned away to hide her smile.

"Stop it," Matilda said, chuckling as she moved to take Kitty's place and slipped her hand through Alice's arm. "You're both as bad as each other. It's hardly subtle."

"Sorry," Alice said, hoping it wasn't as obvious as Matilda made out. "I need to speak to him though, as soon as possible. Do you think it can be contrived?"

"Of course," Matilda said at once, before giving her a searching look. "What's happened?"

"Oh, Tilda." Alice sighed and shook her head. "What hasn't happened?"

With relief, Alice told her of the events of last night after Nate and Matilda had left her.

"The odious beast of a man!" Matilda exclaimed, appalled by her story. "Though how you can call such a creature a man I don't know, and beast is an insult to animals. He's a vile cad and a bully. My God, Nate will kill him when he hears this," she said, her words not bringing Alice a deal of comfort. "But, however did you get away from him?"

"You'll never believe it, Tilda." Alice shook her head, still having trouble believing it herself. "Montagu rescued me."

Matilda stopped in her tracks, her blue eyes wide with astonishment. "What?"

"I know." She laughed a little, knowing her own bewilderment was reflected in her friend's expression. "I was never more surprised. Who would ever believe I would be relieved to see the Marquess of Montagu? But I was never so grateful to anyone. Oh, Tilda, I shudder to think what might have happened if he hadn't been there, and he dealt with Edgar like he was dirt. It was rather splendid to watch. He all but crawled away from the marquess on his belly."

"Well," Matilda said, her voice a little faint. "It seems the man has his uses."

"Yes." Alice smiled a little and looked up at Matilda, who appeared pensive in the light of this information. "Perhaps he isn't as bad as we believed? Oh!" she added in a rush, remembering too late just why Matilda despised him so. "Not to say he isn't a villain too, of course."

Matilda's lips quirked a little and she gave a wry chuckle. "Oh, indeed, a villain to his core, but a civilised one, at least."

***

It was perhaps another half an hour before Matilda contrived to wrest her brother from Mr Stanhope's and St Clair's company. Though it was too improper for Alice and Nate to stroll together unaccompanied, the three of them dawdled until the others were a good distance ahead and then Matilda hung back a little farther to give them some privacy without actually leaving them alone.

"Is something wrong, love?" Nate said, the moment they could speak.

Alice nodded, though she decided now was not the time to share all the events of last night with him. Matilda's words on his likely reaction had given her pause and reason enough to be cautious.

"My parents have instructed me I shall marry Mr Bindley. They are arranging a meeting with him and his parents as soon as may be to discuss the particulars. It is to be a short engagement," she added, her voice bleak and heavy with anxiety and her hand tightened on his sleeve as she looked up at him.

Nate's free hand covered hers. "Tell me you'll not do it, Alice," he said, his voice rough, his gaze searching hers.

"Of course not!" she exclaimed and then ducked her head as she realised she was drawing attention to them both. "I'd rather die," she added with some heat, though less volume.

"And…." Nate hesitated, and she looked up to see him take a deep breath. "And what of me, Alice?"

She smiled at him and all at once her shyness returned with full force and she was compelled to look away and study the ground at her feet. "I-I thought perhaps you… you might have a question for me, Nate?" she said, so anxious now her voice was little more than a whisper.

Nate paused, turning to her, his gaze intent.

"Keep walking," she urged, tugging at his arm. "People are looking."

"Damnation," he muttered. "I'd like to do this properly, but I can hardly get to my knees in the middle of Kensington Gardens."

Alice smiled at him, her heart soaring and whatever he saw in her eyes must have reassured him.

"Alice, darling, please. Please will you do me the honour of becoming my wife?"

"I will," Alice replied, finding her reply was not difficult to find, in fact the words came easily without a trace of doubt. Perhaps things would not be as simple as they appeared now, and perhaps they had much to learn about each other, but she knew Nate's heart and she believed it to be true, and honourable. Everything else would come.

Nate let out a shaky breath and turned to look at her. "This is intolerable. I need to kiss you."

Alice couldn't help but laugh at the sincerity of his complaint and he returned a rueful smile.

"Don't tease, love. I'm in agony here."

"I'm sorry," she said, leaning into him a little. "But the more pertinent problem to overcome is how we shall achieve a marriage at all. I'm assuming Gretna Green," she added.

"Good heavens, no," Nate replied, so obviously horrified at the idea she was a little dismayed.

"But Nate, how else are we to achieve it in time? We must be married at once."

"Marrying me will be scandal enough," he said with a glower. "I'll not subject you to the ignominy of an anvil wedding too." They walked in silence while he considered. "We'll marry at St

Paul's Church in Covent Garden. If we get a common licence, there is no need to read the banns."

Alice let out a sigh of relief. "Yes, I'm over twenty-one so there is no permission needed. We'll need witnesses, though. Do you think we can manage it?"

"I do," he said, excitement glittering in his eyes. "But can you get away?"

"I will, somehow, but when?" she said, finding it hard to breathe. Excitement, fear, and a dawning realisation that she really would disoblige her parents and marry an unsuitable man made her feel quite giddy.

"It's Sunday tomorrow, dash it all," he cursed, frowning with annoyance. "I'll not be able to make the arrangements tonight, so it must be Monday morning. I'll arrange it for eleven a.m."

Alice's hand tightened on his sleeve and she could feel the colour leaving her cheeks as she imagined her parent's reaction to the news.

"Can you do it, Alice?" Nate asked, and though she did not look at him, she could feel the heat and weight of his gaze upon her. "Can you go against everything they want and marry a man they think beneath you?"

Fire scalded her chest at that. "You're not beneath me," she said, such anger in her voice that Nate's eyes widened a little. She let out a breath, allowing the rage to leave her, and smiled at him. "You're not beneath me," she said again, gently now. "You're a good and kind man and I believe you'll be a loving husband, though…."

Nate frowned, ducking his head to meet her eyes.

"What is it?" he asked, daring to reach out and touch a finger to her chin, turning her to face him. "Tell me. What is it that makes you hesitate?"

"I'm not hesitating," she said with a soft little laugh. "I'm marrying you."

Though there was hesitation, if not in her heart, then in her mind.

"Alice," he said, her name on his lips sending a shiver of awareness down her spine. Good heavens, by Monday afternoon she would be this man's wife. She shivered again. "Alice, if we are to marry, we will have each other's hearts for safekeeping. How can I do that if I don't know what troubles you, what makes you afraid?"

She drew in a breath, knowing she had to confide this, her only real fear for their future, the only thing that could truly break her if she'd made a mistake in trusting him with her heart. Alice lifted her eyes to his and dared to speak her mind. "What if it's just an infatuation, Nate? What if you tire of me, or... or grow bored?"

For a moment, there was a flash of anger in his eyes and she quailed a little.

"Is that what you think of me?" he asked, the hurt in his voice unmistakable.

Alice regretted it at once, regretted making him unhappy, but it didn't change the fact she needed an answer, an honest one. "I *think* you are everything I dream of, I think it enough to marry you, Nate, but the truth is this has all happened so fast. Too fast. If things were different, we would have more time. If things were different, you could court me and I could be certain of everything I think, before I speak those vows before God." She stared at him, willing him to see that she trusted him, but she would have the truth, no matter what it may be. "The world has shown me the face of Nathaniel Hunt and he is a reckless libertine. You have shown me the face of the man beneath the façade, and I have fallen in love with him, but how did Alice Dowding, perpetual wallflower, catch such a man? How does she keep him?"

His breath caught and he stopped, staring at her, and Alice knew people were looking but she couldn't move either, trapped in his blue gaze. "You love me?" he said, his voice rough.

Alice smiled. "I do."

He laughed, a breathless rush of amusement that made his lips curve and his eyes sparkle.

"Do you want to know how to keep me, Alice?" he said, lowering his voice to a whisper.

She nodded, wanting to know that above all things.

He leaned down and she shivered anew as his breath fluttered warm against her neck.

"Love me," he said. "Don't ever stop." He lifted his head and smiled at her, sincerity shining in eyes that were just a little too bright. "I'm yours alone, Alice, I'll never give you reason to doubt it."

Alice's heart was expanding, she felt certain of it. It filled her chest, pushing at the confines of her ribcage as she stared upon this extraordinary man who had changed her life with a kiss in the moonlight.

"If you two carry on like this, we'll never keep it quiet," Matilda muttered, moving closer and elbowing her brother. "You do remember you're in a public place?"

"Oh, I remember," Nate said with a heavy sigh. "But I'm finding it hard to care. Tilda, say hello to your soon-to-be sister."

Alice smiled as Matilda looked between them and then gave a heartfelt sigh. "Thank heavens," she said, and then gave a little squeal and ran to clutch Alice's arm. "I'm so excited!"

To Alice's delight, her joy seemed genuine and whole-hearted, and knowing that Matilda would stand beside her gave Alice courage.

"Tell me everything," Matilda said, bubbling over with excitement and having just as hard a time as they had at keeping her voice down. "Where and when is the happy event to be? We have so much to arrange."

Nate laughed and looked between his sister and Alice, and the happiness in his eyes made her throat tight with pleasure.

Chapter 17

Dearest Alice, I'm so excited to see you and the rest of our Peculiar Ladies. Helena has excelled herself with this ball. It will be glorious.

—Excerpt of a letter from Her Grace, Prunella Adolphus, Duchess of Bedwin to Miss Alice Dowding.

28ʰ June 1814. Baker Street, London.

Alice stared at herself in the mirror. She thought she looked a little different somehow. Oh, she was still small enough to go unnoticed in a crowd and for many of her acquaintance to pat her on the head and chuck her under the chin, as if she were twelve years old and not a woman of two and twenty. There was certainty in her eyes, though, a straighter line to her back, a more determined lift to her chin. Nathaniel Hunt loved her, and, on Monday morning, she would leave this place in secret and she would be his wife.

Little Alice Dowding, who had stammered and blushed her way through life, never putting a foot wrong or doing or saying a thing to disoblige anyone, would please herself. She would not marry a vile man who would make her unhappy so her parents could climb a little higher in society. She would face their wrath, their retribution and their condemnation, which she did not doubt would come. Alice would look them in the eyes and explain her reasons and they could accept them—and her husband—or they could disown her. It would be their choice, just as Nate was hers.

Turning before the looking glass, Alice smiled. She had bought this dress in the days after Nate had kissed her, fuelled by desire and a new burst of confidence. The confidence to wear it had, as yet, eluded her. Not tonight.

It was dazzling confection in deep burnt orange, the heavy satin shimmering bronze as she moved. She had even been daring with her hair and allowed her maid to arrange it in a tumble of loose curls, caught here and there with jewelled combs. It was most out of character and made her feel rather wicked.

She *was* wicked, she supposed.

Alice Dowding had kissed a stranger on a moonlit balcony. She'd met in him secret and captured his heart, and soon she would run away and marry him against her parents' wishes.

Wicked indeed.

A slow smile curved over her mouth, a knowing look appearing in the reflection before her as she slid a hand down the decadent satin. Shy, biddable little Alice was gone, chased away by someone bolder and more courageous. This Alice was a woman who knew what she wanted, she decided, looking at the petite but nonetheless voluptuous figure in the glass. *Yes,* she thought, smiling, and Alice rather liked her. She thought perhaps her scandalous grandmother would have approved too.

In the dark of the carriage, concealed beneath a voluminous cloak, Alice kept the secret of her new dress to herself. Her mother had not seen it. She would *not* approve. Already she had disclaimed her hairstyle as less than respectable. Alice had taken that as a compliment and thanked her mother, who gave her a narrow-eyed stare.

"You're in a strange mood this evening," she remarked, giving Alice pause.

That would not do. She must not give her mother cause for suspicion.

"I'm sorry, Mama," she said, contrite at once and rather chagrined that the following lie fell so easily from her lips. "I have rather a headache and all those pins poking at me made it worse. This was the only way I could bear to wear my hair, or I should not have come at all."

"Oh, my dear," her mother said at once, reaching for her reticule. "You should have said. I'll give you my smelling salts. You know how I suffer with my head. No doubt you have inherited my delicate constitution."

Her mother continued to prattle on about her various ailments and her nerves as Alice breathed a sigh that the danger had passed.

She accepted the smelling salts with a pang of guilt, which she forced herself to squash at once. A dutiful daughter would not lie and dissemble, perhaps, but Alice would not end up married to Mr Bindley because she was too polite to refuse him or displease her parents. Those days were at an end. Deceiving them was wretched of her and she knew it, but she would not regret it.

The Duke of Bedwin's magnificent London home, Beverwyck, was lit up and dressed to impress. Alice could well believe that Lady Helena had arranged every last detail of the glorious décor. She had spent little time in the young woman's company, but she seemed to vibrate with energy and high spirits, the kind of woman who must always have a purpose in life, her every second filled with action.

Flowers graced every corner and alcove: white roses and peonies with the faintest blush to their lush petals. The perfume was heady, filling the summer evening with the promise of romance and magic.

As a footman took Alice's cloak, her mother's eyes widened in astonishment as she saw her daughter's gown. With a flicker of anxiety, Alice realised how different it was from her usual pastel colours and muted tones. Before now she would have chosen anything that would allow her to blend in, not to attract attention.

Before her mother could draw her aside and take her to task, however, Alice breathed a sigh of relief as a familiar voice rang out.

"Alice!"

Turning, Alice beamed with delight as her dear friend Prue hurried to greet her.

"Alice, my word, you look... simply magnificent," Prue said, shaking her head in wonder. "What a gorgeous gown."

Miss Prunella Chuffington-Smythe, founding member of the Peculiar Ladies Book Club, was recently—and ecstatically—married to the Duke of Bedwin.

"Your grace," her mother breathed in dulcet tones, sinking into a low curtsey worthy of a queen.

Prue blinked and exchanged a look with Alice, her lips twitching a little.

"Good evening, Mrs Dowding, a pleasure to see you here. I do hope you'll forgive me if I steal your daughter away. We have so much to talk about. Bedwin will look after you."

Prue sent her husband a mischievous look as he stared at her in outrage before hurriedly composing his features to face an ecstatic looking Mrs Dowding.

"Oh, Prue, the poor man," Alice said, mortified as Prue hustled her away. "We must rescue him."

"Nonsense," Prue said briskly, taking Alice down a corridor and into a private parlour. "He'll manage, and I must have a word alone with you before we face the world."

Alice laughed and took a moment to look over her friend.

"Oh, my, Prue," she said, sighing with wonder. "You do look grand. Every inch a duchess."

It was true. Dressed in a dark plum taffeta gown and with a parure set of diamond and ruby jewels adorning her neck, wrist and ears, Prue looked splendid indeed, and remarkably beautiful. She was also quite obviously brimming with happiness.

"Piffle," Prue said, with a snort that reminded Alice that her friend had her feet firmly on the ground. "A bit of silk and some diamonds might titivate the exterior, but I'm still the same old Prue, I assure you."

"I was never gladder of anything," Alice said moving closer to give her friend an impulsive hug. "Oh, Prue, I'm about to do something quite desperately scandalous. Will you still be my friend when the *ton* are gossiping about me over breakfast? Will Bedwin allow it?"

Prue's eyes widened in surprise. "Well, considering it was him they were discussing over breakfast a few short weeks ago, I'll want to know the reason why if he doesn't," she said frankly, before her eyes crinkled with concern. "But whatever are you talking about?"

Alice bit her lip. "You'll not tell a soul?" she asked, smiling as Prue returned an affronted scowl.

"As if you need ask," she replied, huffing.

With a deep breath, Alice prepared to admit all. "On Monday morning at eleven a.m., I will marry the man I love," she said, relieved to get the words off her chest. It was so good to share this with her friend. "Nathaniel Hunt," she added with a flush of pride. "My parents don't know and will probably disown me, but they'll force me to marry Edgar Bindley if I don't, and I won't, Prue. I can't."

"I should think not," Prue said, wrinkling her nose in disgust. "Frightful creature." Her brow creased, though, and concern filled her eyes. *"The* Nathaniel Hunt?" she said, her unease quite apparent. "Matilda's brother, the club owner?"

"Now, now, Prue," Alice scolded her. "Don't tell me you've been listening to gossip."

Her friend flushed a startling shade of red, which rather matched her gown. "No, indeed," she said in a rush, giving Alice a sheepish smile. "Suppose you tell me all about him then, for I'll admit, what I've heard via the tattle-mongers would suggest he's a rake and a libertine."

Alice laughed a little and nodded. "Yes, I know, and I think there is truth enough to make a girl wary, but... oh, Prue, he's not like that at all. It was all Matilda's doing, you see. She arranged for him to help me complete my dare and he did, and...."

She gave a happy sigh as she remembered that night on the balcony, and Prue smiled at her.

"I see," she said, her eyes full of warmth and understanding, and of course Prue did see. A silly dare had changed her life, too. She would understand. "So, Monday you marry without your parent's consent."

Her expression was grave now, and Alice knew what she was thinking.

"Yes, and I know that may cause a rift that will never heal, but that will be their decision, Prue. They need to decide if their daughter's happiness is important, if her choices are her own and more important than stepping a little higher on the social scale. If they cannot forgive me, I shall mourn the loss of them, but I will not regret my decision."

Prue let out a breath and nodded. "Well, you've considered the consequences and accepted them, so I can do nothing more than wish you happy."

She held out her hands to Alice, who took them.

"There is one other thing that might help soothe your parent's ire I suppose," she said with a mischievous grin. "How would it be if the Duke and Duchess of Bedwin were to serve as your witnesses?"

**

28ᵗʰ June 1814. The Duke and Duchess of Bedwin's Ball, Beverwyck, London.

Matilda gave her brother an affectionate, if exasperated, sigh and smacked his hand away from his cravat.

"You look very handsome. Do stop fretting."

"I'm not fretting," Nate retorted as they walked up the steps to the duke's vast home. "I'm Nathaniel Hunt, proprietor of London's most exclusive gaming club. I have nerves of steel and an icy calm that has presided over games worth more money than you can even dream of."

Matilda arched an eyebrow at him, just a little, and Nate sighed.

"Oh, all right, I'm fretting," he muttered. "Is my cravat a disaster?"

"No!" Matilda replied, laughing now. "But it will be if you don't stop yanking at it. Honestly, Nate. All you need to do is smile and dance with a few other ladies and it will all be over."

"I don't want to dance with other ladies," he said, glowering a little. "I want to dance with Alice."

Matilda rolled her eyes. "I think I am aware of that fact, but if you don't want the rest of the world to realise you're about to elope with her, you'd best keep your distance."

"We're not eloping," he said in a harsh whisper, rather indignant at the idea. "Covent Garden is not eloping, and I can't avoid her all evening."

"You're marrying without her parent's knowledge or consent, that's eloping in my book, and I didn't say you had to avoid her.

Just don't stand gazing at her like a mooncalf all night, and only one dance."

Nate scowled. "I can't believe you just called me a mooncalf," he said, looking affronted.

Matilda sighed and took his arm as they walked through the grand entrance into the foyer. "There's really no other word for it, darling," she said, enjoying the touch of colour that rose on his cheeks. Teasing her brother for falling in love was her new favourite thing, or at least it would have been if she weren't so horribly envious.

Not that she begrudged him his happiness, far from it. She was delighted that he'd found his happy ever after, and that it was with Alice... well, that was just wonderful. Matilda had always longed for a sister, and for such a sweet-natured girl as Alice to fill the role was more than she could have asked for. Yet, she lived in her brother's house and understood newlyweds would not enjoy having her around when they only wanted to be in each other's company. She must consider what to do next.

Seeing plenty of familiar faces, she bade Nate a good evening, with a final warning to watch himself, as he moved away from her into the ballroom.

"Good evening, Matilda."

Looking around she saw Lucia approaching her. "My word, Lucia," she said, her mouth falling open in astonishment. "You look... stunning."

There really was no other description. Lucia was small and slender, her glossy black hair coiled into a complicated style and studded with pearls. Her golden skin gleamed in the blaze of the hundreds of candles, and her dark eyes were thickly lashed and full of secrets. The dress she wore tonight was a rather shocking fuchsia pink and Matilda thought there wasn't another woman in the entire ballroom who could have carried it off. The low décolletage showed a daring amount of cleavage and the single, heavy pearl drop that nestled there drew the eye. Lucia clearly wanted to be noticed tonight, and she would be.

Lucia looked Matilda over, returning an appreciative smile. "I must return the compliment," she said. "You are catching every man's attention without even trying."

Matilda squashed the rising bitterness in her chest. "Yes, they're wondering how much they must spend to make me their mistress," she said, not quite vanquishing the emotion from her words or her heart.

Lucia eyes darkened. "Men are vile," she said, and with such venom Matilda stared at her.

"You speak from experience," she said softly.

Lucia snorted and met Matilda's eye. "Don't we all?" She slid her arm through Matilda's. "Come, let us take a turn about the room and show them all what they can never afford."

There was the light of challenge in the gorgeous woman's eyes that Matilda could not resist. She didn't lack the will to face society; if that were so, she would have eschewed the gossip and hidden herself in the country years ago. Yet, she had sought out the wallflowers—and found her place among them—not from fear or lack of courage, but because they had welcomed her without judgement. Without *much* judgement, at least. It had taken time to become friends, but she had, and now she was no longer alone. With Lucia at her side, though, she felt bold enough to take it a step further.

Let them look.

Let them judge.

She had nothing to be ashamed of, no matter what they believed of her. *The Huntress*, they called her, and whispered about her lovers. Yet, no man had ever touched her; she'd barely even been kissed unless you counted a cousin when she was fifteen years old, which she certainly did not. A dry press of lips could hardly be counted a kiss. And then there had been Lord Dawlish, her first beau, the man she thought she might one day marry, until her father had ruined it all. He'd kissed her once or twice: sweet, little innocent kisses full of hope. Her heart clenched.

"I'm not what they believe me to be," she said, a little startled by the words but glad to have said them all the same.

Lucia gave her a warm smile and squeezed her arm a little. "I never doubted it," she said, and then a frown pleated her lovely brow. "I don't know if I can say the same. They think me strange, a foreigner. I do not fit here. I do not belong."

"Of course you belong," Matilda replied at once. "You are among friends here, and we are very glad to have you."

"You're sweet," she said, though her tone was melancholy, giving weight to the storm clouds that seemed to cluster in her dark eyes. "But I belong nowhere. I am between worlds, a little of each and belonging to neither. I hate it."

Matilda acknowledged a thrill of unease at the anger of those last words. Hatred seemed to be something Lucia was well acquainted with, and a fire burned within her that Matilda recognised.

Retribution.

"Lucia," she said, choosing her words with care. "If ever you need a friend, a confidante, I would take your secrets to my grave, so… come to me before—"

"Before I do anything rash?" Lucia spoke for her, meeting Matilda's anxious gaze with such directness she knew she'd been right to worry. "It is too late for that," she said, her voice a low purr of satisfaction. "Though it is far from rash. Reckless perhaps, but I have lived my whole life in preparation of what comes next and I welcome it. Whatever it may be. However it may end. At least, it *will* end."

"Lucia," Matilda began, alarmed, but at that moment a young man approached them. His cheeks were aflame, and he stammered a little as he dared to speak to Lucia.

"S-Senorita de Feria," he said, bowing low. "We met at Lady Faversham's garden party."

"Mr Brampton, of course," Lucia said, gracious now, all trace of anger and fire vanished and hidden behind those fathomless dark eyes. "How could I forget?"

"May I request the honour of the next dance?"

"Indeed, you may," Lucia replied, giving him a smile that made the man look like his knees would buckle at any moment. "In fact, would you do me a service and take me to get a glass of lemonade first? It's most dreadfully hot in here."

"It would be an honour, Senorita."

Matilda watched, disturbed, not only by Lucia's words but also by how she hid her true feelings with such ease. What was going on behind that beautiful façade? Whatever it was, Matilda could only feel trepidation. Not so much for Lucia, perhaps, who had appeared almost invincible as the fire burned in her eyes, but for whatever man had crossed her and earned her vengeance. She had the distinct feeling he may not get out alive.

She stood, immobile, in the middle of the ballroom as the cream of the *ton* moved around her, chattering, gossiping, and laughing. For a moment she felt disorientated, disconnected from the world, and never more alone in her life. That's just foolishness, she scolded herself. She had a loving brother, and soon a sister too, and many friends. She was not alone, yet an abyss yawned at her feet.

Her skin prickled, awareness surging through her, the knowledge of eyes on her, of being watched. The weight of a cool gaze slid over her flesh, as obvious as a caress. She did not look around. She did not need to. Matilda knew who watched her.

"Tilda! Yoo-hoo!"

She turned at the exuberant call, knowing who it was before she saw Bonnie yelling across the ballroom like a hoyden. All the old tabbies tutted and muttered their disapproval as Bonnie ran towards her, skirts all a-rustle and hair escaping its pins. Matilda grinned, loving her unfettered enthusiasm for life, and her refusal to be primped and moulded into something she wasn't.

"Hello, darling," Matilda said, greeting the girl with genuine pleasure. "Are you having fun?"

Bonnie pulled a face. "Not yet, are you? Have you found any eligible men to dance with? No one ever asks me."

"Oh, well that won't do," Matilda said, with a tut of disapproval. "Let me see, who should you like to dance with?"

"Oh, St Clair," she said at once, a mischievous glint in her eyes. "He's perfection, isn't he? So handsome." Bonnie put a hand to her heart and rolled her eyes up in her head, pretending to swoon.

Matilda suppressed a violent desire to snort with laughter and dragged Bonnie away from an especially disapproving matron who was staring at them both with horror.

"Well, he is very handsome," Matilda allowed, tugging Bonnie from the centre of the ballroom as the dancers gathered for the first set. "So, I shall see what I can do."

"Oh, lovely!" Bonnie exclaimed, grinning. "You're such a good sport, Matilda," she said, before adding with a sigh. "I don't suppose you could persuade him to offer for me too?" she added.

Matilda bit her lip. "I think that may a bit beyond me," she admitted.

Bonnie made a face and turned in a circle as they walked, looking around and batting a large ostrich feather out of her way as a dowager lady's rather large coiffure impeded her view.

"Bonnie!" Matilda exclaimed, and hurried her on before the woman could cause a scene. Bonnie flounced after her without so much as batting an eyelid.

"If I don't get a proposal soon, or at least the sniff of one—"

"Gordon Anderson?" Matilda guessed with a sympathetic smile.

Bonnie nodded and made a gagging face which made Matilda snort after all. "Gordon Anderson," she agreed with a heavy sigh. "He of the reek of the cowshed, the temper of a starving ferret, and the manners of a ram."

Matilda covered her mouth with her hand to hold back her laughter. Bonnie's descriptions of Gordon Anderson were so outrageous and dreadful that all the Peculiar Ladies had confessed to a longing to see the man in person. They must see such a monster of human creation with their own eyes.

Bonnie made her hands into fists and placed them on her hips, sticking out her chest in the way a wild highlander might and affected a very thick Scottish accent. "I'll tan yer bum if ye don't keep a civil tongue in that empty head of yours, Bonnie Campbell."

Matilda's mouth dropped open, as did a dozen or more people about them who'd witnessed her little impression. Matilda flushed and grabbed her by the wrist, hauling her out of the main room and into the corridor.

"Bonnie," she said, torn between scolding her and laughing her head off. "He never really said that?" she asked instead, a little disbelieving.

"Oh, aye, he did. Word for word," she said with a huff, her own accent slipping through with her anxiety.

Unlike Kitty, who had been known to accentuate her own Irish brogue in polite company, Bonnie had gone to some lengths to eradicate hers to give herself the best chance of catching an

English husband. Though she'd not curb her tongue nor her appetite for life, she'd made concessions. They all made concessions.

"He's a bully and a great lummocking heathen," she said, uncharacteristically gloomy. "I must find a husband before Morven forces me to marry him. We'll murder each other before the honeymoon otherwise," she added with a dark tone.

"Well, that would never do," Matilda said. "I'll see who I can introduce you to this evening."

Both women paused as Kitty came flying around the corner, red-faced and breathless, and ground to a halt.

"Oh," she said in surprise. "Hello."

"Hello," Bonnie and Matilda said in unison, exchanging suspicious glances.

"Whatever are you doing?" Bonnie asked, scrunching up her nose as she looked Kitty over. "You look like you've been running for miles."

"Oh," Kitty said again, flushing a little harder and trying to smooth down her dress and tidy her hair. "Nothing," she said, before adding with a touch too much nonchalance. "Did you see a man come this way? A tall fellow, hair like a copper pot?"

"Kitty," Matilda said, narrowing her eyes at the young woman and feeling rather like a mother hen. "What the devil are you up to?"

"Nothing!" Kitty said, folding her arms and huffing. "Only I was certain he came this way. I didn't imagine it, or him. I'm sure I didn't."

"Well, he didn't, so you must have," Bonnie said, moving to take Kitty's arm. "Perhaps he's gone for refreshments. I say, speaking of, I'm famished, aren't you? Shall we check? Come along, Tilda."

Matilda's stomach rebelled at the thought of food or facing the crush of the refreshments room.

"No, thank you. You two run along and do *try* to stay out of trouble. I'll go back to the ballroom."

"Yes, Mama," Bonnie said in a singsong voice, before ducking a curtsey and then running away with Kitty, the two of them snorting with laughter.

Matilda shook her head with chagrin and decided she felt about a hundred years old. At twenty-five, she was the oldest of the Peculiar Ladies. A spinster. The title rankled. Perhaps it was better to be scandalous than dusty and forgotten at the back of the shelf. The girls' laughter echoed down the hall, and she smiled. Had she ever been that full of fun and laughter? She couldn't remember it.

With a sigh, she hurried back to the ballroom, unwilling to be discovered alone and set more tongues wagging. She was within mere inches of her goal and about to step through the door, when it opened from the other side and the Marquess of Montagu appeared.

Good God, she was doomed.

"Oh!" she said, quite unable to hide her annoyance and irritated by the way her heart pounded. "Why must you forever be turning up like a bad penny?"

He closed the door behind him, his expression as rigid and unchanging as ever. The man might as well have been cut from marble.

"A sovereign, surely?" he said, his voice dripping condescension.

Matilda snorted. "Oh, naturally," she said, her lip curling a little with disdain before moving to hurry past him. He made no attempt to stop her and her fingers grasped the doorknob before she realised she had to say something.

"Damnation," she muttered.

"Cursing now? How unladylike," he observed, as she turned back to find those strange grey eyes watching her with a glimmer of amusement. She shivered under their scrutiny. They were too pale, almost silver and rimmed with black; they made him seem less than human.

"Well, thanks to you, I'm no lady," she said, with fire fuelling her irritation, facing him and feeling the strangest thrill of exhilaration as she did so. Try as he might, this man could not crush her. Even her fear of him seemed to be diminishing with each encounter, though she did not know what it was she did feel. "Though, unlike some, I have not forgotten my manners. I must thank you, it seems, though the realisation sticks in my throat," she said frankly.

He watched her, neither confirming nor denying her statement.

"And therefore, you curse," he said, his head tilting to one side a little. "You do not enjoy being in my debt?"

"An understatement, I assure you," she said, allowing a tight smile to reach her lips. She wanted to rattle at the bars of his exquisite self-control. He was always so immaculate, so self-possessed. He made her feel reckless, out of control, as if he was a perfect sheet of white paper and she was a lit match, charring his pristine edges. She wanted to set a fire beneath that cool exterior and watch him burn.

The marquess's eyes fell to her mouth and rested there and all at once *he* was the match and she felt the lick of flame. She was suddenly too aware of him, of his proximity. Despite her hatred for the man, there was no denying his beauty, although it was dangerous to behold, cold and pitiless like an endless expanse of snow and ice, or the gleam on a blade you never saw coming.

"Thank you for what you did for Miss Dowding," she said in a rush, needing this to be over, to be out of his company at once. "I don't know why you helped her—for a second time, indeed—

195

unless perhaps you do have a shred of common decency in that icy soul of yours but, whatever the reason, I'm grateful."

He watched her a moment longer, utterly still, unnervingly so.

"I regret to disillusion you, but there is no shred of decency. You know better than that," he said, his voice as quiet and even as always. Emotionless. "You know *much* better than that," he added, his gaze returning briefly to her mouth. "Well enough to understand my motivation, my pleasure in having you in my debt. Dissembling does not suit you. Between us, there should always be honesty." His gaze lingered on hers for a long moment. "Good evening, Miss Hunt."

Matilda caught her breath, the strangest sensation running over her as he turned and walked away from her without a backwards glance.

"Devil," she whispered, discovering she was trembling as she turned back to the door and hurried away.

Chapter 18

Matilda! What news! I'm ready to burst with it, aren't you?

—Excerpt of a letter from her grace, Prunella Adolphus, Duchess of Bedwin to Miss Matilda Hunt.

28ᵗʰ June 1814. The Duke and Duchess of Bedwin's Ball, Beverwyck, London.

Nate glowered over the ballroom and crossed his arms. Alice was dancing again. What the hell happened to her being a wallflower?

He felt like a small boy who'd discovered buried treasure just at the moment the bigger boys had arrived to shove him out of the way. *Stop being an ass*, he muttered, trying to school his features into something less murderous. She would marry him tomorrow, and then, tomorrow night….

He let out an uneven breath.

It was ridiculous that a man of his years and experience should be such a nervous wreck, but it was nonetheless true.

When he'd seen Alice tonight, his chest had constricted, his throat had grown tight, and such a rush of emotion had assailed him he'd not known what to do or say, certainly not without giving himself away. He'd seen nothing so glorious in all his life. Her hair was a cascade of fiery curls and the dress glowed like embers on a winter's night. She burned like a flame, stealing the air from the room, from his lungs and scorching him, branding his flesh, even though he not even touched her. God, he longed to touch her.

"Put your tongue away Hunt, for heaven's sake."

Nate started as the duke sauntered up to stand beside him.

"Bedwin," he said, noncommittal, wondering if the man knew who he'd been watching.

"I hear congratulations are in order."

Nate's head snapped around at that, terror at the idea that someone had discovered them making his heart beat fast.

"How the hell did you ever trounce me at cards, man?" Bedwin said, shaking his head with a pitying expression. "Your every emotion is writ large on your face and, before you break my nose, please remember my wife is your beloved's best friend."

"Oh," Nate said, the tension leaving him in a rush.

"Quite," the duke replied, lifting a glass of champagne from a passing waiter and handing it to him. "For heaven's sake, do try looking a little less intense. I half expect you to start writing bad poetry or some such nonsense."

Nate opened his mouth to reject such a ridiculous assertion and realised he could do nothing of the sort. Rubbing a weary hand over his face, he gave a groan. "I'm losing my damn mind."

"I know," Bedwin replied cheerfully. "Happens to the best of us, I'm afraid. Speaking of the best of things, I'm your best man. Hope you don't mind?"

The duke snorted as Nate blinked. "I beg your pardon?"

"The ladies have organised us," he said, grinning at Nate's confusion. "To be fair, knowing a little of Mr and Mrs Dowding, Prue has the right of it. Having us as witnesses to the happy event should ease the shock just a little."

Nate let out a breath. "That's very decent of you, Bedwin, truly. I... I don't know what to say."

"Nothing to say, and call me Robert." He gave Nate a wry look. "I owe you for all the nights you poured me into a carriage instead of letting me stay and make a bloody fool of myself at *Hunter's*. You could have fleeced me for a deal more than you did."

Nate shook his head and gave a short bark of laughter. "You make me sound almost charitable. I'll have you know I bought a house in the country on your losses alone."

The duke grinned at him, looking thoroughly unrepentant. "I'm glad to hear it," he said, clapping him on the back. "Now, if I am correctly informed, the next dance is a waltz and a certain young lady is waiting impatiently for you to claim it."

Nate did not need asking twice, and hurried along in the duke's wake as they strode across the ballroom.

***

"Alice, look at me," Prue commanded. "Alice!"

Alice did try. She honestly did, but her gaze was riveted to the man crossing the ballroom towards her. Every feminine part of her quivered as he grew nearer, and she clutched at Prue's sleeve, aware she was blushing.

"Alice," Prue said, not disguising the laughter in her voice now.

"Is my mother watching?" Alice said, helpless to look away.

"No," Prue said with a sigh. "Helena is distracting her, which is just as well. Heavens, the two of you can't get married soon enough. You're making me blush, and I'm a married woman."

"I know," Alice said with a heartfelt sigh, "but just look at him."

She had no idea if Prue did look—actually, Alice rather hoped she'd keep her eyes on her own husband—because Nate filled her senses.

Tall and blond and elegant, resplendent in his evening black with a snowy white cravat at his throat, he looked every inch the perfect gentleman. Yet, there was something rather wilder about him, something that set him apart as being… not *quite* a gentleman. Far from dismaying Alice, it was this slightly raw edge that made her heart pound and the blood fizz in her veins. She knew he was a good man, a kind one, yet there was just a tiny bit of wickedness in his eyes, enough to have stolen her away from a ballroom and all but ruined her with his recklessness. Not that she regretted it.

Not for a moment.

"Miss Dowding," he said, his expression stern and unsmiling, though that challenging glint of wickedness danced in his eyes. "I believe this is my dance."

"So it is, Mr Hunt," she said, rather impressed that her voice was steady when her insides were a trembling puddle of mush.

She allowed him to move her onto the dance floor and even kept breathing as his hand rested at her waist. Then the terrible man lowered his head and whispered in her ear.

"This time tomorrow night, I'll have you in my bed, Miss Dowding."

She stumbled the first step, treading on his toes as he gave an unrepentant chuckle of laughter that rumbled through her.

"Wretch," she said with a huff, feeling the blaze of her cheeks like she stood too close to a fire. "You did that on purpose."

"I did," he admitted, glancing down at her. "And you started it."

"Whatever do you mean?" she asked, perplexed as he moved her into a complicated turn that she had to concentrate on before she could press him again. "Well?"

"Well?" he repeated. "What do you mean by coming out tonight looking like a blasted goddess? Every man here wants you, and you've danced with half of them. I'm hard pressed to know who to call out first," he grumbled, and though she knew he was teasing, she realised it was only in part.

"You're jealous?" she said in surprise, having never expected such a thing from him.

"Of course I'm bloody well jealous," he said, looking adorably sulky. "Matilda glares at me if I so much as look in your direction and I have to sit here and suffer every fool who stares at you like you're the last cake on the plate. It's intolerable."

It was impossible not to smile at him, and she hoped Helena was still enduring her mother's conversation, because she knew her heart must be in her eyes. With every bit of courage she possessed, Alice lowered her gaze and her voice.

"I can't wait to be in your bed, Nate," she said, the words low and husky.

Nate stumbled.

It was only for a moment, and she doubted anyone but her could tell, but she could, and she couldn't help her triumphant burst of laughter. Colour touched his cheeks, which was most endearing of all, as he huffed and looked sheepish.

"That was a dirty trick," he muttered as Alice bit her lip, staring at his cravat with determination to hold her amusement in check. "And you'll pay for it tomorrow night."

When she dared look up at him, that wicked light was back in his eyes, giving weight to his words. She shivered in his arms, a delicious thrill of anticipation that made her sigh.

"Oh, God, stop looking at me like that," he protested, sucking in a deep breath, "or we'll not make it till tomorrow. I shall abduct you from the blasted ballroom and it will be an anvil wedding and ruination *en route*."

"Sounds divine," Alice said, undisguised longing behind the words.

"Have mercy, love," Nate replied with feeling. Deciding he'd best make her breathless to stop her talking, he swept Alice into a complicated series of dizzying turns that did just that.

Smiling, she simply enjoyed the sensation of flying in his arms, and dreamed of the day to come.

***

It was long past midnight by the time Alice joined her mother in the carriage home.

"Well, you were certainly popular tonight," her mother said, looking her over, not entirely approving. "You've been hiding your light under a bushel, I see. With how you were tonight you might have caught yourself a title, you know," she said with a frustrated sniff. "Still, what's done is done."

"What do you mean?" Alice asked, frowning a little.

"That Mr Bindley is coming tomorrow to propose to you, of course," she said, giving Alice an impatient look. "We told you it would happen soon enough."

"What time tomorrow?" Swallowing down a bubble of anxiety, Alice struggled to keep her voice nonchalant.

"He's coming to dine with us, so I told him to arrive a little early. You can accept his proposal and then we can celebrate over dinner."

"Oh," Alice said in relief, as her mother's sharp eyes fixed on her. "Oh, it's only that I shall be out in the morning. I've arranged to see Prunella," she added, knowing her mother would never keep her from an appointment with a duchess. "Bedwin is coming too."

"The duke *and* the duchess," her mother said, preening at the idea. "Well, naturally you cannot disappoint them. Just make sure you are home in time for Bindley."

Alice mumbled something incomprehensible and then pretended to doze. Lying to her mother was not something she enjoyed doing... well, perhaps just a little, she admitted. However, she was not past realising it was a dishonest and wretched way to go on, but *needs must when the devil drives,* she thought with a sigh, and then grinned. *Or when Mr Bindley comes calling.*

***

"Come on, a night cap before you leave," the duke said, ushering Matilda and Nate into a private sitting room as the last of the guests dispersed.

Nate sat down with a sigh, as Matilda settled beside Prue.

"Are you all right?" Prue asked, reaching out to touch Matilda's cheek. "You look rather pale."

Now Prue mentioned it, Matilda seemed a little out of sorts. He'd been so preoccupied with his own upcoming nuptials that he'd not seen much of his sister.

"Oh, I'm fine," Matilda replied, a smile at her lips which was not altogether convincing. "Just weary, that's all."

"Montagu didn't bother you, did he?" Bedwin asked, turning to look at her with a frown.

Nate sat up with alarm, his anxiety not soothed by the flush of colour at Matilda's cheeks.

"What the devil was that bastard doing here?" Nate demanded, anger and worry making him speak out of turn.

"Nate!" Matilda exclaimed, glaring at him. "Who his grace invites is hardly our affair."

Bedwin handed Nate a glass of brandy, an apologetic expression in his eyes. "I didn't invite him," he said with a rueful smile before sitting down. "And do, please, call me Robert," he said to Matilda. "I can only apologise," he added, still looking at her. "He was not invited, but you do not exclude the Marquess of Montagu if he turns up on your doorstep."

"But you're a bloody duke," Nate said, outraged. "You outrank him."

"Rank and power are not at all the same thing," Robert said, serious now. "Montagu is not a man you make an enemy of. His enemies have a nasty habit of disappearing. Besides which, he was so damn scrupulous in begging my pardon that it would have seemed churlish to refuse him. He said he'd not be here above an hour, and that he was just...." He frowned, apparently searching his memory for the phrase. "Reminding someone of a debt."

"What the devil did he mean by that?" Nate asked, perplexed, but Robert just shrugged.

"I don't know, and I don't want to, but I pity the poor wretch who owes him."

"Nate," Matilda said, her voice quiet and a little unsteady. "Would you mind if we went home now? I... I'm not feeling terribly well."

Nate put down his drink and sprang to his feet. "Of course, Tilda. Why didn't you say so? My word, you do look peaky."

They made their excuses and Nate took Matilda to his carriage, where she sagged into the corner with a sigh.

"Tilda," he said, once the carriage had rocked into motion. "About Montagu. He didn't bother you, did he? Because if he did—"

"No!" she said, sounding a little exasperated. "No, he didn't bother me. Why should he? He thinks no more of me than a kitchen maid. I'm beneath his notice, you know that."

"I will make him pay you know. Sooner or later."

"No, Nate," she said, sitting up straight at that. "You will not. You will marry Alice tomorrow and have a wife and, soon enough, a home and a family to care for. I won't have you risk that. I am quite content. What is done is done, and you will leave Montagu alone. You heard Bedwin; he's dangerous. If even a duke must treat the man with kid gloves, he's not someone to trifle with."

Nate glowered into the darkness, his jaw tight. He'd say no more on the matter, not to his sister, but somehow, someday, Montagu would pay for his sins.

Chapter 19

*Harriet! You'll never guess what I just heard
about Alice!*

**—Excerpt of a letter from Miss Kitty Connolly
to Miss Harriet Stanhope.**

29th June 1814. Baker Street, London.

"I feel quite dreadfully wicked, just like a character in one of
my own novels," Prue said, grinning widely as her husband helped
Alice into the carriage. "It's very exciting."

Alice, who hadn't slept a wink, and whose stomach was tied in
knots, offered her friend a wan smile.

"I do hope I won't appear in your next story. I think I shall
make a rather woeful heroine," she said, sitting down beside Prue
with a sigh.

"Nonsense," Prue replied with her usual brisk manner.
"You've done the hard bit and got out of the house. There will be
no more subterfuge after this; it can all come out in the open.
You'll feel much better then, take my word for it."

Alice gave a laugh that sounded just a touch too close to
hysteria. "Mother wouldn't stop this morning. Mr Bindley will
arrive tonight to propose, and she was asking me all sorts of
questions about the wedding preparations. It put me in such a
quake I nearly confessed everything." Her voice trembled as the
enormity of what she was doing hit her all over again. "And I've
dragged both of you into my d-drama, and I've not got a thing for
my w-wedding night, let alone a trousseau...."

She snapped her mouth shut, refusing to turn into a watering pot. Anyone would think she didn't want to marry Nate, and that wasn't it at all. Deception and subterfuge were not nearly as much fun as one would imagine, though, especially when she stretched her imagination to include her parents' reaction to the news she'd married Nathaniel Hunt.

"Alice," Prue said, her voice steadying with its calm assurance of good sense. "Do you love Mr Hunt?"

With a deep breath Alice found a smile curving her mouth. "I do."

"And you've not changed your mind about marrying him?"

"No. Not for a moment."

Prue let out a breath of relief. "Well, then," she said, tugging Alice's arm through hers. "Everything is perfect. I took the liberty of arranging some things for you, so your trousseau is not an issue, and Robert has agreed to break the news to your parents in the morning, once you are truly married. He'll arrange for your things to be packed up and sent to you at once."

"Oh!" Alice looked back at the duke, wide eyed. "Oh, no! I... no, that won't do. Not that I'm not grateful. Terribly grateful, but Nate and I must face them together. If we do not, it will seem as if I am ashamed of him, of what I've done, and I'm not, not in the least."

"Well," Prue said, giving Alice an admiring look that warmed her cheeks and made her feel a little less tremulous inside. "How brave you are, Alice, and quite right too."

"Thank God," Robert said with feeling. "I would have done it, of course, Alice, but I confess I was in far more of a quake than you appear to be."

Alice laughed and the duke grinned at her. Suddenly, she felt as brave as Prue believed her to be. Nate was waiting for her, and that thought alone was enough to make her smile and put her anxieties aside. In little more than an hour she would be Mrs Hunt. It could not come soon enough.

****

Nate paced the aisle while Matilda looked on, an expression of affectionate indulgence in her eyes. Pulling out his fob watch, Nate checked it for the fifth time in as many minutes. One minute past eleven. Where was she?

"Nate, it's barely eleven o'clock. She'll be here." Matilda's voice was calm and soothing, not that it soothed him a bit. Nothing would until he saw her here.

"What if she changed her mind?" he said, the idea twisting his guts into a knot. "What if she was too afraid to go through with it, or her mother discovered her plan, or Mr Bindley arrived and—"

"Nate!" Matilda said, smiling at him and gesturing to the sudden shaft of sunlight which had illuminated the gloomy interior as the large oak door swung open.

He exhaled.

There she was, illuminated all around with golden light. *Like an angel*, he thought, too relieved to be nauseated by his own whimsy. By God, she was lovely enough to have wings.

Nate could do nothing but smile like a fool as she walked towards him, and his heart lifted as he saw the reflection of his joy in her eyes. There were no doubts in the summer blue, no hesitation or regret, just happiness.

"Prue insisted we stop to buy flowers," she said, the words shy and a little hesitant.

"Of course," he said, noting the little bouquet of peonies. "I ought to have thought of that. She was quite right."

She smiled up at him, and his heart felt as if it might burst. All the hopes and dreams he'd set aside for so many years and told himself he'd forgotten about crashed into him at once. He'd spent so long convincing himself he didn't want them anymore, because he knew he couldn't have them, that he'd almost believed it. Almost. Until Alice had needed a kiss in the moonlight to give her courage and, in return, she'd given him the courage to remember.

"You're sure?" he asked, needing to hear her say it, although the answer shone in her eyes.

"I am," she said.

So, they turned towards the altar and recited their vows.

***

Alice stepped down from the coach and looked up at the smart house on Half Moon Street that was now her home.

"Welcome home, Mrs Hunt," Nate said, his large hand clasping hers.

She gave a shaky breath and smiled at him.

"Well, turtle doves, this is where I leave you," Matilda said, leaning out of the coach window. "I'm going to stay with Prue and Robert for a few days, but you needn't worry. I shall be moving out. You'll not have a spinster sister hanging about your necks."

"Matilda!" they both said at once, and Nate discovered himself relieved to hear the shock in Alice's voice at the idea.

"You can't think we would turn you out of your home," Nate said, horrified that she should not feel welcome.

"Of course not!" she exclaimed, laughing at them both. "Indeed, you are both so good I know you will insist I stay, but it won't do, I assure you. If you think I want to spend my days walking in on the two of you billing and cooing, you have more faith in my endurance for such nauseating displays than I do."

"Oh, but Tilda," Alice said, genuinely crestfallen. "We are sisters now, and I'd not chase you from your home for anything."

"There, there," Matilda soothed, smiling and quite unruffled. "It is time I established myself in any case. Don't worry, you'll still see plenty of me, enough that we'll bicker like true siblings soon enough, I don't doubt. Nate, I thought I might take that lovely little house on South Audley Street, if you don't mind it? It's been sitting empty since we moved here and it's perfect for me."

"Matilda," he said, his throat tight. "I—"

"Stop it!" she said, her voice stern. "You know very well how much I enjoyed living there."

Nate moved back to the coach and took her hand. His heart ached. Matilda deserved this kind of happiness, far more than he ever would.

"It's all right, Nate," she said with a sigh, squeezing his fingers. "Truly. I'm so happy for you, and I'm looking forward to having a place of my own. It's about time and, with your generosity, I will be able to live like a duchess. Now, run along, children," she said, laughing and making a shooing motion with her hands. "Go and have your happily ever after."

With his heart in his throat, Nate closed the coach door, and watched his sister wave and smile as it rolled out of sight.

Alice slid her hand back into his. "We'll get her to come back, Nate," she said, and he looked down to see the sincerity in her eyes. "And then we'll find her a good man, so she'll be as happy as we are."

Nate lifted his wife's hand to his mouth and kissed the fingers. Matilda's future was still very much his concern, but for now, he had other matters to attend to, and another life to care about, another heart to protect. He swore to do a better job for both the women in his life than he'd ever done in the past.

"Come along then, Mrs Hunt," he said, wondering if the novelty of saying that would ever leave him less than smiling and dazed with the depths of his good fortune. "We have a wedding night to see to."

"It's not even two in the afternoon," Alice said, blushing a little.

Nate snorted and swung her up into his arms. "Darling girl, if you think I'm waiting until darkness falls to make this marriage official, you've really learned very little about me since that kiss in the moonlight."

"Oh," Alice said with a happy sigh. "How lovely."

***

Alice laughed as Nate insisted not only on carrying her over the threshold, but all the way to his bedroom.

"You'll hurt yourself," she protested as he kicked the door open and slammed it shut again.

"If lifting a little slip of a thing like you from the ground will damage me, I dread to think what you are expecting of our wedding night," he said, a trifle indignant as they finally found themselves alone.

"Wedding afternoon," she corrected, as he set her down on the floor. She kept her arms about his neck, having to stand on tiptoe to keep them there.

"Afternoon *and* night," he said, his voice firm, before frowning and looking around. "Where is it?" he muttered. "Oh, here we are." With a boyish grin he disengaged her hands and moved across the room. Alice admired the view as he bent and then hefted a solid looking footstool over his head. "I've had one put in every room," he admitted.

"Oh, Nate!" Alice laughed, as he placed it before her and held out his hand. She took it and stepped up, sighing with pleasure as she found herself eye to eye with her handsome husband. "I love you," she said, finding it easier each time the words left her mouth.

Nate sighed and closed his eyes, leaning his forehead against hers, sliding his arms about her waist and pulling her close. "I love you too."

They stayed like that for a long moment, and then his eyes flickered open, a rather devilish light evident. "Aren't you going to kiss your husband, then, Mrs Hunt?"

Alice bit back a smile. "Aren't you supposed to lead the way?" she said, attempting to look chagrined. "Why is it you always make me do all the work?"

"Because you're more daring than I, love," he said, his voice low and intimate, making her shiver with longing. "And you're so good at it, too."

"Hmm," Alice said, wondering why she didn't feel more afraid of what was to come, or why she wasn't dying of nerves or shyness. "At kissing, perhaps. I've had a little practise at that. A handsome stranger taught me on a moonlit balcony, you see."

"A stranger?" he said, sounding scandalised by the idea. "What kind of wicked, wanton creature have I married, by God?"

"This kind," Alice whispered, pressing her lips to his.

He sighed against her mouth, allowing her to lead, to nip and taste and tease his lips, tantalising him with the tip of her tongue as pulled her closer.

"What a lucky wretch I am," he murmured, as Alice giggled and deepened the kiss. "Remind me to thank that handsome stranger if ever we see him again."

To her relief, he took the lead thereafter, as for all her newfound boldness and confidence, she didn't really have any very certain ideas of what was to come. Prue had whispered a few reassuring words to her, but there had been no time for confidences or revelations.

Nate's hands fell to her buttons, fumbling a little, which was both amusing and reassuring. At least her sophisticated husband wasn't totally unmoved by events. She trembled with anticipation as her gown fell to the floor, followed by petticoats and stays until she stood in only a fine cotton shift. Alice trembled, expecting a final unveiling and unsure if she was relieved or disappointed when he returned to stand before her, and a swift grin flashed.

"Your turn," he said, gesturing at his buttons when she returned a blank look.

"Oh!" she said, a little surprised, but pleased to take a turn.

She had been dying to know what lay beneath all those pristine layers of starched cotton, linen, and luxurious silk. Ever since the day she'd turned up at *Hunter's* and seen him in such disarray, his shirtsleeves rolled up to reveal powerful arms, she had longed to see more of him. Now her longing was reality and she made swift work of pushing the fitted jacket from his shoulders and unbuttoning his waistcoat. With more enthusiasm than finesse, she yanked his shirt from his waistband, and he chuckled.

"Such impatience," he said, laughing as she gave a huff of frustration.

"I've told you before, you wear too many clothes."

"An error I'll try hard to rectify at every opportunity," he said gravely, before pulling his shirt over his head and allowing it to drop to the floor.

Alice caught her breath and stared at him. Broad shoulders and a lean muscled torso filled her vision. Sandy blond hair covered his chest and narrowed to a line that trailed in an intriguing manner beneath his waistband.

"Have pity, love," he said, as she realised he was breathing hard now, the rapid rise and fall of his chest illustrating his impatience. "Touch me," he added, by way of explanation, a desperate edge to the demand.

Well, that was a request she had no problem indulging. Her fingers were burning with the desire to do just that. She raised her right palm and set it tentatively upon his chest, feeling the rapid thud of his heart beneath. Glancing at him, she saw his eyes were intent, a look burning in the darkened depths that made her feel he was holding a great deal in check, allowing her to explore him.

Alice thought she ought to reward such patience and raised her other hand to lie beside the first. Slowly, she slid her hands over his skin, learning the shape of him, the contours of muscle, the satiny skin and the rough rasp of coarse hair beneath her fingertips. Finding her own breath a little erratic now, she followed a path down his sides, pleased by the fine shiver that ran over him. Her fingers traced along the waistband and settled upon the buttons there, undoing them one by one as Nate leaned into her, nuzzling into her neck.

His breath was harsh against her skin, matching her own as she pushed breeches and smallclothes from his narrow hips.

"My," she said, unaware she'd spoken at all, as Nate gave a soft bark of laughter. Emboldened by the rather frantic look in his eyes, she trailed her finger through that coarse hair again, stroking back and forth as he shivered and her hand drifted lower.

"Is it all right to... to touch you?" she asked, unsure of what he expected of her. Was it unseemly to be so intrigued?

"Of course," he said, the words roughened with desire. "I want you to touch me, everywhere, however you wish. I want to do the same." He looked at her, a question in his eyes and she nodded, smiling.

"Yes."

He let out a shaky breath. "I would never hurt you, but—"

"I know," she said at once, not wanting to think on it too much. "Prue explained a little. I trust you."

A large hand cupped her cheek and she turned her face into it, closing her eyes. "You can tell me no, Alice," he said, his thumb stroking her skin softly. "Never be afraid to, or to tell me yes," he added, a wicked glint in his eyes as he leaned in and nipped at her earlobe. "Or harder, faster, *more*...."

Alice felt her breath catch at the possibility of ever daring to say anything of the sort, though the idea was less unnerving as he trailed kisses down her neck, setting fires as his lips touched her skin.

"Or, please, Nate, don't stop," he added, almost purring with satisfaction as her breath caught. "I'd like to hear that one."

"Please, Nate," she whispered, but he chuckled and moved back.

"I interrupted you," he said, challenge lighting his eyes now. "You were mid exploration." Taking her hand, he slid it down his torso to rest upon the golden hair above his groin, where his arousal was evident now. "Don't stop."

Alice took him at his word and allowed her fingers to trail over him. Her breath caught. She was enraptured by skin that was so fine, softer even than her own. She curled her fingers about him, testing the weight and the unexpected hardness beneath the silk.

Glancing up, she found Nate had closed his eyes, his breathing deep and even, as though he was controlling it with care.

Alice explored a little further, fascinated by the heat of his body, by the pleasing curve of the blunt head and the heavy, yet delicate feel of his balls as she cupped them in her palm.

"Alice," he said, her name a low moan as she looked up at him again.

"Show me how," she said, eager to learn.

His eyes flicked open, dark with desire. "Get these bloody boots off me first," he said, sounding rather agitated. "I need you in my bed now."

With rather more enthusiasm than she suspected was deemed appropriate for a virgin bride, Alice leapt from the stool and tugged at his boots, throwing them to the floor with careless abandon. Next, she wriggled the breeches and drawers down, trying not to stare too much at the very male part of him which was impossible to miss at this angle.

Kneeling before him she leaned back, gazing with wonder up the impressive landscape of his body. Nate looked back at her, wonder of his own shining in his eyes, a slight smile curving his mouth.

Later, she might wonder at her own audacity, at what on earth had possessed her, but in that moment it seemed the most natural thing in the world to want to please him, to kiss him, and she leaned in, pressing her lips to the soft skin at the apex of his thigh.

His breath caught, an agreeable sound she wished to hear again, so she nuzzled him there, breathing in the scent of musk and soap and warm, male skin. Alice turned her head, glancing up to find his gaze fixed on her. She thought perhaps he was holding his breath as she pressed her mouth to the softest skin. His arousal jerked under her touch and he muttered a curse.

"Enough!" he said, the word shaky as he leaned down and grasped her arms, hauling her up to him. She was lifted, carried to the bed and set down upon the edge where he made short work of stripping her of her shift. For a moment he just stared, breathing hard.

"Lay back," he said, barely whispering the words though they surged through her.

She did as he asked, aware of his heated stare upon her, devouring her, seeking out all the secret places even she did not know as well as his eloquent gaze seemed to understand them. He lay down beside her, leaning on one elbow.

"How I have longed to touch you this way," he said, resting a reverent hand upon her hip and sliding it over her skin, over her waist. "That first night on the balcony you changed me. You owned me from the moment my lips touched yours, before even. From the moment you asked me to kiss you and promised you wouldn't tell if I kissed you first, I wanted to run away with you. I wanted to take you away from the stupid ball and bring you back here and keep you all to myself."

"You have me now," she whispered, quivering with longing as his warm hand cupped her breast.

"I do," he agreed, smiling as he stared down at her. "I do," he said again, and then lowered his mouth and captured her nipple. Alice made a startled sound and clutched at his head, hands tangling in his thick blond hair as she sighed. He caressed her with his tongue, circling the nipple and tormenting a little with gentle scrapes of his teeth, then licking and sucking first one breast and then the other as she squirmed with pleasure.

He made a low sound of amusement and she felt it move through her, tugging at her womb. Her body was clamouring, parts of her she'd barely acknowledged before now awakening and demanding his attention. *At last,* they seemed to cry, *oh, yes, at last.*

Nate lifted his head. "I want to taste you everywhere," he said, the low tenor of his words turning into liquid heat inside of her.

"E-Everywhere?" she queried, a little doubtful.

"Mm-hmm," he murmured. "Especially where you most need me. Where do you ache for me? Tell me."

Alice stared at him, blinking. "I-I," she stammered. Surely that was a rhetorical question? "I... don't know."

He tsked at her and shook his head.

"No?" she said, feeling her cheeks flame.

"No, you little fibber," he said, laughter in his eyes, though not the mocking kind. This, with him, was warm and safe and rather intoxicating, drawing her into intimacy, asking that she trust him. "Does your body ache for me, Alice? Does it throb and cry out for my touch?"

"Yes," she admitted, wondering if the scald of her cheeks could burn the bedding.

"Tell me where," he coaxed, bending to kiss her mouth. "Tell me and I'll make it better. So much better."

Alice whimpered and shook her head, mortified to find his request so impossible, but he just smiled and kissed her again.

"Then show me," he said, his voice gentle.

He moved back, watching as Alice swallowed and lifted one hand. She had to do this much; she would not allow her own stupid shyness to stop her from enjoying her marriage bed. It had kept her from so much pleasure throughout her life; it had to stop now.

Slowly, and hardly daring to breathe, she trailed a hand down her body, between her breasts, down her stomach. The look in Nate's eyes gave her confidence that this was what he wanted from her.

"Oh, God, yes," he murmured, the words spoken on a harsh breath as he stared at her hand moving lower. "Alice," he whispered, soft and so full of desire her confidence grew. "Show me."

Torn between shame and searing desire, Alice let her hand rest between her legs, covering the little triangle of fiery curls.

"More," he rasped, moving down the bed. "Show me."

With her breath caught in her throat, Alice widened her thighs, captivated by the look in her husband's eyes, by the blatant need.

"Is this where you want me?" he asked, touching a gentle fingertip to her curls. "Please say it is," he begged her.

"It is," she managed and then gasped as he lowered his mouth to her skin, kissing her inner thigh, moving closer as she continued to hold her breath, feeling giddy and wanton and out of her mind with desire. He parted her curls with careful hands and then his mouth was on her again and she was beyond coherent thought.

There was nothing beyond this room, beyond this bed, beyond the wet heat of her husband's mouth upon her private skin. Her world shrank, coalesced, and reshaped itself to that shimmering pleasure beneath her flesh, the point where he caressed, teased, and licked until she was nothing more than a quivering expanse of nerves and sensation.

Alice sought for something to hold on to as reality seemed to slip away from her, tumbling her into some strange, dreamlike state. The bedclothes rumpled beneath her grasping hands as she arched into Nate's mouth with abandon. Seeking her own pleasure with shameless moans and cries, Alice called his name as he'd wanted her to do as light glittered and shone behind her eyelids and the pleasure broke and sparked through her blood like fireworks.

"Alice, Alice, oh love."

She was only dimly aware of his voice, of the caresses and kisses that covered her as he moved up the bed, until his body pressed against hers and she awoke from the dreamlike place he'd sent her to. His skin seared hers, so hot, the weight of his body so exhilarating as he encompassed her, surrounded her.

Clutching at his shoulders, she wrapped herself around him, gasping as his erection nudged against flesh that was still aching with pleasure, slick with desire.

"I'll be careful," he promised, easing a little inside her. "Tell me if I hurt you."

Alice nodded, still a little dazed and grateful for it, for the way her limbs felt heavy and pliant, though that sated, weighted astonishment was leaving her as his body entered hers. So strange, and yet not strange at all as she held him to her. He moved slowly, with as much tenderness and care as he'd promised her as he joined them together.

His groan of pleasure fanned the embers of desire still hot in her blood, simmering beneath the surface as he heated her from within once more. Lifting his weight from her, he braced himself

219

on his arms, looking down at her as he moved. He filled her completely as she gasped and clutched at him, surprise, pleasure, and pain merging all at once.

"Alice?" he said, her name as unsteady as his breathing.

"I'm all right," she said, releasing a breath and giving a surprised little laugh at the realisation they were as close as two people could ever get. "Don't stop."

"Thank God," he said, making her laugh again with the fervent nature of his words.

He was so beautiful, she thought, wondering how many scandalous couples were making love in the light of a summer's afternoon. Though the curtains were partly closed, a little sunlight entered the room still, glinting on his golden hair and burnishing his skin. Her hands roamed his body, unable to stop touching him, to stop exploring him as that strange, dreamlike state beckoned again. Alice closed her eyes, chasing sensation as it tugged at her, urging her closer as his body moved inside her.

She arched and moved with him instinctively, following where he led, trusting him to show her the way, except that glittering peak remained just out of reach, no matter how she reached towards it.

"Nate," she said, the word a plea, a cry for help. "Nate, don't stop, please… please… I can't."

"I know," he said, moving a hand between her thighs, seeking the source of her pleasure and guiding her towards the edge. His thumb caressed her so gently, yet that was all Alice needed to find the brightness dazzling her once more as she clung to him.

"Yes," he said, a triumphant, joyful exclamation that filled her senses before he joined her, shuddering and crying out as he found his own pleasure, filling her with it, with his body, his love, as they clung together and gasped for breath, laughing and overwhelmed in each other's arms.

Chapter 20

My word, Prue!

My word!

—Excerpt of a letter from Mrs Alice Hunt to her grace, Prunella Adolphus, Duchess of Bedwin.

The 29ᵗʰ June 1814. Half Moon Street. London.

"What time is it?" Alice asked, her head pillowed on Nate's chest.

"Why?" he asked, his voice still lazy and sated. "Going somewhere?"

She snorted and shook her head, turning to press a kiss to his skin, still a little giddy that she could do such a thing. "Don't be silly. It's only…."

Nate shifted, moving her head onto his arm as he turned on his side so he could look at her.

"Only?"

"Only Prue said she'd sent my letter to my parents at five-thirty, to give them time to cancel Mr Bindley's visit. I don't want to cause them any more embarrassment than I must."

Nate made a harrumphing noise that suggested he cared little for their or Mr Bindley's embarrassment, but otherwise held his tongue.

"Do you think they'll come here?" she asked, trepidation as scenes of her furious father hammering on Nate's front door filled her mind and made her stomach twist.

"No," he said, kissing her nose. "The deed is done, and I believe you told them we'd call tomorrow. Besides which, my staff have instructions to tell anyone with the temerity to ask that Mr and Mrs Hunt are out of town and are not expected back before tomorrow afternoon. They'll never get past Jenkins in any case; most terrifying butler in London. He even scares me."

Alice gave him an indulgent smile. "Mr and Mrs Hunt," she repeated, grinning. "How wonderful that sounds."

"It does," Nate said. He reached out and tugged at a burnished curl, his expression growing serious. "There will be plenty who don't agree though, love. I'm not good *ton*, you do understand that?"

She snorted and rolled her eyes. "Much I care for that. Besides which, you are invited to many of the best places. Matilda, too."

"That's because a lot of very powerful men owe me a great deal of money. Displease me and I might cut off their credit, or even call in their debt. That doesn't mean I'm a welcome presence. They tolerate Matilda and I because they have little choice."

"But Matilda told me your mother was a viscount's daughter," she said, frowning. "I can't claim anything like that."

"Yes, and my father's great-uncle was an earl," he added with a shrug. "And my father caused a scandal by losing all our money and dying in penury, leaving his two children in the gutter to scrabble with the rats. I clawed our fortune back with hard work and the running of a less than respectable establishment."

"But *Hunter's* is the most exclusive club in London," Alice protested.

"*Now*," Nate said pointedly. "It wasn't to begin with, and I worked at all aspects, including throwing the louts out and breaking noses when required. Mud sticks, Alice." There was a thread of anxiety to his voice now and when he looked up, she could see it in his eyes, something a little vulnerable, a little bit unsure. "You could have done better than me," he said.

Alice stared at him for a moment. "You know," she said, reaching out and tracing the edge of his jaw. She could feel the rasp of whiskers just appearing, and enjoyed the rough edge under her fingertips. "Before I met you, I told Prue I wished she could write a hero for me, that she could conjure him up and make him real. Do you know what I asked for?"

Nate shook his head, a curious look in his eyes. "A handsome prince? A duke?"

"No!" she said with a huff of laughter. "Ridiculous man, as if I would. I asked for a kind man who never treated me like a child." She trailed her fingertips over the curve of his lips. "A man with a devilish smile," she whispered, leaning forward to press her mouth to his. "A man who was just the right amount of wicked."

He closed his eyes and sighed, opening to her kiss.

"I think I might know someone who fits that description," he said against her mouth, and she could hear the smile in his voice.

"So do I," she said. "It's that stranger in the moonlight again."

"Hmm," he said, nipping at her ear and making her squirm. "Well, you'll just have put up with me until you see him again."

Alice laughed as he rolled her onto her back and settled into the cradle of her thighs. "I can do that."

***

Matilda wiped her eyes and gave her nose a vigorous blow. "Stop it, you foolish creature," she muttered to herself. "You will not turn into a watering pot. You're better than that."

She'd asked the driver to take her on a tour somewhere, wherever he pleased, knowing she needed a little time to compose herself. Prue and Robert were engaged to visit friends this afternoon, so she would join them for dinner. They'd asked her to accompany them, assuring her their friends would not mind, but Matilda had refused. How tired she was of being the gooseberry. Seeing Nate and Alice so happy together had been wonderful, and yet she was heartsick. How could she be envious of them? It was wicked of her. Not that she wished them any ill, far from it. She was genuinely happy for them, but....

But.

There was no way on earth she would return to live in a house with a couple of newlyweds. It would be rubbing salt in the wound, and eventually she would say something spiteful and hate herself for it. No. She needed to get out and establish herself. A companion would have to be found. No doubt some humourless creature, dried up and fossilised. With a start of shock, Matilda realised what a dreadful and unfair thing that was to think of another unmarried woman. She was perilously close to being considered an aging spinster herself, and she didn't even have the benefit of an unblemished reputation. How could she make judgements about women who found themselves in such circumstances through no fault of their own?

Burdened with an excess of self-loathing, guilt, and a healthy dose of the blue devils, this brought on another round of sobbing until she'd soaked two lace edged hankies.

"Really, Matilda," she scolded herself, disgusted with such a display of self-indulgent pity. "Pull yourself together."

It was just as well she'd not gone with Prue and Robert, she thought with a rueful sniff.

Noticing a flash of green beyond the coach window, Matilda got the attention of the driver and asked him to pull over. The confines of the coach were smothering and, more than anything, she wished to be out of London. Memories of summers in the country as a child crowded her mind, making her sick with longing for a time when her life had been carefree and safe. A time when she'd had everything she'd ever dreamed of. She longed to be surrounded by trees and grass and birdsong, and away from the cruelty and glittering painted beauty of the metropolis.

The enclosed patch of green surrounded by trees was hardly the idyll she sought, but it seemed like a little oasis of calm and it might help her wretched heart settle itself a little.

As one of the postilions handed her down, she realised it was St James' Square. Some of the grandest and most sought-after homes in the city enclosed the little green, and Matilda gave a laugh. Good grief, not exactly the rural country scene she longed for, but still the cool green beneath the canopy of the trees called to her, an irresistible pull on what was becoming a hot afternoon.

"I'll only be a moment or two," she assured the coach driver.

"Should you like Charles to accompany you, Miss Hunt?" he asked, gesturing to the man who'd helped her down.

"Oh, no," she said, not wanting to be watched in case she was taken with another fit of the dismals. "It's unnecessary. I'll not go beyond the square."

Moving past the railings, the path led her to the centre where a large, shallow pond glittered in the afternoon sun. On a grand plinth in the middle of the water was a statue of William the Third on horseback. Matilda sighed and tried to allow her lungs to unlock enough to draw a deep breath as she walked the periphery of the basin. How lovely it would be to kick off her shoes and paddle in that cool water. She smiled to herself as she imagined how that would be viewed by the illustrious residents of the square. You could likely be transported for such audacity. Feeling therefore a little daring, Matilda looked about herself to ensure she was alone, before crouching down and trailing her fingers in the water.

It was deliciously cool. She sighed with pleasure and dabbed her damp fingers against her cheeks, which were still flushed from her outburst in the coach. Matilda sighed and allowed a few drops to trail down her neck, shivering a little as one slid into her décolletage.

"Miss Hunt. I would say what a surprise to find you here alone, but... that seems to be our destiny, does it not?"

Matilda whirled about, standing so quickly that she stumbled. A strong hand grasped her waist, steadying her. Horrified, she found herself face to face with the Marquess of Montagu.

Oh, good Lord.

The day had only needed that.

The heat of his palm burned through the fine muslin of her summer gown, branding her as her heart skipped and her breath hitched. Before she could exclaim or move back, he removed his hand, returning it to the heavy silver-topped cane he carried.

"What are you doing here?" she asked, frustrated to discover her voice unsteady.

One pale, blond eyebrow rose just a little. "I live here," he said, with a somewhat sardonic curve to his mouth. "If I may return the question?" he said, an enquiring note to his voice, though there was a glint in his eyes that was calculating, disturbing.

His attention drifted to her neck and the little trickles of water sliding over her skin. Matilda blushed, aware of the quality of his gaze as he followed the trail of a droplet down her throat.

"I...." She began and then stopped. Really, she ought to have some scathing comment for the man, some insult or rejoinder to remind him of her animosity, but she was too tired. Sorrow and fear for the future had eaten away at the backbone on which she so prided herself. "I saw the green," she said, a little startled at the exhaustion in her voice. "And I... I just wanted...."

She shook her head and gave an uneven laugh. Good God, what was she thinking? Perhaps she'd cry on his shoulder next.

"It doesn't matter," she said, reminding herself of just who she was speaking with. "Forgive me for trespassing. I should certainly not have done so if I'd known you lived here."

With relief, she heard the words sound as cool and indifferent as they ought to be but, before she could leave, the marquess had reached out and caught her arm, stilling her.

Matilda gasped and looked down at the elegant gloved fingers resting upon her wrist.

"It's a public place, you cannot trespass." He watched her a moment longer. "You've been crying," he said.

There was neither sympathy nor satisfaction in his tone, more a statement of fact.

Damn him. She would not allow him to know of her private feelings, her weaknesses.

Not him.

"Weddings always make me cry," she said brightly. Nate would want news of their marriage to spread; she may as well help things along. "My brother," she added before he could ask. "He married Miss Dowding this morning. It was very romantic."

Montagu said nothing, just continued scrutinising her, those strange grey eyes so intent she felt they could look inside her, through her. He could find his way beneath her skin and unearth her every secret, her every weakness, all of her.

His hand remained at her wrist, though she'd made no move to pull away from him. Her skin burned beneath those long fingers, even though her spencer and his gloves separated his touch from her flesh. She felt seared by it.

"Good for her," he said at length. "And what of you?"

Matilda stiffened, not wanting to have this conversation with anyone whilst her emotions were still so raw, but least of all him. "Whatever do you mean?"

"You know precisely what I mean," he said, the words clipped and a little annoyed at her deliberate prevarication. "Where will you go? You'll not want to live with a happy couple."

"Good heavens, no," she said, striving to keep her tone light and amused when all she wanted to do was curl up in a ball and sob. "I have that well in hand, though, I assure you. Please don't trouble yourself."

She managed to sneer a little, knowing damn well he didn't care a farthing for her troubles.

"I could help you," he said, his voice lower now, a look in his eyes that made her heart react with anticipation of his next words. "I could give you anything you ever desired."

She knew what he meant at once, and he knew she understood.

He would make her his mistress.

Fury burned within her.

To her eternal relief, anger chased away the sadness and the self-pity, and she welcomed it, welcomed the familiar heat of rage that this man always brought her. Strange, how such a cold man could make her burn with anger. She wanted to poke at the façade of the perfect gentleman with a sharp stick. Montagu was famous for never, *ever,* losing his temper. He never raised his voice, never showed emotion of any kind. A cold bastard, it was said of him in awed tones.

It was irresistible, the desire to goad him into a reaction.

Matilda took a step closer to him, so close that their bodies almost touched, she could kiss him if she wanted to. Instead she stared into his eyes, calm now as the anger steadied her.

"I'm just considering all the things I would rather do that ever give myself to you," she said in a sweet, breathless tone. "Let me see... die an old maid, oh yes, that's one. Live in the gutter, that's two. Give myself to almost any other man in the world, no matter how lowborn...." She flashed him a coquettish smile. "You know, I could do this all day. It's rather amusing."

He didn't react, did not betray the slightest indication of having even heard the insults. Knowing just how highly he prized his name and impeccable lineage, it was likely the worst litany of things she could possibly have said to him. He didn't so much as blink. The hand at her wrist still held her, but there was no pressure to it. She could have snatched it free but somehow it would have felt like weakness, and she'd not be weak before him.

So, when he reached out with his free hand and touched her cheek, her unsteady intake of breath was infuriating. It was a delicate touch, just a fingertip, as if he was daring to put his hand to something forbidden and exquisite, but she felt it all the way to her toes.

Matilda's breathing grew increasingly erratic. Something hot and uncomfortable uncoiled inside her, a liquid heat that made her skin tighten with awareness. It was nonsensical, this reaction. Since he'd ruined her, she'd become accustomed to rejecting advances from men who thought to take liberties with her. She'd have no compunction with slapping a man's face, nor kicking him in the shins if the occasion demanded it.

It was the perfect opportunity to slap *his* damn face, but she was frozen, immobile, yet burning alive with sensation, and she could not fathom why.

Just as the silence and the tenderness of his hand on her cheek were becoming intolerable with the confusion it brought bubbling up inside of her, he spoke.

"There is something between us." He sounded as mystified by the idea as she was. "I should like to discover what it is."

Matilda forced her gaze to his and felt a jolt of something pass between them, as though to illustrate his words. Her cheeks blazed. She snatched her wrist from his grasp.

"There is nothing between us," she said, feeling a strange flicker of uncertainty in her chest as the words left her mouth. "Nothing but loathing and contempt."

"You disappoint me," he said, his voice quieter than usual, softer. "It is craven of you to deny the obvious, and I have always admired your courage. You have never cowed away from me, never backed down. You have more backbone than most men of my acquaintance." His lips quirked a little. "And I know some rather terrifying people."

Matilda stared at him. She didn't know what to do with such a comment. Her instinct was to rage at him further, but something perverse inside her unfurled with pleasure at his words.

She was mad. There was no other explanation. She would have to be addled to have any desire to please him, insane to recognise the thrill of having his approval.

"I don't care for your admiration, and I don't give a damn for your disappointment."

There was amusement in his eyes now, as if he knew she was lying, knew everything she'd just experienced, all the uncertainty and confusion and heat, and she really did want to slap him. Instead she looked him in the eyes.

"Just so there is no misunderstanding between us," she said, willing her voice not to tremble, "I would starve in the streets before I let you put your hands on me. I'd rather bed a viper."

"A little overdramatic, Miss Hunt," he murmured, tilting his head a little, as if assessing a street performer. "But illuminating and certainly vivid in its descriptive quality."

Matilda flushed, her fists clenching. So much for rattling the marquess's cage; the only person she'd enraged was herself.

"Go to hell," she said, turning her back on him and walking away, despising herself for having allowed him to goad her, when she'd sought to do the same to him.

Someday, she promised herself, someday she would shatter that smug composure of his, and then… then she'd have the last laugh.

Matilda was almost back to the carriage when she heard her name called across the square.

"Miss Hunt. Matilda!"

"Lucia," she exclaimed, more than relieved to see a friendly face, especially one she could vilify every man on the planet to with impunity.

She greeted the young woman, who seemed to grow lovelier every time Matilda saw her. Today, she wore an enchanting gown and matching spencer of emerald green, trimmed with white satin. A spring bonnet of green–and–white satin crowned her black curls, which crowded about her face.

"Oh, I am glad to see you," Matilda said, with real feeling, taking the young woman's arm. Behind Lucia she noticed a footman, standing a discreet distance away and loaded down with boxes. "A little shopping?" she asked, laughing as the poor man juggled the stack in alarm as it slid sideways. The smallest box on the top toppled and Lucia caught it in a deft, gloved hand, and grinned.

"Poor John," she said to the footman, who blushed scarlet. "I'm a terrible trial to him. Speaking of which," she added, taking Matilda's arm, "did I see you speaking with Montagu?"

Matilda fought a blush and grimaced. "You did."

"Oh, there's gossip, isn't there?" Lucia said, her dark eyes alight with mischief. "Do come home and have tea with me. You can tell me everything. I'm only a few minutes' walk from here."

Matilda hesitated.

"Oh, do say you'll come," Lucia begged, looking so earnest that Matilda couldn't help but smile. "Though we're in a terrible mess. There's been some dreadful mix-up with the lease and so we're being evicted. Can you believe it? Boxes everywhere. It's enough to make me want to scream. We shall have to find something else before the end of the week, or I shall be living on the street."

"That's a coincidence," Matilda said ruefully. "I'm moving too. In fact—"

She felt something unwind inside her as she realised it was the perfect arrangement. Lucia would be the antidote she needed to the loneliness of leaving her brother, and the perfect companion for when she was feeling bitchy and less than charitable with the world, especially the male portion of it.

"In fact... how do you feel about coming to live with me?"

Chapter 21

At last, a stroke of good fortune. Thank heavens for Matilda Hunt. She has saved us. I am blessed at least in having such a friend even if curses fall at my feet like raindrops. Lord, I am so tired of putting on this face, of pretending to be something I am not.

Yet … I do not know what I truly am, nor who.

I suppose I never shall.

—Excerpt of an entry from Senorita Lucia de Feria, to her diary.

29th June 1814. Baker Street, London.

"Ready?"

Nate looked down at his wife and covered the hand that was clutching at his sleeve with his own.

"You're creasing a very fine piece of tailoring, love," he said, smiling at her to settle her nerves.

"What? *Oh,*" she said, crestfallen as she stared at where her fingers grasped at his arm. "I do beg your pardon."

He saw the effort she took to unfurl her fingers and stopped her.

"Clutch away," he said, leaning down to kiss her, though they were in full view of the street. "I'm here. I won't leave you. You're not alone. You never will be again."

She gave a sigh, and he saw some of the tension leave her shoulders.

"You always know just the right thing to say," she said, leaning into him.

"Are you sure you want to do this, Alice? I can just as easily go in by myself—"

"No!" she exclaimed, shaking her head with vigour. "No, indeed. I'm not such a feeble creature that I would allow you to face my parents alone. I... I'm just n-not looking forward to it, that's all."

"Shall we wait a bit then? Come back later," he offered, even though he knew she'd not put it off. Alice was far braver than she gave herself credit for.

As predicted, she shook her head, russet curls dancing.

"No. Certainly not. We're here now, so... let's get it over with."

Taking a deep breath, she shot him a rather fraught smile, which made his chest ache with pride, and they walked the final distance to her parents' front door and climbed the steps. Nate had to admit to feeling a little anxious himself. He'd been cast as the villain of the piece before now, rightly or wrongly, but he'd never ruined anyone, *or* married them, which in Alice's case might amount to the same thing in some people's eyes—her parents', for example. Still, he couldn't bring himself to regret it. Certainly not on his behalf, at least. He was a selfish bastard, that's all there was to it. She was his now, and he was never letting her go.

As they were shown into an elegant and richly furnished entrance hall, it was clear enough that the servants had gathered what was going on. The butler was thin lipped with disapproval, and a footman and two female servants just had to cross the hall at that moment, wide-eyed with interest.

"You dare come here?"

Nate gripped Alice's hand as her father appeared in the hall from one of the front rooms. He was not a tall man, but he was broad, with a double chin, thick neck, thicker waistline… and currently a face like thunder. How lovely, delicate Alice could have come from this glowering, red-faced fellow, Nate could not fathom.

"Mr Dowding," Nate said, reminding himself that he had stolen the fellow's daughter, and he had every right to want to string him up by his privates. He'd do his best to keep things civil, for Alice's sake. "I understand that you must be upset—"

"Upset!" the fellow roared, his chin quivering with indignation. "Upset does not quite cover it, sir, and now… *now* you have the temerity to come here and—"

"I love him, Papa," Alice said, letting go of Nate's hand and stepping between them. "And I despise Mr Bindley. I tried to tell you how awful he was, but you wouldn't listen. So, I made my own choice. I'm sorry if you don't like it, but it is done now. Nate is the man I chose. He is a good man, a kind one. He's also exceedingly rich," she added, a comment which Nate was aware she made only to soothe her father. "He owns *Hunter's*, you know."

"Of course I know!" he retorted, getting redder in the face with every moment. "The young jackanapes has denied me membership these past two years."

"Well," Nate said, smiling a little. "I could hardly deny my father-in-law membership, now, could I?"

There was a moment of calm, during which Nate felt there was a glimmer of hope, and then it all went to hell as Mrs Dowding arrived on the scene.

She appeared at the top of the stairs, like an actress in some overblown melodrama, and swooned.

"Mother!" Alice cried, and hurried up the stairs.

The woman crumpled on the top step, but didn't fall, which to Nate's cynical eye appeared more calculation than luck.

"Alice," the woman said faintly, as Alice brought her around with smelling salts. "Oh, my baby... my poor ruined daughter...."

"I'm not ruined in the least," Alice replied, her voice tart. "I'm married."

"To him!" the woman wailed in a sensational fashion, pointing an accusing finger down the stairs. "That... that *villain*."

"Oh, for heaven's sake, now you're just being silly," Alice said, remarkably unimpressed by her mother's histrionics. "He's not a villain. Not even close, so there's no need to turn it into a Cheltenham tragedy."

Nate looked up at his wife with pride. God, she was magnificent.

She helped her mother to her feet and guided her down the stairs.

"Now," Alice said, her voice stern. "We shall go and sit in the parlour and discuss this like rational people."

A knock at the door gave the butler an excuse to enter the fray once more, looking down his nose at the entire family now. Nate was just thinking the farce couldn't possibly get any worse, what with a red-faced, furious father and a hysterical, swooning mother, and then Mr Bindley arrived.

Ah, the jilted lover. It had only needed that.

The fool was carrying a bouquet of roses and an expression of concern.

"I just c-came to see if Miss Dowding was m-more herself today," he enquired, all solicitousness, until he looked around and became aware of the rising tension in the room.

"Oh, my poor boy...." Mrs Dowding wailed, embracing Edgar in a move that horrified him as much as it amused Nate.

He almost felt a twinge of sympathy. Almost, but not quite.

"Mrs D-Dowding," the young man exclaimed, frozen in place while Alice's mother crushed his roses and sobbed.

"I'm afraid you're too late, old man," Nate said, rather enjoying himself now. "Alice married me yesterday morning."

Mrs Dowding emitted another howl of woe, while Mr Dowding tried to prise her off Mr Bindley. Alice just stood back watching the goings on with a look mild disgust until Nate caught her eye. Her lips twitched.

At that moment, however, Mrs Dowding released Bindley from the hold she had on him, and the spurned Romeo flung down his roses with fury before throwing himself at Nate.

"You blackguard!" he cried, enraged, momentum giving him rather more force than came naturally as he barrelled forwards.

Surprised, Nate crashed to the floor and Bindley followed him down, pummelling and flailing his fists like a wet hen with a great deal of show and very little impact.

"Oh!" Alice cried in outrage and ran to help, trying to drag Mr Bindley from Nate.

Nate, who didn't dare throw a punch for fear of Bindley flinging himself backwards and hurting Alice, was a little stymied.

"Alice, get back, love," he huffed, unsure whether to laugh or to get truly angry until Mr Bindley finally got lucky and struck him a blow to the chin. "Right, you little weasel, that's quite enough of that." Nate drew his knee up in a sharp gesture which made Bindley shriek like a scalded cat and fall to a heap on the floor.

"A... a gentleman... would never...." Bindley gasped, clutching at his private parts while his eyes watered.

"We've already established I'm no longer a gentleman," Nate replied as he got to his feet and glowered down at Bindley. "You might bear that in mind the next time you come near my wife, or consider allowing her name to pass your lips. I promise you'll regret it."

"You're welcome to the frigid little doxy," Bindley snarled, unsteady as he struggled to his knees and clutching at a gilded console table to get to his feet. "I'd never have looked at her if not for the money. She smells of trade and desperation."

There was a cry of horror from Mrs Dowding, who was realising Mr Bindley was not as nice a young man as she'd imagined. Nate, however, was beyond incensed, and knocked him down once again with a strike that likely broke his nose.

Bindley howled and crashed back into the console table as a china vase smashed to the floor and wood splintered in all directions.

"You," Nate said, snarling at the outraged looking butler with such ferocity that the fellow leapt forward to do his bidding. "Help me put this scuttling creature in the gutter where he belongs."

Between them they hauled a moaning Mr Bindley out of the door, where Nate hailed a hackney carriage and shoved him inside. Although he had little compunction about leaving the wretched excuse for a man in the street, they needed no further scandal.

By now thoroughly irritated, Nate strode back into the house, picked up his hat and turned back to his parents-in-law.

"Right," he said, his tone brusque. "I'm your new son-in-law. It's done and there's nothing you can do about it. Now, I'm sorry that it came about the way it was and I apologise for the clandestine nature of our marriage. It was underhand and badly done, and I understand you are well within your rights to be upset, but we felt we had no choice." He paused and took a breath, trying to tamp down his emotions and sound calm and reasonable. Well, calm, anyway. "That," he continued, "is the last time I will apologise for who I am or what I've done. I love your daughter and I will do everything in my power to make her happy. If that's not good enough for you, well, that's too bad, but bear in mind I'll not allow you to make Alice suffer for her choice."

There was a definite edge to his words, and he gave Mr Dowding especially a hard look that threatened retribution.

Mrs Dowding gave a little sniff and reached for Alice's hand. "How dare Mr Bindley say such things about you? I was never more insulted."

Alice smiled and patted her mother's hand. "Never mind, Mama. I tried to tell you he really wasn't a very kind man."

To her credit, the woman nodded her agreement, though she said nothing more.

Nate looked to Mr Dowding, who was still red-faced with indignation, though who it was aimed at now, Nate wasn't sure. The fellow let out a deep breath.

"Reckon we both need a drink," he said, glowering a little, though Nate took it as the overture it was clearly meant to be.

"I would appreciate that, sir."

Mr Dowding grunted and gestured at Nate to come into his study. "Go and take tea in the parlour, you two," he said over his shoulder to his wife and daughter. "I need to speak to my son-in-law in private."

The words were somewhat begrudging, but Nate glanced back at Alice and winked at her. It was a start.

"Now then," Mr Dowding said, closing the door to his study. "About my membership...."

Chapter 22

Dear Harriet,

Did you know Lucia will be living with Matilda? Can you imagine two such beautiful creatures under one roof? They'll have men beating their door down!

I wonder how it would be if I lived with you? There would be no swooning suitors, I'm afraid. Could I bring my cat? He's frightfully bad tempered, in fact, we're both horrid in the morning. I'd give it three days before you murdered me in my sleep …

—Excerpt of a letter from Miss Kitty Connolly to Miss Harriet Stanhope.

1st July, 1814. Upper Walpole Street, London.

Alice grinned as the girls all whooped and clapped as she entered the room. Ruth showered her with rice, which pattered over the polished wood floor, and Kitty promptly slipped over on it. She sat on her behind with an undignified, "Ooof!" and then burst into laughter, which set everyone off again.

"Come here, you dreadful creature," Harriet said, hauling her to her feet and tutting, though there was obvious affection in her tone.

"Well, it's not my fault," Kitty objected, almost going over again and taking Harriet with her. "Ruth set me up."

"I do beg your pardon, Kitty," Ruth said, torn between laughter and mortification.

Happily, Kitty seemed to take such indignity in her stride and wasn't the least bit offended.

"So, how is married life?" Bonnie asked, dragging Alice to a settee and sitting her down. "Tell us everything!"

Alice blushed crimson and caught Prue's eye. "I c-couldn't possibly," she stammered, laughing and shaking her head. "Besides, it would spoil the surprise."

Bonnie made a sound of disgust. "I don't want any surprises from Gordon Anderson, I thank you," she said, folding her arms and glowering. "And the way this season is going, he's inescapable."

"Oh, but surely your guardian will give you a little longer, Bonnie?" Ruth asked in concern. "You're only two and twenty, hardly on the shelf yet."

"I don't know," Bonnie said, the words heavy with foreboding. "But I will have the devil's own job persuading him the expense of another season is worthwhile when he has good old Gordy waiting in the wings."

Ruth leaned over and squeezed her hand in sympathy. "Is he really that bad?"

"Worse," Bonnie muttered.

"Oh, dear." Ruth bit her lip, looking anxious. "Well, the season is almost over, perhaps, but there will be plenty of house parties and events over the summer." She picked up a large platter of iced buns and handed one to Bonnie. "So, it doesn't mean your chances are at an end."

The girl took a bun, staring at it morosely. "It does if I have to go back to Scotland."

The women all looked at each other, and back to Bonnie. Marrying a man one didn't even like, let alone love, was far from unusual, but a fate they all feared. Alice had no trouble in sympathising with her predicament.

"Well then, you must stay with me," Ruth said, suddenly decisive. "We will be going to the country. Papa has bought a new house," she added, flushing a little and avoiding everyone's eye.

Alice hid a smile of sympathy. Ruth's father was an extremely wealthy man, but no amount of money could buy breeding, and the *ton* were not kind to those who didn't belong. The *ton* saw the man only as a vulgar climber, a Cit, or a mushroom, and the way he collected artwork, jewels, and houses only added to their contempt for him.

"We will certainly go to St Clair's for the summer ball," she added, looking excited at the prospect. "So, we shall see Kitty and Harriet, and… oh, a whole host of eligible young men. And then there will be garden parties and dinners, and all sorts of social events. There, you see. Plenty of time yet."

Bonnie let out a breath and leaned over to kiss Ruth's cheek. "Thank you," she said, with such sincerity that Ruth beamed at her.

"You're welcome. In truth, I shall be glad of your company."

"Well, this is all well and good, but I still have not smoked a cigar nor drunk a glass of cognac," Lucia pointed out. She was arranging her skirts with a prim moue of displeasure on her exquisite face, and everyone laughed as she'd obviously intended.

"When are you going to do it, Lucia?" Alice asked, remembering the nerves and downright panic that had assailed her at the idea of kissing a stranger on the balcony.

"I thought at the Earl of Ulceby's ball," she said, smiling a little.

"Oh," Alice said in surprise, a little frisson of anxiety running down her spine. The man might have been her father-in-law, if not for Nate. "You're going to that?"

"Do you mind very much, Alice?" Lucia asked, sudden sympathy in her eyes.

"Oh, no," Alice said in a rush, shaking her head. "Not in the least, only Lord Ulceby is not a nice man, and… do watch out for his son, Edgar Bindley. He's a spiteful cad."

"With a broken nose," Matilda murmured before taking a sip of her tea. Alice glanced at her and grinned.

"I know," Lucia said, her dark eyes glinting with something secretive that might have been anticipation. "That is why I chose them. I should not like to steal anything, even as silly as a cigar and a drink, from a man I esteemed."

"Do you esteem any man?" Matilda asked, the direct question rather shocking the group as everyone stilled.

Lucia did not seem affronted, however, and merely considered the question. "No," she said simply.

Everyone laughed, assuming she was being amusing again, but there was something in her eyes that told Alice she meant it. There was an air about Lucia that gave her pause. She was beautiful and graceful, yet never at ease. Something raw and untamed lived within her, like a wild creature gone utterly still in the moment before it pounced. Alice shivered at the idea and turned to Matilda.

"Will you go to the Ulceby ball?"

"I suppose so, to keep Lucia company and out of too much trouble, if nothing else," she said with a wry laugh. "I assume they won't banish me at the door for being related to Nate, as the earl owes him too much money."

"The earl owes everyone money," Alice said in an undertone. "I can't understand how he can possibly afford to hold such a lavish ball. Father had a rather frank discussion with him when they believed I was to marry Edgar, and he says they're on the brink of bankruptcy."

Matilda nodded. "I know. I've heard much the same, and Nate cut off his credit over a year ago, but a man like that has his pride. He'd rather die than have the world see he cannot live as he wants."

"But it's all for show," Alice said, uncomprehending of how a man could beggar his family and squander their fortunes, their futures.

"It's a sickness, I think," Matilda said, her voice soft. "I was angry with my father, for a very long time but... but he was so sorry for what he'd done. So full of remorse. He said demons had possessed him, and... I can almost believe it."

Alice frowned. She didn't believe in demons, and could only think a man who could ruin his own family so utterly was weak, but she could not pretend to understand it, so perhaps she was too hard.

"It is a sickness for some," Lucia said, making them both start as they'd not realised she was attending their conversation. Her voice sounded hard, cold, and unforgiving. "But not for Lord Ulceby. He is a cruel, greedy man, and one day he will pay the price for it."

Alice stared at Lucia, at the glitter of certainty in the young woman's eyes, and a prickle of foreboding slithered down her spine once more. There was a private edge to her words that made Alice believe Lucia was speaking of some specific event, and one to which she was privy. She glanced at Matilda, who held her cup suspended in mid-air, her expression so arrested that Alice knew she'd heard the threat in the words too.

"Well, then," Ruth said, breaking the strange atmosphere with her cheery, no nonsense voice. "These cakes will not eat themselves. For heaven's sake, tuck in, ladies."

Oohs of pleasure murmured around the group as various trays of delicate pastries were passed back and forth.

"You know," Prue said, giving Lucia and Kitty a sly glance. "Both Alice and I are married because of our dares. So, I think you two ladies should prepare yourselves."

The group laughed and made sounds of encouragement, all except the two ladies in question. Kitty looked as if she might cry and Lucia folded her arms, a scowl darkening her face.

"I would never give a man such power over me. I shall never marry. Never."

Kitty, by contrast, blinked hard and scrambled to her feet. "Would… would you excuse me, please?" she said, and rushed from the room.

"Whatever did I say?" Prue asked, perplexed. "I know I'm good at putting my foot in my mouth but—"

"I'll go after her," Harriet said, putting down her plate and following Kitty out the door.

"I suppose we all have our secrets," Matilda said softly.

After the meeting, Alice and Matilda bade Ruth goodbye and found Nate waiting for them with the coach.

"And how were the Peculiar Ladies today?" he asked, a glint of amusement in his eyes.

"Very well, thank you," Matilda said, giving her brother a warning glance, which Alice knew he'd ignore

"And which book was the subject of discussion today?" he asked, with an enquiring air.

Alice and Matilda exchanged glances, and both burst out laughing.

"What?" he asked, looking between them with a disgruntled expression. "It is a book club, isn't it?"

Alice took his arm. "Yes, dear," she said, her tone soothing. "Sort of."

"What the devil does that mean?" he asked, suspicion lacing the words. "What do you lot get up to if not discussing books? No!" he said, suddenly raising a hand before either of them could speak. "On second thoughts, I think I'm safer off not knowing."

"See?" Matilda grinned at Alice. "He can be trained."

Nate glowered at his sister and looked about to reply with some suitably piquant comment when they both saw Matilda's expression freeze. Though Alice would have thought it impossible, she both blanched and blushed at the same time. The colour leached from her skin, leaving two scarlet spots blazing on her cheeks.

Alice and Nate turned to follow the direction of her gaze, and Alice gasped as she saw the Marquess of Montagu further down the street. He and Matilda stared at each other, as though drawn by some invisible force, unable to look away.

Nate took his sister's arm. "Come along, Tilda," he said, his voice gentle, but firm, as he guided her to the coach and handed her inside.

Once everyone was settled, Nate rapped on the ceiling and the coach rocked into motion. Matilda seemed calm enough now, though Alice couldn't help but notice how her gaze travelled to the window, and watched as they drove past the marquess, who was still standing on the street.

"Now that the two of us have been suitably disposed of," Alice said, taking Nate's arm and exchanging a worried glance with him. "We can concentrate on getting you a husband."

Matilda looked up at that, something that might have been alarm in her eyes. "What?" she exclaimed. "Oh, good heavens, no. I thank you. If there is any husband hunting to be done, I'll do it myself. They don't call me *The Huntress* for nothing, you know," she quipped, smirking at them.

"Don't do that," Nate said, with such tenderness that Alice felt a lump in her throat. "You're better than all of them, Tilda, but somehow, somewhere, there's a man worthy of you, and we'll find him. I promise."

"Yes," Alice agreed, shifting to sit beside her and taking her arm. "And then you'll be as happy as we are."

Matilda snorted at that, giving Alice a look of mock affront. "Not if you find me a husband like him, I won't," she said, with all the indignation of an offended sibling.

"Well, I like that!" Nate retorted, folding his arms. "I'll have you know I'm an excellent husband."

Alice laughed and moved back to sit at his side, quite unable to disagree with that statement as she leaned into him and put her head on his shoulder. "Yes, you are," she crooned, as though soothing an irritable child. "A very excellent husband."

Nate made a harrumphing sound and pulled a face at his sister, who laughed.

"Oh, very well," Matilda said, rolling her eyes at him though they were filled with laughter. "I admit it. You're a wonderful husband and you're both revoltingly happy, and I couldn't be more thrilled. Now, for heaven's sake, get me home before I have to endure another moment of it, or I won't be responsible for the consequences."

Once Matilda had been safely escorted home, Alice snuggled up in her husband's arms.

"She will be all right, won't she?" she asked, still worrying over that strange scene with the marquess.

Nate nodded. "We'll make sure of it," he said, smiling at her. "Tomorrow, I will go through everyone on my client books, and everyone else I know, and compile a list of eligible men. Then, my darling, we will start entertaining. Surely if we throw enough dinners and parties we can find *one* good man?"

"That's a marvellous idea," Alice said with relief. "You're a wonderful brother too, you know."

"You'll make me blush," Nate said softly, shifting a little to look down at her. His eyes darkened in a manner that did something quite similar to Alice. She wasn't entirely surprised when he tugged at the satin ribbons of her bonnet and cast it aside. "Now," he said, that beguiling voice working its magic on her insides and turning her into a quivering wreck. "Let's see just how wonderful a husband I can be."

Alice sighed as he pulled her close and kissed her, his hands wandering and caressing in a shocking manner she really ought to protest about, though she didn't have the slightest intention of doing so.

After all, what was the point in wishing for a man who was just the right amount of wicked, and not enjoying it?

Eager to find out what happens with the next member of The Peculiar Ladies Club? Well... read on for a sneak peek!

Girls Who Dare– The exciting new series from Emma V Leech, the multi-award-winning, Amazon Top 10 romance writer behind the Rogues & Gentlemen series.

Inside every wallflower is the beating heart of a lioness, a passionate individual willing to risk all for their dream, if only they can find the courage to begin. When these overlooked girls make a pact to change their lives, anything can happen.

Ten girls – Ten dares in a hat. Who will dare to risk it all?

To Break the Rules
Girls Who Dare, Book 3

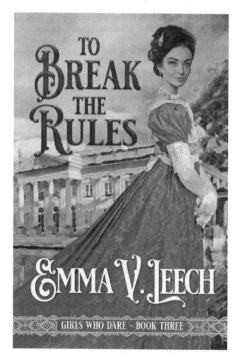

An irresistible enigma ...

Senorita Lucia de Feria is possibly the most beautiful woman in the world and beyond a doubt the most beautiful that Viscount Cavendish has ever seen.

Yet this mysterious beauty is up to something, something that has Cavendish convinced that her motives are less than pure.

The viscount needs no further motivation to spend time in lovely Lucia's company, but desire and intrigue make for unholy temptation.

A dangerous lover ...

Lucia is not everything she seems to be

Lucia has secrets ... secrets one man would kill her for.

Now, with revenge in her heart and a fortune at stake, she's close to having it all or losing her life.

At every turn, Viscount Cavendish is there, with his pirate smile and those wicked blue eyes.

A daring circle of friends ...

When an unusual book club brings The Peculiar Ladies into her life, Lucia is charmed and lured into feeling she belongs for the first time. Between her new friends and a man she is in danger of falling for, her plans are all going awry.

This beautiful Senorita has spent her entire life longing for vengeance, but she never expected to find something she cared for more along the way.

Lucia cannot afford distractions, friends or a suspicious nobleman. Yet suddenly she has all three.

It might be time to break her own rules.

Chapter 1

*Am I foolish, to be so intent on revenge,
to risk everything I have for the chance
of retribution? Perhaps, but everything I
have is a lie, and sooner or later the
truth will find me. At least, when the
inevitable happens, I will have the
satisfaction of having made him pay.
That will be my legacy.*
**—Excerpt of an entry from Senorita
Lucia de Feria, to her diary.**

The 1st July 1814. Upper Walpole Street. London.

Lucia watched in amusement as the Peculiar Ladies made a fuss of a blushing Alice. A few days earlier the young woman had defied her parents and married Nathaniel Hunt, owner of the exclusive and notorious Hunter's, a gambling club frequented by the richest men of the *ton*.

That Alice, of all people, should have stood up and defied her parents was astonishing, as she was the shyest among their group. Lucia couldn't fault her choice, however. Nate was handsome and rich, and clearly besotted with his new bride. Faced with a choice between him and the *Honourable* Edgar Bindley, there was really no contest. Honourable was a word that neither Edgar nor his vile father had any concept of.

The Earl of Ulceby, Lionel Bindley was a greedy and selfish man who cared for nothing and no one. Lucia knew this. Her friends had no idea of her link to Ulceby. Indeed, the man himself would not know her if he passed her in the street, but she knew him. Her position at the fringes of good society was tenuous at best. Her funds, such as they were, had been used in their entirety to establish herself during this one season, to make herself a well-known figure, and therefore one not easily disposed of once the truth was out. She had no illusions that she would be welcomed into society then, no matter her financial situation. People who were friends to her now would no longer receive her, and she reminded herself daily to keep them at a distance.

Every morning as she stared at a reflection of a woman with no place in the world, she reminded herself of her objectives, of what she sought to achieve. Friends did not enter that equation. Her life was given over to one abiding desire.

Revenge.

She had rules to abide by, to make as many acquaintances among the *ton* as she was able, whilst allowing no one close.

Today, the Peculiar Ladies were gathered in the luxurious home of Miss Ruth Stone whose father was of the merchant class. Rich to the point of vulgarity, he sought to enter the ranks of the *ton* but found doors closed to him on all sides. They might not be able to ignore his wealth, but they'd never overlook his lack of breeding. Now his daughter was of age he'd pinned his hopes on her snaring an impoverished nobleman.

Unbeknown to Ruth, her father had been one of the men who had pursued Lucia the most relentlessly, intent on making her his mistress. Finding him hard to dissuade no matter how many times she refused him, Lucia had changed tack and befriended his daughter.

Ruth was no fool and ran the household as her bird-witted mother had little on her mind further than spending her husband's money. As she had hoped, staying with Ruth as her guest for a few days had shielded Lucia from Mr Stone's interest. Despite her loathing of the man who was a manipulative creature, she'd seen enough to realise he respected and loved his daughter and would not willingly invite her censure. A word from Lucia could make his life very uncomfortable at home.

This was what men were, though, how they worked. They saw what they wanted and did whatever they deemed necessary to get it, caring little for who might stand in their way. Only one man had ever shown any care for Lucia, and even he could not protect her when it had mattered.

Men were loathsome creatures, self-centred and unreliable at best.

At worst ... they were lethal.

Men flirted with her and Lucia allowed it, drawing them into her circle, giving them hope they might have a chance, but she never let them overstep the mark. The rumours of her parentage were whispered about wherever she went—that her Spanish mother had been a courtesan—and most people expected her to follow suit. In fact, the woman in question had been Portuguese not Spanish, but English men were ignorant and careless, and it was the least of the things about her that were not as they appeared.

The offers from men had become increasingly lavish, ridiculously so, and she was careful not to bruise anyone's pride as she gently rebuffed their advances. That was perhaps hardest of all, when she wanted to spit in their faces and tell them to go to hell. Yet it only increased her exclusivity and their desire to have her. They called her *Señorita Ciudadela* or Miss Citadel, and they laid bets as to whom would be the first to breach her walls.

It disgusted her, but Lucia was playing her own game, and soon she would laugh in their faces when they realised who it was they'd been throwing themselves and their fortunes at with such abandon.

With difficulty, Lucia forced such dark thoughts away and returned her attention to the ladies around her. Ruth had invited Bonnie to accompany her to the Earl of St Clair's summer ball, and Bonnie was alight with pleasure at the invitation. Sadness bloomed in Lucia's chest as she watched them laughing and chattering together. She had seen friendships blossom between the ladies, watched both Prue and Alice as they'd fallen in love and overcome the trials and tribulations of their courtships with support from the women around them. How she longed for that, to rely on an unwavering friendship, but real friendship required truth at its foundation, and that was something Lucia could not give. She was a morass of lies and half-truths and though it would soon be at an end, she was not fool enough to believe the truth would win her any friends.

"Well, this is all well and good," Lucia said, entering the conversation at last. "But I still have not smoked a cigar nor drunk a glass of cognac." She arranged her skirts with deliberation, affecting a prim moue of displeasure expressly to make everyone laugh.

"When are you going to do it, Lucia?" Alice asked her, a glint of sympathetic warmth in her blue eyes.

"I thought at the Earl of Ulceby's ball," Lucia said, knowing that Alice would worry for her. She was a sweet girl and her limited experience of the Ulceby men had given her a healthy fear of the family.

"Oh," Alice said, her surprise and anxiety as evident as Lucia had expected. "You're going to that?"

"Do you mind, very much, Alice?" she asked, wishing the girl had been nowhere near Edgar Bindley. Matilda had confided that Alice had almost been violated by Edgar during a visit to Vauxhall Gardens. If not for the Marquess of Montagu's intervention things could have ended very badly. Mr Bindley had also pursued Lucia over the past weeks, and she could feel nothing but revulsion for him. She'd taken care never to be alone with him, though he was a pale imitation of his father.

"Oh, no," Alice said in a rush, shaking her head. "Not in the least, only Lord Ulceby is not a nice man and … do watch out for his son, Edgar Bindley. He's a spiteful cad."

"With a broken nose," Matilda murmured before taking a sip of her tea. Alice glanced at her and grinned.

"I know," Lucia said. She'd only been too pleased to discover Mr Hunt had broken Edgar's nose. Her own retribution would be bloodless, but far more devastating. "That is why I chose them. I should not like to steal anything, even as silly as a cigar and a drink, from a man I esteemed."

"Do you esteem any man?" Matilda asked, the direct question rather shocking the group as everyone stilled.

Lucia considered her answer, unsurprised by Matilda's directness, it was a quality she valued highly about the woman whom she had recently rented rooms from. "No," she said.

Everyone laughed, assuming she was being amusing again, though Lucia saw nothing to laugh about. Men would use her if she let them, so she would use them before they got the chance.

"Will you go to Ulceby's ball?" Alice said, clearly a little discomposed by Lucia's answer as she turned her attention to Matilda.

"I suppose so, to keep Lucia company and out of too much trouble if nothing else," she said with a wry laugh. "I assume they won't banish me at the door for being related to Nate as the earl owes him too much money."

Lucia's ears pricked as Alice lowered her voice, unaware Lucia was still listening to the conversation.

"The earl owes everyone money," Alice said. "I can't understand how he can possibly afford to hold such a lavish ball. Father had a rather frank discussion with him when they believed I was to marry Edgar and he says they're on the brink of bankruptcy."

Matilda nodded. "I know. I've heard much the same and Nate cut off his credit over a year ago, but a man like that has his pride. He'd rather die than have the world see he cannot live as he wants."

"But it's all for show," Alice objected.

"It's a sickness, I think," Matilda said, her voice soft. "I was angry with my father, for a very long time but … but he was so sorry for what he'd done. So full of remorse. He said demons had possessed him, and … I can almost believe it."

"It is a sickness for some," Lucia said, watching both women startle as they realised she'd been listening. "But not for Lord Ulceby. He is a cruel, greedy man, and one day he will pay the price for it." She could not keep the venom from her words and cursed herself as Alice and Matilda stared at her.

Hold your tongue you fool.

"Well then," Ruth said, breaking the strange atmosphere with her cheery, no nonsense voice. "These cakes will not eat themselves. For Heaven's sake, tuck in ladies."

Oohs of pleasure murmured around the group as various trays of delicate pastries were passed back and forth.

"You know," Prue said, giving Lucia and Kitty a sly glance. "Both Alice and I are married because of our dares. So, I think you two ladies should prepare yourselves."

The group laughed and made sounds of encouragement, but Lucia folded her arms, a scowl darkening her face.

"I would never give a man such power over me," she said, unheeding of her own advice to watch her blasted tongue. "I shall never marry. *Never.*"

Kitty, the other young lady with a dare to complete, blinked hard and scrambled to her feet. "Would … would you excuse me please," she said, and rushed from the room.

"Whatever did I say?" Prue asked, perplexed. "I know I'm good at putting my foot in my mouth but ..."

"I'll go after her," Harriet said, putting down her plate and following Kitty out the door.

"I suppose we all have our secrets," Matilda said softly, turning to look at Lucia and smiling a little. Lucia swallowed and forced a smile to her own lips, reminding herself once more to keep her mouth shut.

***

Fred Davis sighed and rubbed at his neck, turning his head back and forth to ease the ache. He'd been standing on the same spot outside a certain gentleman's club for bloody hours now, but he was damned if he'd give up. Silas Anson was a pain in the arse, but Fred had worked for his father, the old viscount since he was a boy. Now the old man was dead, and his sense of duty would not allow him to leave the son in the lurch.

Whether the fool liked it or not.

From what Fred knew of Silas, never had there been a man more in need of a good valet, nor one less likely to take one on. As Fred straightened and looked down the road once more, that fact was illustrated so vividly that Fred winced with distress.

The new Viscount Cavendish was a bloody shambles.

Towering and broad shouldered, Silas Anson had the kind of figure suited to battlefields and sword wielding heroics. He was not at home in polite company—despite impeccable breeding—and didn't bother trying to fit in. If not for that fact he disdained the *ton* more than they disdained him, he'd probably not be welcome anywhere. However, his cavalier attitude to society made him rather an intriguing figure and one women seemed to take to like felines around a dish of cream. Strangely, Silas seemed to care little for their attentions either and his name had never yet been linked to any woman, respectable or otherwise. The fellow was an enigma.

Albeit a dishevelled one.

His coat was wrinkled, his shirt a long way from the pristine white it ought to be and his cravat made Fred want to wring his hands and weep. As for his boots, they were so offensive that Fred simply couldn't look at them.

"Lord Cavendish."

Silas' head snapped around, a glint of displeasure in his eyes, the startling blue of generations of the Cavendish family fixing on Fred. It occurred to him then that Silas was likely unused to his new title yet as his father was barely cold in the ground. Him and his old man hadn't spoken since Silas was a boy.

The blue eyes narrowed and then widened as recognition filled them. "Davis?"

"Yes, my lord," Fred replied, relieved that Silas recognised him. It had to be fifteen years since they had last seen each other.

"By God." Silas stared at him for a moment, apparently nonplussed, and then startled Fred by holding out his hand. "It's good to see you."

Fred stared at the proffered hand, a little taken aback. Nobility did *not* shake hands with the serving classes, but then Silas had never taken much heed of the rules.

"Still a stickler for proprieties, I see," Silas said, a rather mocking glint in his eyes as his hand remained outstretched. There was challenge in his stance and Fred knew better than to test him. He took the viscount's hand and shook it. "What brings you to this part of town?" he asked, a glimmer of suspicion in the blue now.

Fred took a breath, knowing Silas would likely fight him every step of the way.

"I came to see you, my lord."

"Oh?"

The suspicious look deepened and Silas folded his arms.

"I've been valet to the Viscount Cavendish for over thirty years, my lord. I know every skeleton in the cupboard and few what's buried so deep even your father didn't remember 'em."

"Are ... are you intending to blackmail me?" Silas said, his expression somewhere between outrage and delight.

Fred tutted and rolled his eyes. "No, my lord," he said, with every ounce of dignity he possessed. "I'm intending to work for you."

Silas stared at him in astonishment. "Doing what?"

The question so took Fred aback that he gaped at the man before him for a good while before he could bring himself to answer. "As your valet, of course."

"My valet?" Silas roared with laughter, causing people on the street to turn their heads and stare. Fred shifted, uncomfortably aware the man was making a spectacle of both of them. "By God, that's a good one. I'm not some preening tulip! I don't have a bloody valet."

"No, my lord," Fred said, his tone dry as sand. "That much is evident."

Silas stopped laughing and regarded him a little closer. "You cheeky blighter."

"I speak as I find, my lord," Fred said, folding his arms to match the viscount's. "And you're a bloody disgrace. If those boots have seen a lick of polish anytime this past month, I'll eat my hat."

"I might make you eat it anyway," Silas retorted, clearly nettled by the comment. "I've never heard such impertinence."

"I've known you since the day you was born, my lord, I never blamed you for running off and I've been dead proud of all you've achieved, but you're Cavendish now, you can't run from it any longer and I reckon it's about time someone took you to task."

Fred held his ground, knowing too well the Cavendish temperament after decades of dealing with the man's irascible father. They despised any sign of weakness, the only way to deal with them was not to back down. "The fact is we need each other."

The mystified look in his eyes satisfied Fred.

"What the devil do you mean by that?" Silas demanded.

"I mean, my lord, that you don't have the faintest idea of what your position entails, seeing how you and your father have been estranged this past fifteen years, and I'm too old and set in my ways to go and work for someone else. I'm as much a part of your inheritance as Cavendish House and I'm damned if I'll let you throw away all my years of loyalty."

"You make it sound as if I was tossing you in the gutter," Silas retorted, a thread of anger in his voice now. "As far as I remember I offered you a very generous retirement in light of your loyal service to my father."

"That you did, my lord," Fred admitted, his voice softening a little as he remembered the staggering amount settled upon him. He'd not expected anything like the sum the new viscount had offered him "But the fact is, my work is my life. I never married and I got no kin. What would I do?" There was a note of pleading in Fred's demand he hadn't meant to allow, but Silas heard it the same as Fred did.

A frown of consternation gathered at Silas' brow. "I understand," he said, his voice gruff with unease. Another trait of the Cavendish men was that they'd rather die than speak of anything that smacked of sentiment or emotion. "It's true that I ... I owe you a debt, Davis," Silas said, sounding increasingly awkward.

It was Fred's turn to frown now. "Whatever for?"

Silas' mouth quirked and he huffed out a laugh. "For a thousand little kindnesses when I was a boy. For not letting me starve when the fellow banished me to my room, for taking the time to notice a snot nosed boy when you might have ignored me, and certainly for taking the blame when that bloody vase got broken, by God man, the fellow might have dismissed you for that."

Blushing for the first time he could ever remember, Fred stuttered and shook his head. "I never meant that you owed me nought. That's not why I'm here."

Fred watched, bemused as Silas grinned, showing even, white teeth in a face that was mostly uncompromising and hard. "I know it, and for that alone I suppose I'd best let you have your way, though I warn you now. I'll not put up with primping and fuss. I'm not a doll to be dressed up and paraded about."

"I gathered that much," Fred said, chuckling and shaking his head with dismay.

Silas gave a snort and shook his head. "Oh, to the devil with it. Come along then, it looks like you've got yourself a job."

Fred gave a deep and heartfelt sigh of relief. "Thank you, my lord," he said, meaning it. "I promise I'll not give you cause to regret it."

"Hmmm," Silas replied, though there was laughter in his eyes. "We'll see.

Fred fell into step with his new master, unable to stop his gaze from falling to the shocking state of the man's Hessian's.

"There is one condition of my employment," he said, unable to restrain himself despite his good fortune. "For the love of everything holy, let me polish your boots."

"Bloody hell, I thought you said I wouldn't regret it?" Silas shook his head and sent him an accusing look.

"What possible harm could polishing your boots do?" Fred demanded.

"A great deal," Silas said, perfectly serious. "People might think I give a damn."

Available June 7, 2019 on Amazon and Kindle Unlimited

Pre Order your copy here

To Break the Rules

Want more Emma?

If you enjoyed this book, please support this indie author and take a moment to leave a few words in a review. *Thank you!*

To be kept informed of special offers and free deals (which I do regularly) follow me on *https://www.bookbub.com/authors/emma-v-leech*

To find out more and to get news and sneak peeks of the first chapter of upcoming works, go to my website and sign up for the newsletter.
http://www.emmavleech.com/

Come and join the fans in my Facebook group for news, info and exciting discussion...

Emmas Book Club

Or Follow me here......

http://viewauthor.at/EmmaVLeechAmazon
Emma's Twitter page

About Me!

I started this incredible journey way back in 2010 with The Key to Erebus but didn't summon the courage to hit publish until October 2012. For anyone who's done it, you'll know publishing your first title is a terribly scary thing! I still get butterflies on the morning a new title releases but the terror has subsided at least. Now I just live in dread of the day my daughters are old enough to read them.

The horror! (On both sides I suspect.)

2017 marked the year that I made my first foray into Historical Romance and the world of the Regency Romance, and my word what a year! I was delighted by the response to this series and can't wait to add more titles. Paranormal Romance readers need not despair however as there is much more to come there too. Writing has become an addiction and as soon as one book is over I'm hugely excited to start the next so you can expect plenty more in the future.

As many of my works reflect I am greatly influenced by the beautiful French countryside in which I live. I've been here in the

South West for the past twenty years though I was born and raised in England. My three gorgeous girls are all bilingual and the youngest who is only six, is showing signs of following in my footsteps after producing *The Lonely Princess* all by herself.

I'm told book two is coming soon ...

She's keeping me on my toes, so I'd better get cracking!

KEEP READING TO DISCOVER MY OTHER BOOKS!

Other Works by Emma V. Leech

(For those of you who have read The French Fae Legend series, please remember that chronologically The Heart of Arima precedes The Dark Prince)

Girls Who Dare

To Dare a Duke

To Steal A Kiss

To Break the Rules

To Follow her Heart

To Wager with Love (November 15, 2019)

To Dance with a Devil (coming soon)

Rogues & Gentlemen

The Rogue

The Earl's Temptation

Scandal's Daughter

The Devil May Care

Nearly Ruining Mr. Russell

One Wicked Winter

To Tame a Savage Heart

Persuading Patience

The Last Man in London

Flaming June

Charity and the Devil

A Slight Indiscretion

The Corinthian Duke

The Blackest of Hearts

Duke and Duplicity

The Scent of Scandal

The Rogue and The Earl's Temptation Box set

Melting Miss Wynter (October 10, 2019)

The Regency Romance Mysteries

Dying for a Duke

A Dog in a Doublet

The Rum and the Fox

The French Vampire Legend

The Key to Erebus

The Heart of Arima

The Fires of Tartarus

The Boxset (The Key to Erebus, The Heart of Arima)

The Son of Darkness (TBA)

The French Fae Legend

The Dark Prince

The Dark Heart

The Dark Deceit

The Darkest Night

Short Stories: A Dark Collection.

Stand Alone

The Book Lover (a paranormal novella)

Audio Books!

Don't have time to read but still need your romance fix? The wait is over…

By popular demand, get your favourite Emma V Leech Regency Romance books on audio at Audible as performed by the incomparable Philip Battley and Gerard Marzilli. Several titles available and more added each month!

Click the links to choose your favourite and start listening now.

Rogues & Gentlemen

The Rogue

The Earl's Tempation

Scandal's Daughter

The Devil May Care

Nearly Ruining Mr Russell

One Wicked Winter

To Tame a Savage Heart

Persuading Patience

Also check out Emma's regency romance series, Rogues &
Gentlemen. Available now!

The Rogue
Rogues & Gentlemen Book 1

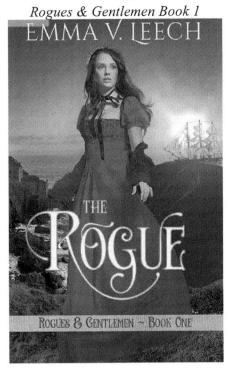

1815

Along the wild and untamed coast of Cornwall, smuggling is
not only a way of life, but a means of survival.

Henrietta Morton knows well to look the other way when the
free trading 'gentlemen' are at work. Yet when a notorious pirate,
known as The Rogue, bursts in on her in the village shop, she
takes things one step further.

Bewitched by a pair of wicked blue eyes, in a moment of
insanity she hides the handsome fugitive from the local Militia.
Her reward is a kiss that she just cannot forget. But in his haste to
escape with his life, her pirate drops a letter, inadvertently giving

Henri incriminating information about the man she just helped free.

When her father gives her hand in marriage to a wealthy and villainous nobleman in return for the payment of his debts, Henri becomes desperate.

Blackmailing a pirate may be her only hope for freedom.

Read for free on Kindle Unlimited

The Rogue

Interested in a Regency Romance with a twist?

Dying for a Duke

The Regency Romance Mysteries Book 1

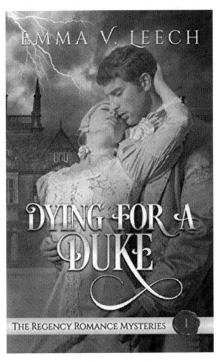

Straight-laced, imperious and morally rigid, Benedict Rutland - the darkly handsome Earl of Rothay - gained his title too young. Responsible for a large family of younger siblings that his frivolous parents have brought to bankruptcy, his youth was spent clawing back the family fortunes.

Now a man in his prime and financially secure he is betrothed to a strict, sensible and cool-headed woman who will never upset the balance of his life or disturb his emotions ...

But then Miss Skeffington-Fox arrives.

Brought up solely by her rake of a step-father, Benedict is scandalised by everything about the dashing Miss.

But as family members in line for the dukedom begin to die at an alarming rate, all fingers point at Benedict, and Miss Skeffington-Fox may be the only one who can save him.

FREE to read on Amazon Kindle Unlimited.. Dying for a Duke

Lose yourself in Emma's paranormal world with The French Vampire Legend series….

The Key to Erebus
The French Vampire Legend Book 1

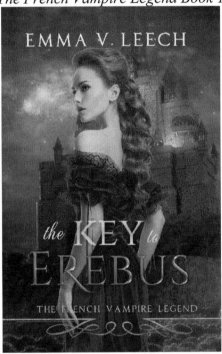

The truth can kill you.

Taken away as a small child, from a life where vampires, the Fae, and other mythical creatures are real and treacherous, the beautiful young witch, Jéhenne Corbeaux is totally unprepared when she returns to rural France to live with her eccentric Grandmother.

Thrown headlong into a world she knows nothing about she seeks to learn the truth about herself, uncovering secrets more shocking than anything she could ever have imagined and finding that she is by no means powerless to protect the ones she loves.

Despite her Gran's dire warnings, she is inexorably drawn to the dark and terrifying figure of Corvus, an ancient vampire and master of the vast Albinus family.

Jéhenne is about to find her answers and discover that, not only is Corvus far more dangerous than she could ever imagine, but that he holds much more than the key to her heart …

FREE to read on Kindle Unlimited

The Key to Erebus

Check out Emma's exciting fantasy series with hailed by Kirkus Reviews as "An enchanting fantasy with a likable heroine, romantic intrigue, and clever narrative flourishes."

The Dark Prince
The French Fae Legend Book 1

Two Fae Princes
One Human Woman
And a world ready to tear them all apart

Laen Braed is Prince of the Dark fae, with a temper and reputation to match his black eyes, and a heart that despises the human race. When he is sent back through the forbidden gates between realms to retrieve an ancient fae artifact, he returns home with far more than he bargained for.

Corin Albrecht, the most powerful Elven Prince ever born. His golden eyes are rumoured to be a gift from the gods, and destiny is calling him. With a love for the human world that runs deep, his friendship with Laen is being torn apart by his prejudices.

Océane DeBeauvoir is an artist and bookbinder who has always relied on her lively imagination to get her through an unhappy and uneventful life. A jewelled dagger put on display at a nearby museum hits the headlines with speculation of another race, the Fae. But the discovery also inspires Océane to create an extraordinary piece of art that cannot be confined to the pages of a book.

With two powerful men vying for her attention and their friendship stretched to the breaking point, the only question that remains...who is truly The Dark Prince.

The man of your dreams is coming...or is it your nightmares he visits? Find out in Book One of The French Fae Legend.

Available now to read for FREE on Kindle Unlimited.

The Dark Prince

Acknowledgements

Thanks, of course, to my wonderful editor Kezia Cole.

To Victoria Cooper for all your hard work, amazing artwork and above all your unending patience!!! Thank you so much. You are amazing!

To my BFF, PA, personal cheerleader and bringer of chocolate, Varsi Appel, for moral support, confidence boosting and for reading my work more times than I have. I love you loads!

A huge thank you to all of Emma's Book Club members! You guys are the best!

I'm always so happy to hear from you so do email or message me :)

emmavleech@orange.fr

To my husband Pat and my family ... For always being proud of me.

Made in the USA
Columbia, SC
17 September 2023